Enemy Beside Me

by

Vicki Fitzer

PublishAmerica
Baltimore

© 2005 by Vicki Fitzer.
All rights reserved. No part of this book may be reproduced, stored in a retrieval system or transmitted in any form or by any means without the prior written permission of the publishers, except by a reviewer who may quote brief passages in a review to be printed in a newspaper, magazine or journal.

First printing

All characters appearing in this work are fictitious. Any resemblance to real persons, living or dead, is purely coincidental.

ISBN: 1-4241-2185-X
PUBLISHED BY PUBLISHAMERICA, LLLP
www.publishamerica.com
Baltimore

Printed in the United States of America

Dedication

To Renee, whose strength and courage inspired me.

Acknowledgements

Special thanks to my teacher, Suzan King, whose encouragement and commitment to her students made an everlasting difference in our lives.

And to my sister, Debbie, for her continual support and assistance.

Prologue

Death has arrived. I've been expecting him, but still, I am intimidated by the power of his presence as he enters my room. He has visited me on previous occasions, though I somehow managed to escape him, knowing his return was inevitable. Fear of him is not an emotion I own. Strange as it may seem, I'm not uncomfortable with him near by. I wouldn't call him a friend, nor is he my enemy. Physically I have never seen him, yet I have learned a great deal about him.

Patiently he sits with me, waiting for me, not knowing if I will accompany him or not. The decision is not his. Is it mine? Is it God's? Death will wait until he knows it is time to go, with or without me. I wonder if it is my unwillingness to go which keeps me from making the journey I was born to undertake.

I lie here quietly while my body rests, not moving nor making a sound. I struggle to move my arms and legs, but they remain lifeless. My eyes do not see, yet my ears hear the voices, though I don't think they can hear me. The words they whisper to me bring comfort. My mother's voice, soft with emotion, and my father's low tones of encouragement. "Please, God, help me answer. I lie here dormant, with no one to assist me, the smell of death strong in this room. How long will death have dominance over me?"

As my mind drifts farther away, I'm aware of the passing of another day. The voices have gone and the room has grown still. For now, I will sleep while death watches me, waiting.

I do not want to die. I feel my will grow stronger. Once more, I will elude him.

Tomorrow they will hear me, somehow I will make them hear me. Goodnight, death, I will not be seeing you tomorrow. This is one journey you will have to make alone. We will meet again some day as we both know. But for now, farewell.

Chapter One

Sarah stood before the bay window which overlooked the sea, amazed at how she never tired of the breathtaking view. The window was partly opened, allowing a cold breeze to fill the room with the smell of salt water.

December evenings in Maine came as no surprise to the people who lived in this small provincial town of Seaside Cove. The icy winds from over the frigid waters of the Atlantic Ocean were no strangers. Snow draped itself across the town, like a blanket covering a sleeping child. It was as if Father Time had stood still while Mother Nature performed at her best, and the whole world looked on in awe at the beauty of her magnificent task.

The cold air chilled Sarah's skin when she walked onto the balcony. Winter had set up its domain for a season as the sun withdrew its warmth. The ocean had a calming effect, which gave Sarah a sense of contentment. She was happy here. Life treated her well and she realized she had taken its blessings for granted.

Brilliant shades of burnt orange and crimson red changed to softer mystical pinks and purples as the sun set. She smiled at remembering how she and her brothers used to stand on the balcony and look at the ghostly images the moon cast on the water believing they were the lost forgotten souls of the unforgiving sea. They were small children at the time, joined together by a close bond which remained between them as they grew older.

Tonight would be Sarah's last night to stand on this balcony, to sleep in this room, for tomorrow her life would not be as she knew it now. Sarah placed her hand on her stomach and thought of how many changes there had been since she found out she was pregnant four months ago. If someone had told her a year ago she would be at this point in her life today, she would have laughed at them. At eighteen fate dealt her an unexpected hand, but willingly she accepted. With her arms wrapped around her slender frame, not wanting to move, she tried to hang onto the present, yet, was drawn into the future.

When she left the balcony, Sarah felt an overwhelming sadness. Inside, she took in every piece of furniture in her bedroom, from the rocking chair her grandfather had crafted with his own hands, to the headboard where she had carved her initials when she was eight years old. The stuffed animals she had accumulated through her childhood years seemed to beckon to her. Her heart ached as she leaned over her bed, and rubbed her hand across the white and pale pink comforter her mother had lovingly hand stitched.

The sadness she was feeling surprised her, for she had not felt this way since the night she had told her parents the news which would change their lives forever. Confident with her decision to marry Greg, Sarah felt her sadness was because she would soon be be leaving her home, her youth, everything she knew and loved. College had always been a dream of hers, and now that dream was only a distant memory. Her parents wanted her to still go after the baby came, but Sarah wanted to be home with her child. Maybe later she had told them.

A faint knock drew Sarah back to reality. "Come in." Sarah looked up as Catherine her mother entered the room. "Sarah, why aren't you ready? Our guests will be here in less than an hour. Can I help you with anything?"

Normally she would welcome her mother's assistance, but she was self conscious of her stomach even though she wasn't showing. "Thank you, Mom, but I'm fine. I'll be ready on time." Sarah sat down in the middle of her bed.

Catherine gracefully approached her and laid a tender hand upon the young woman's shoulder as she sat next to her. "What is it? What's wrong?"

It was not often Sarah remembered seeing fine, tiny lines crease her mother's forehead. Her mother was obviously concerned about her.

"Nothing is really wrong. I guess I'm just tired from all the planning and activities of the last few weeks." Sarah looked away so her mother wouldn't see the tears in her eyes. She was very close to her mother and was able to talk to her about anything until she found out she was pregnant. Raised in a Catholic home where godly principals and morals had been instilled in her, she had known that her parents viewed the church as the final authority. She felt trapped and so alone in what she thought was a hopeless situation. Finding the strength within herself, she put aside all fear of the consequences and blurted out the words she needed to confess.

All her anxieties were put to rest when her parents embraced her. The heaviness she carried was replaced with their love and compassion. How could she have ever doubted their devotion and affection they had shown her whole life? Not once did they condemn or judge her. They shared their thoughts and concerns with her, but remained supportive of her decision to marry Greg. There were other alternatives like adoption or being a single parent. Whatever her decision, they would be there for her. But abortion was not an option.

Her parents had been so wonderful from the beginning, but Sarah still carried a certain amount of guilt. She had betrayed their trust in her and hurt them though they never spoke of it. But sometimes at night, when Sarah passed by her parents bedroom door, she could hear her mother crying softly into her pillow. A picture formed in her mind of how her father must have tried to comfort her mother. But who was there to comfort him?

As she turned back around, Sarah clasped her hands behind her head and laid back on the bed. The ceiling fan above her went round and round reminding her of the windmill on her grandparents' farm.

Catherine leaned back and propped herself up with her elbow. "You sure it's not more than that." She said reaching over to wiped a tear from Sarah's cheek.

"I'm a little sad, I guess. I know I'm only moving across town and I can come visit, but it won't be the same."

"You're right, it won't be the same, but change never is. Sarah, you've had to grow up before you were ready to. Marriage is a big step, especially when you'll be a mother soon, too."

"Mom, I know I haven't talked with you much lately. It's just been hard for me. We've always been honest with each other, for the most part. I need you to be honest with me now." Sarah looked over at her mother with searching eyes.

"I'll try to be honest with you as I can. What is it?"

"You know I love Greg very much, and I want to make him happy. Like the way you've made Daddy happy."

"We do have a good marriage, but we've worked hard to keep it good. When two people come together under one roof, there are going to be differences. Believe me, we've had our share of disagreements," Catherine said thoughtfully.

"How do you know when someone loves you as much as you love them? Men are so different than women. They don't show what they feel like we do. Greg tells me he loves me, but—oh, I don't know. Maybe I'm expecting more from him than he can give me or knows how to give me. At times he seems so distant from me. Like he's there, but he's not there. Does that make any sense?"

"From what you've told me about Greg's parents it doesn't sound like he's had the best example to follow. I don't really know the Winslows, so I can't say who's to blame. One thing I do know, you've got to teach a man how you want to be treated. Your grandmother once told me, a man wouldn't have to live with a nag if he treated her like a queen. Tell Greg what you need, what you want from him. Time will run its course and he'll follow suit." Catherine and Sarah stood up together and faced each other.

"Thanks, Mom. I really do feel better." Sarah sighed with relief as she hugged her affectionately.

"Now, you hurry and finish getting ready." When she reached the door, Catherine stopped and turned toward Sarah. Her voice sounded a little teary. "I love you."

"I love you, too," Sarah whispered, and looked fondly at her mother. With a faint smile, her mother turned and left the room.

Alex Matthews stood in front of the fireplace with one hand resting against the mantle while the other held a glass of scotch. His eyes were entranced by the orange and blue flames. Outside the four walls of his sanctuary, the world was left to deal with the chaotic mess it had created. Inside, solitude and tranquility were the substance of which his world was made.

The library was a place Alex spent numerous hours. Portraits of his father and grandfathers hung between the mahogany bookshelves which extended from the floor to the twenty foot ceiling. A collection of law books accumulated over the years filled the shelves to capacity. Cherry wood furniture accented by burgundy and beige tones throughout the room drew Alex to the warmth it projected.

Alex cherished this house and could not imagine ever living anywhere else. He was born here as was his father, and his father's father. The estate had been in the Matthews family for four generations. This was more than just a home to him—it was part of his heritage. Because the trees were two hundred years old towering over seventy-five feet tall surrounding the estate, it was christened "The Pines."

With a sound determination, the old grandfather clock chimed out the quarter hour. The time was 6:15, and by this time tomorrow the house would not be the same, for a part of his life was taking on a new meaning. His only daughter whom he adored, would leave to begin her life with another man.

As her father, Alex had been the one to care for her and protect her from a world that could be less than caring and nurturing. Over the years as she grew from a child into a young woman, he had been there when life handed out the good times as well as the hurt and disappointment. They had spent hours together talking, sharing their ideas and dreams, and just having fun together. Sarah had grown up right in front of him, but in his eyes she was still his little girl.

Tears welled up in his eyes as memories of Sarah's childhood drifted across his mind. He could see her first steps, hear the first time she called him Daddy. The aching in his heart was ever present. If he could only turn back the hands of time for just one day. But it was too late. Time had run out. And now, he no longer would be the man in her life. The season had come when he must let her go to share her life with Greg.

Although he had made a decision to be supportive and put his feelings toward Greg aside, Alex was still angry. His hand gripped the mantle as he downed the rest of his scotch. Greg had taken advantage of Sarah and robbed her of her innocence. Alex had checked around and discovered Greg had quite a reputation with the female gender. The effort he made to discourage the marriage only drove a wedge between him and his daughter. Sarah was determined to go through with the marriage, so Alex kept his opinions to himself. Sarah's happiness meant the world to him and he wanted their relationship to be restored.

As he left the library, Alex saw Catherine coming down the stairs. With hands on her hips, she pretended to look annoyed. "Alex, you're not ready either." A few long strides brought him to her side. He extended his hand to escort her down the remaining stairs. She took hold like a lady accepting a gentleman caller's invitation.

"Now, Cath, you know I'm as quick as the younger generation. I'll be ready in a flash." He winked at her and bowed ever so teasingly.

"Moving kind of slow, gramps. You better hurry or it will be your bedtime soon," she said in a sultry voice.

Alex pulled her with ease into his arms, changed the mood and held her in a sensual embrace. While his fingers stroked her hair, he whispered in her ear, "Bedtime, mmm, that's a pleasant thought." Alex drew her in closer and moved his mouth up her slender neck to her inviting lips, kissing them passionately before he released her.

She blushed, which gave her a childlike quality he had been drawn to from the first time they had met. Regaining her composure, she smoothed out her silk shirt as she stepped back, bumping into the wood banister. Alex tried to hide his amusement without success.

"Oh, you," she said with a laugh as they walked down the stairs together hand in hand.

"How bout a quick drink before dinner?" Alex led her into the den and walked over to the wet bar.

Catherine settled on the love seat and rested her arms on the back of the sofa and watched Alex fixed the drinks. "Well, it'll have to be a quick one. The Winslows will be here soon." She sighed and turned around diverting her attention from Alex to the embers which burned and crackled in the fireplace.

Alex sat beside her after he placed a martini in her hand. The way she stared without blinking, he knew she was deep in thought. "What are you thinking about?" He put his arm around her shoulders while he admired her face. She was even more beautiful by the fire.

"Oh, I don't know." Catherine leaned forward and set her drink down on the coffee table. "Well, that's not entirely true." Catherine stood up and walked over to stand in front of the fireplace and then turned to face Alex.

"You're not worried about tonight are you?" Alex laid his head back and put his feet upon the coffee table.

"I wish it were that simple," she said as she crossed her arms and began to tap her fingers on her elbow.

"Can't be too serious, can it? So what's up?" Alex remained on the love seat following her with his eyes while she walked back and forth in a repetitious manner.

"I know there's a lot of mixed emotions in this house right now. I keep telling myself that's all it is. But I was upstairs with Sarah earlier this evening and I think she is even sensing something. Maybe it's just last minute doubt and reservations. I don't know. I just wish there was something we could do."

Alex stood up abruptly and set his glass down hard on the table next to Catherine's drink. His face tensed as he approached her, shoving his hands deep into his pant pockets. Alex was angry and the evidence came out in his voice. "Catherine, I've lost track of the times we've had this discussion, with and without Sarah. The wedding is tomorrow. What do you think can be done now!" Alex removed his hands from his pockets and threw them up in the air as he turned away and walked over to the large bay window.

Alex knew Catherine looked to him for the answers, as did his clients. His clients did not always take the advice of their attorney, and neither had Sarah. Alex put his hands back into his hip pockets and looked out into the darkness. "Sarah is doing exactly what she wants and we both know it. I tried to talk to her, but she refused to listen. I wasn't able to change her mind then." Alex turned back toward his wife without moving from the window. His jaw flinched as he looked at her. "And it's a little too late now, don't you think?"

The hurt expression on Catherine's face bothered Alex. He was upset at the situation and not her, but when she brought this whole mess up he took his anger and frustrations out on her. Her face turned a light shade of red which revealed her embarrassment as she spoke in a gentle voice. "I'm sorry. I shouldn't have said anything."

Alex walked over to the wet bar and stood behind it placing his hands on the bar. He continued as if he did not even hear her apology. "If I had my way, Sarah wouldn't be marrying Greg, not tomorrow, not any day. I don't think he's good enough for her and I don't trust him. He pursued her, used her and then wanted to walk away when she got pregnant." Alex slammed his fist down on the bar and startled Catherine. "I wish to God he'd walked away and kept going.! I'm not sure why he wants to marry our daughter, but I doubt it's for love."

His jaw tightened as he left the bar and walked toward the fireplace. Catherine moved out of his way and sat back down on the love seat. As he tossed another log on the fire, he grabbed the wrought iron poker and repeatedly stabbed the wood angrily. With one final thrust, Alex placed the poker back in the stand and finished off the rest of his drink in one gulp. Without even bothering to look at Catherine, he walked swiftly out of the den. There was not much time left to change his clothes and this conversation was over as far as he was concerned.

He could feel his wife's eyes on him when he walked away. A part of him wanted to go back to her and take her in his arms and apologize. But he needed to cool down first. Later that night he would somehow make it up to her. They had a good relationship and knowing her like he did, she was forgiving him as he went up the stairs.

When he reached the top of the landing, Alex noticed Sarah's door was partly opened. Hopefully she had not heard the previous conversation downstairs. Just to see her sitting at her vanity was all he needed to make him forget his anger. Slightly turned from the mirror, she sat still, and gazed into the ocean. He was taken back at how young she was, yet so lovely. His heart was full of pride and admiration as he watched her.

Her emerald green eyes were identical to her mother's, as was the same auburn hair which caressed her delicate shoulders. Graced with poise that suited her 5'4" petite frame, she was a mirror image of Catherine.

Alex held onto the door frame to keep from entering her room. He longed to wrap his arms around her and never let go. But that would only happen in his dreams. The time had come to let her go, to become the woman he knew she would be. Alex swallowed hard to keep back the tears which stung his eyes while he stood there silently. Next to his wife, Sarah was the love of his life. If it was in his power, he would do anything for her.

Alex's knuckles were white when he released the door frame. Softly backing away from her door his mouth quivered as he whispered under his breath, "I love you." He headed toward his bedroom while his heart was being ripped away. He realized she needed her time to be alone, to bring this part of her life to a close as they all must. At his bedroom door, Alex stopped and turned, looking back at Sarah's door once more. With a downcast expression he shut the door firmly, closing a final chapter in his life.

Chapter Two

Marina Winslow paced back and forth impatiently, clicking her fingernails together. Frank glared at her with annoyance because she knew this habit irritated him immensely.

"Quit making that god awful noise!" Frank said with a scowl on his face. Marina ignored him as she kept up the ritual. He glanced down at his watch. They were suppose to be at the Matthew's at 7:00 and he didn't want to be late.

"What's taking Greg so long up there in his room?"

"How should I know?" Marina said with a snap. She became more agitated each time he opened his mouth.

"Well, you know everything else he does." Frank was used to her behavior and he could go the distance with her. Twenty years of marriage had proven that.

"Obviously not! If that were true he wouldn't be in the mess he's in today." Marina's voice was full of bitterness as her words sank their teeth into Frank's heart.

Frank knew where this was going and was not anxious to get there. "There's no time for this now. We have gone over this a hundred times and got nowhere. It won't be any different now. Now shut up and let it go!" Frank got out of the chair while he rubbed his lower back. The broken spring had poked him way too long, which caused him discomfort. And for some reason he could deal with his wife better when he was standing up.

Marina stopped pacing and turned to confront Frank. "Let this go! Greg's life is ruined and you talk like he just lost his job or something. I was insane to think I could expect anything different out of you. Why can't you stand up and be a man?" She crossed her arms and glared at him.

Frank's temper began to rise. His patience with Marina was on thin ice and she knew what would happen if he crossed that line. Like a panther that closed in on its prey, he advanced toward her. He was over six feet and could be intimidating. He did not like to be aggressive, but he could only take so much from this woman.

"What would you rather Greg have done? Abandoned Sarah and the baby? Not own up to his responsibility? He's doing what a man should do." Frank felt his blood pressure start to rise so he began to settle back down. Speaking in a calmer tone he backed away from her and said, "Marina, you know as well as I do Sarah didn't get pregnant all by herself."

"I don't care what you say! Sarah Matthews seduced my son with those green cat eyes of hers. The way she enticed him with her expensive clothes and all that money, Greg didn't stand a chance!"

Frank's eyes widened in shock. "What world are you living in? You can't really believe all this nonsense you're saying. Sarah is a sweet, kind girl who our son pursued.

All the other girls he dated fell all over him. They threw themselves at him, but not her."

Tired of the argument, he went to the kitchen to get a beer out of the refrigerator. But she followed after him, close on his heels with hands on her hips.

Marina gritted her teeth before she lashed out. "That's bull crap, Frank! She used her angelic face to trick him into bed with her. That innocent front of hers doesn't fool me, not for a second. With his good looks and potential she knew a good thing when she saw him and sunk her hooks into him. Her mind was set on him and she didn't care how she got him!" With a flip of her hand in Frank's face she turned back toward the dim lit living room.

"Is that how you did it, Marina? How you got me to marry you?" Frank said accusingly, his eyes mocking her. He stood up straight and raised his shoulders back ready for battle.

As if a barricade blocked her path, Marina stopped dead in her tracks and whirled around to face the man she loathed. Her navy blue eyes turned a shade of smoldering gray, her mouth dropped opened and then closed with teeth clenched together. Angry tears streamed down her cheeks as she swallowed hard.

"That's a lie! A bold face lie and you know it!" Marina was so angry that she shook and lunged at Frank, jamming her index finger against his chest. "You know I was on the pill. Was it my fault I became a statistic!" There was fire in her eyes now. "How dare you say that to me, like you had no part in it!"

Frank's beer spilled onto the front of his shirt and the floor as he grabbed her wrist to jerk her finger away from his chest. "Back off, Marina!" He only held tighter when she tried to pull her wrist from his grasp. "I mean it!" Frank finally released her and shoved her out of his path. The kitchen towel he picked up was ragged and worn out, not much use in cleaning up the beer.

Marina rubbed her wrist. "You think you can just push me around. Well you can't." She stormed out of the kitchen back into the living room where she knew he would follow.

Frank threw the towel on the counter top leaving the mess on the floor. Still angry he followed her. "I won't apologize to you because you don't deserve one. What you do deserve, I didn't give you. I'm sick and tired of your accusations of Sarah. My folks thought you got pregnant on purpose. See how it makes you feel? But you're doing the same thing to her. Greg had just as much to do with the conception of this child as she did. It's a shame it happened, but it did. End of story. Besides, Sarah comes from a good family and he's getting a better chance than a lot of people who end up in this situation."

Marina was not about to change her mind or opinion. "Greg wanted her to have an abortion and she refused. She would have stayed a single parent, but no, you wouldn't hear of it. You insisted he marry her, for God's sake. He doesn't even love her, but you wouldn't listen."

Frank reached his level of tolerance, and he was going to put a stop to this. He advanced toward her in three swift steps. "I will only say this one more time and then I don't ever want to hear of this again." She looked away but did not move.

"I mean what I say so you'd better listen." His voice was loud again as he stepped in front of her. "You can't expect a devout Catholic to abort a baby. That's totally against what they believe. In their minds they might as well be separated from God. It is an unforgivable sin to them."

Marina raised her shoulders back and held her head haughtily. "Oh, she was a real good Catholic girl, now wasn't she." She laughed maliciously.

"Like you're a saint." Frank glared at her scornfully until she looked away. "I think Sarah was very gracious not to expect Greg to marry her, but it's his responsibility. Bringing a child into the world comes with a lifetime commitment. I didn't force Greg to marry her. Like I could force Greg to do anything. He was man enough to own up to what he did. Love has nothing to do with it. If you remember, I didn't love you either. Greg will learn to love Sarah through the years like I've learned to love you."

Marina's almond shaped eyes narrowed to a squint, glaring at Frank with contempt. "Is that what you call this, love? Look at us Frank! For once in your life take a good look around you."

She was right. There wasn't any love left in this marriage. Whatever love he felt for her once, died a long time ago. Marina killed any chance they might have had. She knew it, but would never admit her part in the destruction of their marriage.

Frank was exhausted from being on a merry-go-round which was destined to never stop. "I'm not doing this, Marina. Our son's wedding is tomorrow. What's done is done and you have to accept this."

Her face had become harder. No way in hell was she budging. The wedding was only hours away and Frank was not going to let Marina ruin Sarah's day. Marina had made his life miserable, and as long as he was alive, he would not let her do the same thing to Greg and Sarah.

Without a word, Marina stepped around Frank. She picked up her London Fog coat and imitation alligator purse off the recliner and walked toward the front door. At the hallway mirror she checked her makeup and hair. Then she yelled up the stairs toward Greg's room in her sweetest voice. "Greg, it's time to go. We'll be waiting in the car."

She buttoned her coat and put on her gloves, and turned back to Frank who watched her every move. With her gloved hand around the tarnished door knob, she spoke in an arrogant tone. "Brace yourself, darling. This will be one evening you won't forget." In an instant she disappeared into the cold, black night, slamming the door behind her.

Chapter Three

The door bell rang at 7:15. Sarah stood quietly at the top of the stairs unnoticed by her mother who hurriedly checked her appearance in the entry way mirror. Catherine smoothed her French twist and bit her bottom lip nervously. Poor mother, Sarah thought to herself as she sympathized with Catherine. There is no way she could ever prepare herself for Greg's mother.

Sarah felt a little guilty for not telling more than she did. The few times Greg had taken Sarah to his house the experience was anything but joyful. Marina had been openly rude and harsh. In addition to her own encounter with Greg's mother and everything he had told her, she knew Marina was a ruthless, cold and uncaring person except for her obsessive love of her son.

Unaware of her own actions, Sarah drew a deep breath along with her mother as Catherine opened the door. "Good evening, Mr. and Mrs. Winslow, Greg. Please come in." Catherine graciously extended her hand. "I hope you didn't have any trouble finding our place. When the nights are this dark the roads can be almost invisible."

"We found your house okay, though the roads were kind of slick. Had to drive slower." Frank took her hand in his and shook it warmly.

"Let me take your coats," Catherine said.

Sarah came slowly down the stairs, noticing how Marina's eyes widened when she looked around at the surroundings, especially the crystal chandelier that hung down from the twenty foot ceiling. Her parents had exquisite taste and even though Sarah saw the decor everyday, she knew the house was impressive. But she doubted Marina would ever admit she was impressed.

Josephine, the Matthew's housekeeper, came up quietly behind Catherine. "I'll take those for you, ma'am."

"Thank you, Josephine," Catherine said.

"Hello, everybody," Sarah spoke sweetly and approached their guests.

"You look lovely, Sarah." Frank stepped over to her and kissed her lightly on the cheek.

"Thank you, Mr. Winslow." She blushed slightly.

"None of this Mr. Winslow stuff. It's Frank." He smiled warmly at her.

Catherine led them into the den, calling, "Alex, the Winslows are here." Alex came into the den and extended his hand. Sarah wished her mother could be more relaxed like her father.

Not visible to anyone, Frank put his fingers in Marina's back and nudged her to take Alex's hand. Awkwardly she put forth her hand, barely grasping his. Her handshake was cool like her stare.

"Why don't we have a drink before dinner?" Alex said, walking over to the wet bar. Frank chose a large overstuffed chair by the fireplace while Marina sat on the forest green leather couch away from him.

"Sounds great," Frank said enthusiastically.

Sarah was glad to see that Frank seem to feel so at ease in her home. Although she didn't live at the Winslow house, she knew the atmosphere here was probably a nice change for him.

"What's your pleasure?" Alex asked.

"Bourbon will be fine," Frank said.

"Bourbon! When do you ever drink bourbon, Frank?" Marina sneered at her husband and then turned her attention to Catherine and Alex. "Frank's a beer drinker. Our refrigerator at home is full of beer. Well, it's full until Frank empties it. Then he has to go out again to restock it. Isn't that right, honey?"

Heat began to rise at the base of Frank's neck. He tensed as he pulled the collar away from his neck. He spoke with a forced calmness and managed to laugh. "Marina, likes to exaggerate. We kid each other about whether I spend more money on beer than she does on cigarettes."

Sarah bit down on her lip to keep from laughing out loud. She wished she could get off the couch and go pat Frank on the back. Marina's attempt to embarrass her husband back fired right in her face. Greg had told Sarah his mother didn't like anyone to know she smoked, let alone the fact she was a chain smoker.

"I guess we all have our vices." Catherine laughed lightly with Frank while Alex continued to pour the drinks.

"Yes, we all have our vices." Marina smiled, showing straight, white teeth, though not a true perception of the fangs they represented, Sarah thought.

Frank shifted his weight as Alex handed him the bourbon. "Thanks." Silence briefly fell upon the room while drinks were tasted and everyone attempted to make themselves comfortable. Frank held onto his glass while balancing it on the arm of the chair as he looked around the room. "Mrs. Matthews, you have a charming home. I can see by the furnishings that you have a good eye for color."

"Thank you, and please call me Catherine. No need for formalities. After all, tomorrow we'll be somewhat like family."

Marina leaned forward suddenly with her hand across her mouth and coughed repeatedly.

"That's right. Family." Frank repeated and flashed a wide grin at Marina. Her eyes watered while she continued to cough. Sarah knew what a perfectionist Marina was about her appearance and how embarrassed she would be if her mascara began to run.

Alex looked over to Marina, already standing, ready to assist her. "Would some water help?"

"No, thank you. I'm fine." Marina wiped the corners of her eyes and leaned back into the couch. Sarah wished she was sitting anywhere but next to her future mother-in-law. Being this close made her very uncomfortable. She felt like Marina watched her every move, waiting for her to make a mistake.

Marina crossed her shapely legs and placed a well manicured hand on her knee. "That's a lovely fragrance you're wearing." She addressed Sarah insincerely. "It becomes you. What's it called?" Marina's cold eyes looked hard into Sarah's soft emerald ones.

With excellent posture, Sarah held her own and said, "It's the newest fragrance from Elizabeth Taylor's collection. It's called "Passion."

Marina leaned forward to pick up her drink and began to sip. Giving her attention back to Sarah, she spoke in a condescending tone. "Passion. How appropriate. Your and Greg's passion is what brought all of us here together tonight."

"Marina, that will be enough!" Frank leaned forward in his chair and gave her a look that made Sarah glad she was not on the receiving end.

Marina looked indigent. "I didn't mean anything by it and had no intention of offending anyone." Before anybody else could speak, she looked at Sarah with a forced, tight lipped smile. "Sarah, dear. If I offended you, I apologize."

Totally composed, Sarah looked straight at her and spoke with maturity. "No I wasn't offended. It's no secret as to what brought all of us together."

Even though she handled the situation very well, there was tension in the room. Sarah was thankful, yet relieved when her father spoke up.

"There's no harm done. I think I can speak for all of us when I say this is an awkward situation for our two families. Difficult as it may be, what's done is done and I think we should try and make the best of this for our kid's sake."

Sarah so admired her father. She knew how hard this was on him and she was proud at how he was handling the whole thing. She threw him a "thanks, Daddy, you're the best" look when he glanced her way. Alex had been, and would probably always be her hero.

Frank eased his way through the tension like walking through fog. "So, Sarah are you getting nervous with your wedding only being a few hours away?"

Marina butted in before anyone had a chance to stop her. She looked at Sarah with the same cold, indifferent eyes. "Yes, you must be beside yourself with so many details to think about. You know when Frank and I got married, thanks to my mother, I didn't have to bother with all those worrisome details. Why, you must be especially worried, wondering if your dress will look tight."

Out of the corner of her eye, Sarah saw the stern look on Frank's face when he looked harshly at Marina. But she doubted Marina cared. She was obviously enjoying herself in her efforts to humiliate Sarah, and no one, especially Frank was going to take this piece of satisfaction away from her.

With a pleasant expression froze on her face, Sarah looked only at Marina though she felt all eyes on her. No matter what this woman tried to do, Sarah was determined to get along. She knew Marina blamed her entirely for the pregnancy, yet she hoped when the baby came, a healing would come also.

"Thank you for asking, but everything is just perfect. I haven't had much time to worry. Mom's been so wonderful to take care of every detail. And my dress fits fine."

Alex winked at Sarah when she looked over at him. She refrained from smiling for she didn't want to add any fuel to Marina's fire. Her Daddy played all kinds of mind games in the courtroom and Marina was just another small fish in a big pond. Sarah could hold her own for she had a good teacher.

Saved by the bell, Sarah thought, as Josephine entered the room to announce dinner was ready. Marina was the first to rise and follow Josephine with Sarah and Greg next to her side. As the housekeeper led the way toward the dining room, Sarah became upset though she didn't visibly show any signs, when she saw the way Marina looked at Josephine. Just because she was short and heavy, and waddled slightly did not give Marina the right to look at her like she was a pathetic creature. You're not that attractive, Sarah thought, noticing how her future mother-in-law smiled at her own slender reflection as she passed by a mirror.

Alex was seated at the head of the table with Frank sitting on his right side. Marina sat next to her husband, but only in body. Sarah wondered, how could you could live with someone and completely ignore him. There wasn't any emotion between them, like two strangers passing in the night. Marina only spoke to Frank when he addressed her, and her tone was anything but friendly.

Sarah liked Frank. He was easy to talk to and seemed genuine. His face had a hardness that softened when he smiled. She watched her father and Frank as they talked to each other. Both men were handsome in different ways. Frank's sandy blond hair combed straight back accented his hazel eyes, while her Daddy's dark brown wavy hair made his blue eyes appear darker than they were.

How Frank ended up with Marina, who was nothing like him, was a total mystery to Sarah. It was apparent she took great measures with her appearance. Her makeup was flawless although she wore too much. Sarah had to admit she was an attractive woman, but her eyes were cold, void of compassion and kindness. There was a darkness about Marina which was eerie.

"So, Frank, Sarah tells me you manage an automotive shop," Alex said before he took a bite of clam chowder.

"Yes, I'm the supervisor over at Rykers Auto Repair. Been there twenty three years. Started working there while I was a senior in high school," Frank said proudly.

"That's pretty impressive. Shows a lot of stability. Something you don't see much of anymore." Alex smiled as he savored the flavor.

"Kind of have to be stable when you don't have experience doing anything else." Marina said mockingly and continued to eat her chowder.

Catherine's face was aghast as she looked at Marina. Sarah could not understand why a wife would want to embarrass her husband like this, to try and humiliate him. She felt sorry for Frank.

"Frank, you must be a very good mechanic. I bet after twenty three years there's not a car you can't fix." Catherine smiled earnestly at Frank with a twinkle in her eye. Sarah was glad when her mother spoke up. Frank was a guest in their home and she figured her mother felt obligated to defend him even if it was against his own wife.

"You ever have a problem with your car, I'd be happy to look at it for you. No charge, of course." Frank looked pleased and grateful.

The dinner of roasted pheasant and wild rice was divine. Conversation was light while everyone relished the meal. Marina seem to examine everything on the table. She acted like she was an art dealer. Sarah could tell Marina's manner bothered her mother even though she didn't show it.

"Catherine, I've been admiring your dishes. This is the best imitation of Wedgwood china I've ever seen. Where did you ever find these?" There was an unmistakable challenge in Marina's voice.

Slowly putting her fork down on her plate, Catherine picked up her glass and sipped the wine. "Well actually, they're real, not that it matters. I liked the dishes and I got them at a good price." Sarah could see that her mother was trying to remain civil, but she heard the irritation in her mother's voice.

With a cynical laugh, Marina said, "Well, we both know what's a good price to you would be an extravagance for me." She took a drink of her wine and gloated.

Alex's hand found its way under the table to his wife's hand. She subtlety gritted while his thumb rubbed the top of her hand. "If everyone is finished why don't we go back into the den."

Frank looked relieved and stood up. "Catherine, dinner was great. I can't remember when I've had a home cooked meal as good as this one. It was a real treat."

"You act like I never cook. Just the other night I made a delicious brisket." Marina's eyes were blazing at Frank.

Sarah was a little surprised when Greg spoke out. All through dinner he had been fairly quiet. He answered questions when spoken to, but he seemed to be almost observing everyone as though he were studying them under a microscope. He was pleasant enough to her parents, but he kept his distance from them at the same time. This was not the first time she had noticed this when he was around them. When she asked him about it, he just said it took him awhile to get to know people and open up.

Sarah remembered thinking how strange his answer was, because all the times they were out on dates, Greg was the life of the party where ever they were. She had told herself he was probably uncomfortable around her parents because of the situation with the baby.

"Mom, you don't hardly ever cook. We order in most of the time or go pick up something," Greg said matter-of-factly.

Marina turned on Greg with hostility. She was angry and all eyes were watching and waiting. "I didn't hear anyone asking for your opinion and you're never home to see if I cook or not." She turned back around before he could respond.

Greg attempted to lead Sarah off to the den, but she stood firm. "I wonder why I'm never home." Sarah knew Marina heard him though she acted like she didn't.

A little more composed, Marina's voice was so sweet to the point of being sickening. "Yes, it was a good dinner, but Catherine and I both know, anyone can have a spectacular meal on the table every night if you have someone else to prepare it."

Her mother was a gracious, elegant woman who had dealt with all sorts of people in her charity work. She was kind and caring, but she could be tough when she had to. When Catherine opened her mouth to speak, Sarah was not sure if the gracious, elegant woman was going to answer, or would the woman who could hold her own retaliate. But for right now she wouldn't find out for as her father stepped away from the table he whispered something in her mother's ear. She was not able to hear, but whatever he whispered kept her mother from saying anything at all.

With a closed-lipped smile, Catherine followed Alex out of the dining room, accompanied by Frank and Marina. Sarah looked at Greg bewildered as they also followed everyone to the den.

The remainder of the evening conversation was focused on the wedding. The antique grandfather clock chimed 10:30 and Frank covered a long, suppressed yawn with the back of his hand. "I guess we better get going. Tomorrow is a big day for all of us and it's getting late." Alex and Catherine rose from the loveseat as Frank walked toward them. He shook both their hands warmly and said, "Thanks for a wonderful evening. You've made us feel so welcome and at home. After the wedding is over and things get back to normal, we'll have you over for dinner."

"We'd love to come," Catherine said sincerely.

Alex put his arm around his wife's shoulders as he spoke to Frank and Marina. "Speaking for the both of us, I want to thank you for being so kind to Sarah and accepting her into your family. That means a lot to us. I know the circumstances have been somewhat awkward, but our kids can't lose with the four of us helping them, now can they?" Alex words were more of a plea than a statement.

Frank nodded his head in agreement and turned to face Marina. A spoken word was not necessary for his eyes said enough. She stepped forward as if undertaking a grim task. "Thank you for an interesting evening." She was nonchalant and turned to Greg, speaking in an authoritative way. "Greg, come on. It's late and you need to get a good night's rest to prepare yourself for tomorrow."

Sarah saw Greg's jaw tighten and his eyes narrowed. When he spoke, the irritation was evident in his voice. "Good God, Mom, you act as if I'm going before a firing squad."

Marina threw Greg a look she was famous for and then glared at Sarah for a second. Sara did not blame Greg for ignoring his mother as he turned his attention to her parents. "Thanks for the meal. The food was great." Greg shook Alex's hand but avoided eye contact with him while he gave Catherine his most captivating smile.

Taking Sarah by the hand he said, "Walk me to the car." His tone was short and it surprised Sarah. Alex cast Greg a harsh look which did not surprise Sarah either. She knew how her father felt about Greg and anything he might say or do in a negative way wouldn't set well with her Daddy.

Outside the air was brisk and cold. Patches of ice were on the sidewalk and Sarah slipped trying to keep up with Greg. If she had not had a hold of his arm, she would have fallen. "Greg, please slow down. The sidewalk is slick. I almost fell. Remember the baby." The wind was freezing and it was hard to catch her breath.

"Like I could forget." Greg mumbled the words and continued a little slower down the brick steps toward the car.

Sarah was out of breath when they reached the car. She stood next to Greg trying to shield the wind. She spoke between short breaths. "Why are you in such a hurry?" The moon was not out and the only visible light was from the porch light which was a good distance from them. Between the dark and the wind which blew Greg's straight dark brown hair across his face, Sarah was not able to see what was in his eyes.

"God, I can't stand them!" His voice was angry, and she knew he was referring to his parents. Rarely he spoke of his parents, but when he did, it was always with malice.

"I know things were a little tense in there a couple of times. But I thought everyone handled it okay," Sarah said with reassurance and took hold of his hand, squeezing gently.

"A little tense!" Greg jerked his hand from hers and turned to face her. He was so close she could feel his breath. "You don't have a clue, do you? Maybe that's a little tense for your family, but not mine. What went on tonight was mild compared to what goes on at my house." Bitterness coated his every word.

Sarah shivered as the wind whipped around her body. She wanted to go back to the house, but she couldn't leave Greg like this. "Sometimes people say things they don't mean. Even my mom says her and Daddy have had their share of problems, but they've worked through them." Sarah reached for his hand, but he pulled away and shoved his hands in his coat pockets.

"Don't be so stupid! I'm not talking about words that hurt here, Sarah. You don't get it, do you?" Greg look hard at her and then up toward the front door as his parents came out. "Never mind. It doesn't matter." He sounded hopeless and her heart went out to him.

"This does matter and you didn't have to call me stupid. I want to understand, but how can I if you shut me out?" Sarah grasped his arm and held tight so he couldn't pull away.

"Maybe stupid was the wrong word. More like naive. You live in a dream world. You think everyone's family is like yours. They're not." Greg was not as angry now, but the hardness was still present. He leaned back against his parent's car crossing his arms which forced Sarah to let go of him.

"We're getting married tomorrow. Please don't let tonight ruin our wedding. This will be the last night you'll live with your parents. I'm going to make you happy, Greg. You'll see." She tried to be affectionate and kiss him, but he remained cold and indifferent and turned his head away. Hurt by his rejection, Sarah stepped back. Throughout their relationship Greg had never treated her this way until now. His behavior troubled her and she was not sure what to say to him. "I'm going back to the house." She paused for him to reply, but he kept silent. "I'll see you tomorrow. I love you." With tears in her eyes, she made her way cautiously back up the steps to the house.

Halfway up the steps, Sarah turned and looked down at Greg who was still leaning against the car with his head down. Her heart wanted to go back to him even though he pushed her away. She would find a way to break through the walls he built to shut her and everyone else out. The voices on the porch drew her focus back to the house and she continued slowly up the steps.

"Sarah, wait. I'll come help you." She stopped as Alex made his way down the steps to her side. His strong arm went protectively around her waist, leading her up the steps. "Greg shouldn't have let you come back to the house by yourself. You could've fallen." He looked straight ahead, but she knew he was angry. She did not blame him though. Her father was only concerned.

When they reached the front walkway Frank and Marina were about to step off the porch. "Be careful. The sidewalk is slippery. The winding road down the cliff is probably going to be worse. They can be treacherous this time of year. I don't believe the sand trucks have been out yet to cover the ice," Alex warned.

"Thanks for the warning. We'll be careful." Frank waved and started to descend the steps. He tried to put his hand under Marina's arm, but she jerked away.

The Matthews waved once more to the Winslows before they went into the house. "This is one night I wouldn't want to relive anytime soon." Catherine said and turned off the entry way lights. Sarah didn't notice until now how tired her mother looked. Life had been so hectic that it never occurred to her what toil this affair had taken on her mother. After tonight she was probably emotionally tired as well as physically exhausted.

"Yeah, this has been a long night," Alex said, kissing Sarah goodnight.

"Mom, Daddy, thanks for everything. I don't know what I would've done without the two of you. You guys have been amazing through this whole thing and I just want to say how much I love both of you." Sarah wrapped her arms around both of her parents neck and hugged them.

"We love you too, darling. Now you run off to bed. Don't worry about waking up too early. We don't have to be at your hair appointment until 10:30." You try and get a good night's sleep. You have a big day ahead of you tomorrow," Catherine said kindly.

Alex and Catherine watched their daughter go up the stairs. When she reached the top, Sarah turned and looked down at her parents. The only light on was a dim light above the landing, but she could faintly see them with their arms around each other.

The house was quiet, and Sarah stood still to listen to the ocean, who was a silent friend she had come to depend on throughout the years. The sea was a constant reminder of how it never changed even when life around her did. Tears welled up in Sarah's eyes as she turned and walk away. She would be gone from this house after tonight, but not from her family's lives. For as each day passed with the setting of the sun, the night promised to bring forth a new day with hope of a fresh beginning.

Chapter Four

The peaceful morning came to an end when Carter and Will Matthews came barreling through the front door. The hour was 8:00 and the only ones up were Josephine and the family dog, Butch.

The brothers, were fourteen-year old identical twins and for the most part, inseparable. They were tall like their father, measuring 5'11" and still growing. They had their father's dark wavy hair, but their eyes were green like Sarah's though more transparent. The boys loved sports and it showed in their athletic physiques.

Josephine came out of the kitchen with a stern look on her face. "You boys be quiet. Everyone is still asleep. What on earth are you two doing home so early? When do sleep-overs finish at 8:00 in the morning?" Will was the first to burst out with laughter at her appearance. Flour was all over her face and apron, a dead give away of the homemade biscuits she had made.

"Ah come on, Josie." Carter looked at her with a sad, beat down expression. "You're not really mad at us, are you?"

No matter how hard she tried, she couldn't really get mad at the boys. "And besides," Will whispered, "everyone needs to get up." Just as softly as he had whispered, he then shouted at the top of his manly voice, "Sarah's getting married today!"

Carter immediately began to chant just as loud, "Sarah's getting married, Sarah's getting married!" Both boys and Josephine were laughing and playing with Butch when Sarah came down the stairs rubbing her eyes. She wore a white satin nightgown overlaid with lace her grandmother made for her when she turned sixteen. Her long auburn hair was tousled and hung loosely around her face. Sarah stood on the stairs unnoticed as she watched her brothers. Even though they were almost four years younger, Sarah stayed close to them. She attended all their sport events, helped them with their homework, and gave sisterly advice when needed.

She would miss hearing their loud voices in the morning and the way they teased her about the recipes she tried out on the family's stomachs. A little teary eyed, Sarah pushed her hair back over her shoulders and walked down the stairs.

"Good morning, Josie." Sarah leaned forward and planted a kiss on her forehead. "Can't you two monsters ever learn to be quiet in the morning!" She laughed and pinched both their cheeks.

"Oh, Sis, we are what we are," Will said like he was hurt.

"Come on, all you ragamuffins. Into the kitchen and help me finish breakfast."

Obediently, the siblings followed her to the kitchen. The white marble floor in the open foyer was cold beneath Sarah's bare feet and she welcomed the warmth from the kitchen fireplace.

"I'm making Sarah's favorite breakfast foods, chocolate chip pancakes covered with maple syrup and whipped cream. I've stirred up some homemade biscuits with gravy and sausage links on the side topped off with freshly squeezed orange juice." Josephine beamed at the pure delight on their faces.

"Josie, you didn't have to go to all this trouble for me, but I'm sure glad you did."

Sarah hugged the woman affectionately like she would her own mother.

"Honey, there isn't anything I wouldn't do for you, "Josephine said and patted the young woman on the back.

"Hey, what's all this racket in here? You'd think someone was getting married or something." Alex said teasingly when he and Catherine came through the door.

There was laughter and talking while the family sat around the table to enjoy the celebration feast Josephine prepared. This would be a memorable morning for the Matthews and they wanted to cherish every second. Breakfast time had always been an important event when everyone was together. As the children grew older, it became more difficult to be together at meal time. So Catherine started a tradition where at least they shared breakfast as a family.

Sarah rested her chin on her hand and gazed out the window. The upper part of the window was stained glass and the sun shone brightly through, awakening the colorful prisms as they danced across the wall. The kitchen/breakfast room was her favorite room in the house. There was not any wall in front of the solid oak kitchen table, only a window which allowed the full beauty of the ocean to be seen in all of its glory. The fireplace was warm and inviting with glowing embers. In the warmer months, the French doors were opened to permit the cool breeze from the ocean to flow freely through the house.

Sarah and her mother had shared private times in this room. There were tears and laughter, serious and silly moments that brought them close together. As a young child, Sarah had accompanied her mother when she did volunteer work at the Dale Evans School for children with Down Syndrome. With a tender heart like her mother, her love for the special children grew over the years. When she turned sixteen she made her mother proud by becoming a volunteer.

She already longed in her heart for what she knew would change. A part of her was ready to grow up, but another part yearned to stay a child protected by her parents' loving environment. She was determined to raise her child the way she had been raised. Her mistake was not her parent's fault. She had decided to make a wrong choice even when she knew it was not right. Unfortunately, making a wrong choice not only hurt her, but the people she loved the most.

Sarah looked up at the clock on the wall as the bells chimed 9:00. In nine hours she would walk down the aisle. She had numerous appointments throughout the day, which began with her hair appointment.

With hands clasped behind his head, Alex leaned back in his chair. "So, what's on my two girl's agenda today?" Alex asked, winking at his wife and daughter.

Sarah's eyes twinkled when she looked at her father, for she knew he was hoping he wouldn't be needed. The wedding plans seemed endless and they were all ready for them to be over.

"Sarah and I just have girl things to do today. Things that would only bore you. You and the boys do whatever you like. But don't forget. We must be at the church no later than 4:00. The photographer wants to start taking pictures by 5:00, so we need to be dressed and ready to go."

"Okay, okay, I can take a hint. I know when I'm not wanted." Alex said with a rejected tone to his voice, but Sarah knew he was relieved he did not have to go. He kissed wife and daughter good-bye and left the kitchen to go upstairs to get dressed.

Josephine scooted the rest of the family out of the kitchen except for Sarah. She was busy cleaning up the kitchen and Sarah could not figure out why she had wanted her to stay. Time was slipping away and she knew Josephine had some errands to run before she had to be at the church. As the last dish was put away, Josephine opened the door to let Butch out into the backyard where he could find warmth in his heated kennel. She closed the door against a strong wind which blew through the kitchen.

Sarah laughed as napkins and papers flew off the countertop. Her and Josephine squatted down to pick up the things when Sarah saw the tears flowing down the woman's face. "Josie, what's wrong? This is supposed to be a happy day." She put her arm around Josephine's shoulders and knelt beside her.

"Oh, honey. I'm so sorry. I told myself I wasn't going to do this." She wiped her face with her hands and then placed her hand on top of Sarah's hand. "I'm just going to miss you so much. You know I was here when your parents brought you home from the hospital. I had just come to work for your family shortly before you were born. You were so tiny and helpless. I knew the minute I saw you that I wanted to watch you grow up, so I stayed on all these years and here I am getting ready to watch you get married." She sniffled again as Sarah squeezed her hand.

"Now you're going to make me cry. I'm going to miss you too. You've been like a second mother to me." Tears welled up in Sarah's eyes as they embraced. They stayed in each others arms and remained silent as they held one another. Sarah always knew when the time came to leave home, this day would be difficult, but she did not realize until now how much the separation would hurt.

Sarah gently released Josephine and kissed her on the cheek before she stood up. No words were exchanged, only faint smiles between the two. Sarah turned and left the kitchen. She felt like she was being pulled apart by two worlds that she wanted to be a part of both. If she could only get through this day without falling to pieces emotionally, Sarah knew she could take one day at time to adjust to her new life.

With determination, Sarah went up the stairs ready to face life and all the changes she would encounter each day. For she knew in her heart that strength and courage would carry her through and that was all she could ask for.

The car door rattled after Marina slammed it shut. This had been a stressful day so far but she had not expected it to be any different. The hairdresser kept her way too long and her hair still was not fixed the way she wanted. She could have done a better job herself and now she was going to have to redo it. Incompetent people annoyed her and patience was not a virtue she possessed.

The front door stuck, only adding to her irritation because Frank promised to fix it weeks ago. With a final push from her shoulder, the door flew open. Marina kicked her shoes off at the door and took cigarettes out of her hand bag before tossing the purse onto the couch. She sat down in the recliner and put her feet up while she lit her cigarette. Frank hated smoke in the house, but he was at work and she would have the room aired out before he returned. Not that she cared what he thought, but she was not in the mood to fight with him. With closed eyes she inhaled deeply. She tried to block the wedding out of her mind without success. She didn't know how she was going to get through this evening. Frank warned her more than once not to cause a scene.

She had tried to reason with her son, but he wouldn't listen, not this time. Marina had made a mistake in marrying Frank, and Greg was about to do the same thing. Frank was not who she thought he was when she married him. His only ambition to be a mechanic and work for someone else did little to benefit them for the past twenty years. They lived on a measly salary in a small house in the older part of Seaside Cove.

Inhaling the last ounce of nicotine, Marina raised herself from the recliner. With no enthusiasm, she opened the two windows in the living room. There was enough breeze today which would quickly draw the smoke out of the room. Marina heard Frank's truck back fire as the vehicle pulled into the driveway, warning her he was home unexpected. She should have known he would be home early today. Quickly she grabbed her cigarettes and ash tray and hurried up the stairs. She was in no mood to talk to him and she hated the way he smelled of grease when he came home from work. The offensive odor was just another reminder of one more thing she despised about her husband.

More than once she had entertained the idea of leaving Frank and this dismal life behind, but had stayed for Greg's sake. But now, that was no longer an obstacle she had to contend with. She smiled at the thought of Frank as he would come through the front door to find her gone. No explanation, just gone. The thought lifted her spirits and she hummed a Frank Sinatra tune as she closed the bathroom door.

The maintenance man let Catherine and Sarah in at the back of the church. The time was 4:15 and the florist had arrived only minutes earlier. The smell of gardenias filled the air with an intoxicating fragrance. These flowers were to be placed throughout the church in various arrangements. Sarah had wanted her wedding to be special in every way, and her mother's creativity was put into each detail.

The hallway which led to the designated dressing room was in the opposite direction of where the main sanctuary was located. When she realized how far she would have to walk in her wedding dress with her long train, Sarah hoped the floors were clean. The thought of her gown soiled with dirt horrified her. She bent down running her fingers along the smooth floor, relieved when she turned her fingers over to find no evidence of dirt or dust.

The lights hadn't been turned on yet, and upon entering the room, Sarah stepped back and let out a gasp. She had come in contact with what appeared to be a ghostly figure, but when Catherine flipped on the light switch she saw that her apparent ghost was a faceless mannequin that wore her ivory cream Victorian wedding dress.

"You definitely have the wedding jitters." Catherine laughed and carefully moved the mannequin out of the way.

"I guess I'm more nervous than I thought." Sarah sat down at the dressing table and stared at her reflection. With her hair pulled up in a cascade of curls, she appeared to be older than her mere eighteen years. To become a woman was not an easy transition, for in some ways she still felt like a child. Sarah looked deep into her own eyes in search of herself. This was a moment of truth. Time had prepared her for today and she was ready to be Greg's wife and a mother to her unborn child.

Catherine walked up behind Sarah and placed a string of pearls around her neck and hooked the tiny clasp. Sarah's fingers gently touched the delicate pearls. "Oh, Mother, they're lovely!" Her emerald eyes sparkled as she admired them.

"I wanted you to have these and I was waiting for the right time. These were your great grandmother's and your grandmother gave them to me on my wedding day and now it's my turn to give them to you." Catherine leaned over and kissed her daughter on the cheek.

Sarah held her mother's hand for she knew if she spoke, the tears she fought to hold back would flow freely. No words were necessary as Catherine looked into Sarah's misty eyes. Carefully the wedding gown was removed from the mannequin. Catherine held it up so Sarah could step into the dress. The last button was fastened when there was a knock on the door. Catherine opened the door and did not recognize the young man who stood there.

"Hi, I'm Ben Seiler, the photographer." He smiled and held out his hand. "I can see the bride is almost ready, " he said looking over Catherine's shoulder.

Catherine shook his hand warmly. "Yes, she's just about ready."

"If everyone else is here, we can get started in about fifteen minutes, if that's okay with you?" Ben asked.

"Yes, that will be fine. I will go round up everyone and meet you in the sanctuary."

Catherine walked down the hall as Ben shifted the camera strap that hung on his shoulder.

Ben glanced at Sarah before he turn to leave. He had taken pictures of all types of brides, but he would have to say this one stood out far above the others. She had a quality about her he had not seen before. Her face was angelic which illuminated a brilliant countenance. She was a vision of loveliness which had stepped out of the Victorian past with all the elegance and charm it possessed. As he walked away he wondered if the guy she was marrying realized how lucky he was. Also, did she have a sister?

Chapter Five

Frank sat patiently on a piano bench and watched Marina while she fidgeted with Greg's white rose boutonniere. Fingers prodded and pulled the baby's breath in an effort to get the small flowers to lay a certain way. His weight shifted from one foot to the other while he glared at his mother with irritation. Marina managed to avoid eye contact with her son in an attempt to unpin the flower from his black tuxedo jacket.

"Mom, leave it alone!" Greg yelled as he jerked away from her. "The rose looked fine until you started to mess with the stupid thing." He faced the floor length mirror to straighten out his lapel.

"Marina, leave the boy alone." Frank pulled his shirt collar away from his neck for the top button was choking him.

"I just want him to look perfect." Marina looked at her son with admiration. He was quite handsome and she told people he got his good looks from her side of the family.

Greg turned away from the mirror and said mockingly, "I like the way I look and what matters is that Sarah will too."

It was obvious from the hardness that invaded Marina's eyes that she understood her son's message loud and clear, but she had a message of her own to deliver. With narrowed eyes she stepped toward him and said angrily, "Don't you get smart with me. I am still your mother and you will treat me with respect! I brought you into this miserable world and raised you. Just because you're going to marry that tramp out there doesn't mean you can discard me like your old football!"

Greg tensed as his fingers clenched into a fist. With eyes like a rabid dog he raised his shoulders back and lashed out at his mother. "Don't you ever say that again! Who are you to call Sarah a whore!" The fire in Greg's eyes matched Marina's, whose hand raised to strike his face.

On impulse Frank swiftly got out of his chair and grabbed Marina's wrist. He stepped between the two of them in the line of fire. "Marina, stop!"

"Are you going to just stand there and let your son talk to me that way!" Her face was red and she made it evident that she had no intention of backing down.

"Keep your voice down. Do you want all the guests to hear?" Frank said with a lowered voice.

Marina jerked her wrist out of his grasp. Tiny beads of perspiration formed across her forehead while she fanned herself with her hand. "Answer me! Are you going to let him talk to me that way!"

"What do you expect after what you said about your son's bride. How is he supposed to react!" Frank tried unsuccessfully to stay calm.

"Be a father for once and make him show me some respect. I'm his mother and I deserve his respect!" Marina spoke angrily. She blotted her forehead, careful not to smear her makeup.

"Now you want me to step in and be the father," Frank said sarcastically. "He is twenty years old, molded in your image and now I'm supposed to undo all the damage you've done!" Frank looked at Marina, his eyes full of bitterness.

"Shut up! Both of you, just shut up! You both make me sick!" Greg's face was altered by his hatred. "You want to talk about respect. I don't respect either one of you!" He focused his attention toward his mother and glared at her with hostility. "You've run over Dad my whole life with your control and your high and mighty attitude. What he did was never good enough for you!"

"And you!" Greg's hostility increased when he addressed his father. "You let Mom do whatever she wanted. Why didn't you stand up to her! You're not a man, you're a coward! Then when she pushed you too far, you hit her!" Greg laughed bitterly. "And I'm supposed to respect the two of you! Like the way you two respect each other. Is this one of life's lessons I'm supposed to learn? Well I certainly learned my lesson on respect, now didn't I." Greg gritted his teeth and walked out of the door, slamming it behind him.

With her lace gloved hand tucked securely around Alex's left arm, Sarah stood still in the hallway. Her head was in a whirlwind from all the commotion but thankful to be able to stand there, if only for a second. Carter and Will had run back and forth to report on the continued guests which had arrived.

This wedding was the talk of the town. Sarah's family had not intended for this to happen, but the wedding had become a society affair which attracted all of Seaside Cove's finest. Since her father owned a prestigious law firm and her mother headed up numerous charity bazaars and luncheons, the task to minimize the guest list had been somewhat difficult. Greg's family accounted for about one fourth of the guests which consisted of Frank's co-workers, family and a few friends.

The wedding coordinator, Mrs. Jamison, walked with quick steps, her high heels clicked up and down on the wood floor as she came down the hallway toward Sarah. "Five more minutes and you will need to make your way to the sanctuary. There are two granite pillars at the back of the sanctuary. This is an overflow section where you'll stand and wait until you're given the cue to walk down the aisle. The guests won't be able to see you while you watch the wedding procession. She spoke professionally, aware of every detail.

Mrs. Jamison's expertise fingers fluffed Sarah's veil and checked her appearance for anything amiss. "Well, Sarah, it's time." With a motherly smile she put her finger under Sarah's chin. "You look enchanting. Like you've stepped right off the pages of a fairytale."

Sarah took a deep breath and said, "I'm ready." Her left hand held a bouquet of white roses and baby's breath close to her midriff. Slowly she began to walk with her father close by her side. Upon approaching the sanctuary door she heard the most soothing music which flowed from the orchestra pit. The violins and flutes were like lovers who had become one in harmony. The music calmed her nerves while she waited at the pillars.

The wedding procession was perfect. The bridesmaids stepped in perfect time with the instrumental notes. As the music changed directions, Sarah stood very poised and felt somewhat more confident. The guests rose then, and turned toward the aisle to await her arrival. Except for the music, the room was quiet and motionless. All eyes were fixed upon her as she began her honored walk to the altar.

With each step she took, the aisle seem to grow longer. She felt her father's hand tightened over hers as they reached their final destination and stood before the priest. Her father's fingers trembled as he slowly lifted her veil. She held his eyes briefly before he kissed her on the cheek and then lowered her veil. Words could never express what her Daddy must have felt right now, but through his eyes, Sarah saw her father's heart. As Greg moved to stand by Sarah's side, Alex placed her hand into Greg's hand. It was a gesture they all understood.

Throughout the ceremony Sarah felt like she was on the outside looking in. She was here with Greg, but her heart was also with her Daddy. The vows were joining her and Greg, but they brought separation between her and her father. As Sarah turned toward her husband to proclaim her vows to give him her heart and to stand by his side throughout his life, she saw her father close his moist eyes as their marriage was sealed in Heaven, forever.

By 10:00 the band was winding down, even though some guests remained on the dance floor. The reception was almost over as everyone waited for the departure of the bride and groom. Carter and Will lingered by the food table and nibbled on the leftover cakes and finger foods. The boys were tired and ready for this wedding to be over. This had been a long day for the Matthews family.

Catherine removed her plum satin pumps and began to rub her feet. A long time had passed since she had danced and her aching feet were now paying the price. Even with the weariness her heart was happy. The wedding had gone splendidly, and Sarah looked radiant. Relieved that she could finally sit down for a moment, she looked over at her husband's empty chair. This day had been hard on him though he never let on.

For herself, Catherine felt as if she were blessed with an additional son into the family, but for Alex, he felt he had lost a daughter. As time passed, Catherine knew Alex would get used to idea of his daughter's marriage. Maybe if she were older than eighteen he might feel differently, but she doubted it. Change was not easy for her husband and he would have to adjust once again for soon they would be grandparents and another dimension would be added to their lives. Reluctantly, Catherine put her shoes back on and dragged herself to her feet to mingle with the guests.

The knock startled Sarah as she slipped out of her wedding dress. "Who is it?"

"It's Dad. May I come in?" Sarah and Greg laughed quietly as they hurriedly finished.

"Sure, but wait just a minute. We're almost ready." Alex rested against the wall to wait. What would he say to her? He had hoped to say good-bye to her without Greg's presence. As he pondered what to do, the door flew open.

"You can come in now," Sarah said.

Alex could see how happy they were. "I wanted to be the first to congratulate the new couple." He shook hands with Greg as Sarah wrapped her arms around Alex's neck.

"Sir, I can't thank you enough for all you've done for us. The wedding itself was wonderful and then to send us on a cruise ship to the Virgin Islands for our honeymoon."

"There's no need to say anything. The best thanks you could ever give me is to make Sarah happy and be a good husband." Alex looked at Greg, waiting to hear his reassuring words.

"Sir, you have nothing to worry about. I'll treat her like a queen." Greg sounded convincing enough, but Alex sensed there was something not right, although he could not put his finger on it. Greg was hard to read and he had a way of keeping everyone at a distance. After they returned from their honeymoon, Alex would make an effort to get to know him better, for Sarah's sake.

He didn't want to come across as a possessive father-in-law, so he asked politely instead of telling him. "Greg, would you mind if I borrowed your bride for a minute before you both leave?"

Greg grinned boyishly at Sarah and Alex. "Sure, no problem. I wanted to go tell my folks good-bye before I left. You know how mothers are." Alex somehow doubted that Greg was sentimental about anything, especially his mother.

Alex patted him on the back. "If I don't see you before you leave, have a great time."

"Thank you, sir, we will." Greg paused at the door and looked at Sarah before he left. Alex thought he remotely saw something distant in Greg's eyes, but then it vanished for Greg's grin revealed nothing before he walked out the door.

"Oh, Daddy, thank you so much. This has been a wonderful day." Sarah squeezed her father's neck tighter. Alex laughed and lifted her off her feet to hold her. She was feather light and he wanted to hold her forever.

"I can't hardly believe my little girl is a married woman." He released and held her at arms length to look at her. She glowed like a snowy mountain on a moonlit night. "You've become a lovely young woman, Sarah. Not just your outward appearance, but in your heart also. I hope Greg knows how lucky he is."

"Daddy, you're just prejudiced."

"Yes, I guess I am just a little." Alex smiled hugging her one more time. "But that's a father's right." He turned his head toward the music which floated through the door. The band was playing a Rod Stewart song for their final number. He stepped back with an extended hand out to Sarah. "Madam, may I have this dance?"

"How could a girl refuse such a charming, handsome gentlemen. Sir, I would be delighted." Sarah bowed gracefully and took her father's hand.

The dance was slow and Alex held his daughter close. "Do you remember the first time I taught you to dance?" His voice was soft as he reminisced.

"How could I forget. I walked all over your feet." Sarah laughed and laid her head against his shoulder. They were in perfect step together as the words of the song circled around them, Have I told, you, lately, that I love you. Have I told you, there's no one else, above you.

Alex's cheeks became moistened from the tears that fell from his sorrowful eyes. Neither one spoke as they moved with the music. Alex lifted his hand gently from her back and placed it on the back of her head while he stroked her hair. When the music came to an end, he held her quietly, continuing to sway back and forth. With his lips pressed against her hair, he whispered softly, "I love you with all of my heart, Sarah, forever."

Sarah stopped and lifted her face toward her father. She took his face in her delicate hands and kissed him tenderly on the cheek. With a sad smile she said affectionately, "Forever, Daddy."

Hand in hand she walked him over to the door. He opened the door and turned, looking into her glistened eyes. Slowly, he released her hand and looked at his daughter with a sad expression, although he knew their hearts were joined together by the love they shared for one another. Alex walked through the door saying to himself, "Forever."

Chapter Six

With the ship in full view, Greg and Sarah ran down the walk way which led to the entrance. "Sarah, hurry! We'll miss the boat!" Greg was out of breath as he pulled Sarah by her arm.

Unable to catch her breath, Sarah stopped. She tried to speak between breaths. "I can't go any faster. Besides they're not going to leave without us." Having taken two cruise vacations with her family, she knew there was time allowed for late comers.

Sweat rolled down Greg's face while perspiration stains formed on his polo shirt underneath his arms. With a nod of his head, Greg turned and led the way up the ramp followed by Sarah. Excitement filled the air as they boarded the Royal Princess. Passengers made their way to their assigned cabins with anticipation of dreams of grandeur.

As they were escorted up to the fifth level where the bridal cabin was located, Sarah couldn't help but notice the expression on Greg's face. The Royal Princess was the top of the line and she could tell her husband was impressed. When they reached their cabin, the purser stepped aside and opened the door. Alex had not discussed the accommodations, but knowing her father as she did, Sarah was not surprised with what she saw. The cabin was luxurious beyond belief and she was happy when she saw how pleased Greg looked.

"Man, oh man, your father sure knows how to do things right."

"Yes, he does." Sarah's voice was full of love and appreciation for her father.

Four times the size of a traditional cabin, their cabin was a suite which consisted of a large sitting room where fresh yellow roses adorned a round mosaic table. A king size captain's bed gave the bedroom a commanding presence. The bathroom was enhanced with the same yellow roses which sat on a marble vanity across from a double sized heart shaped Jacuzzi.

In front of a porthole window was a wet bar where a bottle of non-alcoholic champagne sat beside two champagne glasses.

"Greg, look." Sarah held up the bottle as he approached. "We're on our honeymoon, but too young to drink the real stuff." Not that she really cared. She had tasted champagne before and didn't care much for the stuff. The bubbles went up her nose which left a burning sensation. She set the bottle back down and laughed.

"Not a problem," Greg said proudly pulling his wallet out of his back pocket. Sarah was confused when he slid two laminated cards out from under his driver's license. He held the cards in front of her face where she could read the information clearly. The faces that stared back at her were hers and Greg's. Her eyes grew big as she gave Greg a puzzled look.

"Where did you get these?" Sarah didn't know quiet how to react.

"These babies are our tickets to independence. They're fake ID's. You didn't actually think we would come on this cruise and not live like adults, did you? We wouldn't have even been able to get into the casinos or all of the shows." His tone was condescending as he spoke to her.

"You don't have to speak to me like I'm a child. You should've told me before you got them. After all, I am your wife." Sarah crossed her arms and leaned against a wing back chair.

"Then I suggest you act like a wife. It's time to grow up and quit being so naive. Children don't get married. And besides, I'll be twenty-one in six months. You could say I'm celebrating early." Greg laughed and kissed the ID's.

"What if we get caught?" Sarah did not feel right about this and she was apprehensive. What would her parents think if they found out. She did not want to cause them any more disappointment than she already had.

"We won't get caught. They won't even question us." Greg looked at her with irritation. "Let's get ready for dinner."

She still wasn't convinced as he turned to head toward the bedroom and pulled off his shirt. She had hoped to eat dinner together in their cabin. They had spent their wedding night at the Sun Harbor, a fabulous resort hotel in Seaside Cove. Early that morning they had caught the red eye flight to Miami to board the Royal Princess which made for an exhausting two days. Reluctantly, she followed suit to take a quick shower and change her clothes.

The dining room was almost full when they arrived. Soft music blended with the sound of laughter, filling the room with gaiety. Heads turned as Sarah and Greg passed by. They were an attractive couple, well poised and neatly groomed. Dressed in an elegant white silk gown which draped her slender, shapely figure, she resembled a goddess.

Greg wore a pair of black dress slacks with a white dinner jacket. His hair was combed straight back which gave him a look of sophistication. With broad shoulders, a square jaw line, and the way he held his head high and slightly back, there was an arrogance about him. Sarah was proud to be on his arm, to be Mrs. Greg Winslow.

Dinner was exceptional and Sarah would have liked to linger and talk with the other passengers at the table. But Greg was anxious to hit the casinos and see a couple of the shows. They excused themselves as they rose and left the table.

There were three casinos on the ship and Greg wanted to go to all of them. The first casino they went to was full of people who were drunk or in the process of getting drunk. The lights were bright and flashy, and the music was so loud, Sarah could not even hear Greg talk. The slot machines were noisy and it didn't take long for the sound of clanging money to get on her nerves.

She grew weary while she watched Greg play the slot machines, so Sarah decided to find a table and sit down. Spotting one in a far corner, she made her way through the crowd with some effort. Bodies reeked of alcohol and smoke, making her feel queasy. Relieved to be removed from the inner circle, Sarah sat down and relaxed against the chair with her arm upon the table.

She looked at her wedding ring sparkle under the bright lights. The diamonds were small, but lovely. She knew Greg didn't have a lot of money and he bought her what he could afford. Even though she was raised in a family where there was a considerable amount of money, Sarah had been taught not to take money for granted and she had learned about wise investments and spending.

It made her uncomfortable to see Greg throw money away at the casino. The wedding present to her and Greg from his parents was money, but he'd never told her how much. But she was pretty sure the casino was getting a good chunk of it.

Tired of the foul smells and the loud noise, Sarah decided to take a walk around the deck. Some fresh air would do her a world of good. Greg remained steadfast in front of the one armed bandit, hypnotized, and she doubted he would even miss her. Her honeymoon was not going as she had hoped, but maybe she was expecting too much. A romantic at heart, Sarah had been enchanted with fairy tale love stories since she was thirteen.

The ship was enormous and it took her a while to find the deck. But the smell of the ocean guided her. Sarah ran her fingers along the railing as she walked toward the back of the ship. There was no one out here but her. But who would be out at 1:30 in the morning.

Sarah placed her chin in her hand while her elbow rested on the railing. She looked down into the depths of the ocean as the stalwart propellers glided the mighty ship through the powerful sea. The full moon glowed upon the water, giving the ocean an enchanted effect as a chandelier of stars shimmered across the luminous sky.

"The night's lovely, isn't it?"

Sarah jumped as she turned around.

"I didn't mean to startle you. I couldn't help but notice you out here all by yourself." His voice was kind and appealing with an Italian accent.

"That's okay. I just wasn't expecting anyone else to be out her but me." Sarah couldn't help but admire his striking appearance. Dark eyes were separated by a Roman nose. His jet black hair was pulled back in a short ponytail.

"The hour is very late for a beautiful young woman to be out here by herself." He was even more handsome when he smiled.

Sarah turned a light shade of crimson and hoped he didn't notice. "Well, I'm not really by myself. My husband is in the casino and I came out for some fresh air." She looked at him shyly.

"American men. I will never understand them. In Italy, if a man was fortunate enough to have such a beautiful wife, he would never leave her alone."

She blushed once again, and said, "I should be getting back. My husband will wonder where I am." Sarah began to walk back toward the front of the ship with the stranger by her side.

"Would you like me to escort you back inside?" White dazzling teeth once more captured Sarah's eyes.

"Thank you. You're very kind, but that won't be necessary." His attention flattered her, but at the same time she felt uncomfortable. Sarah smiled as she glanced past his shoulder. Someone was approaching at a distance, but she was unable to make out who the figure was.

"As you wish." He stepped back and bowed slightly though he never took his eyes off her. He turned and walked away and passed the figure who still came.

When Sarah was able to see that the figure who quickly walked toward her was Greg she smiled at him. But her smile faded as Greg grabbed her roughly by the arm and pulled her to him. The smell of alcohol rolled off his breath, but she was more disturbed by the anger in his eyes. They blazed as his fingers dug deep into her upper arm.

"Where have you been? I've looked everywhere for you!" His face was only inches from hers, which allowed her to see the fury in his eyes.

"Greg, you're hurting me. Please let go." Sarah winced with pain as the hardness of fingers pressed against her bones. Tears moistened her eyes as she looked away.

"I see it didn't take you long to find company." He spoke accusingly to her. He tightened his hold which took her to another level of pain.

Her arm throbbed as she pleaded tearfully. "I only spoke to him for a second. He was concerned that I was out here by myself." Sarah almost fell backwards when Greg abruptly let go of her arm.

"You're either lying to me or you're just plain stupid! The days of knights in shining armor are gone. This is the nineties. He wasn't concerned for you! He wanted to go bed with you!" Greg's words were slurred and she knew he was drunk.

Sarah did not believe him, but she was so shocked, she didn't know what to say.

"Don't you ever do this again! Do you understand?" Greg's eyes were glazed over and he roughly took her by the hand.

Too angry to speak, Sarah nodded her head while being jerked along. She was embarrassed and hoped they wouldn't see anyone from their dinner table. What would people think of the newlyweds now? By now the muscles in her arm burned and she could barely move. Tears filled her eyes as they approached their cabin.

Sarah closed the door behind her while Greg headed straight for the bathroom and slammed the door. The sounds of vomiting were loud and clear while she stood still in the middle of the room. She wanted to run and hide, but there was no place to go. Her arm was painful as she wrapped her hand around her arm.

Across the room was an antique wall mirror that projected Sarah's despaired image. Stunned by her own reflection, Sarah walked closer to the mirror. Makeup mixed with sticky tears had streamed down her cheeks. The creamy, smooth skin on her arm was tarnished with ugly black and blue finger impressions.

When the bathroom door opened, Sarah turned and faced Greg who walked into the bedroom naked and stood in the doorway, looking at her with sluggish eyes.

"What are you waiting for? Let's go to bed." There was no emotion behind his words. They were mechanical, meaningless.

Obediently she followed him. She undressed as slowly as possible, to prolong the inevitable.

The room was dark, but the moon gave enough light through the porthole, and where she could see him on the bed. His body looked hot and sweaty, and smelled of alcohol. The thought of sleeping with him made her feel sick. Sarah held the satin nightgown next to her body and watched him breathe. They were long deep breaths.

Quietly, Sarah pulled the nightgown over her head and waited again. The breaths came at a steady pace and Greg had not moved. She wrapped her arms around herself, and called out softly, barely above a whisper, "Greg." For what seemed like an eternity, she waited and then called again a little louder than before, "Greg."

With a sigh of relief, she picked a pillow up off the bed. Quiet as a mouse, Sarah pulled out one of the drawers under the captain's bed and removed a goose down comforter. While she held her breath, Sarah tiptoed out of the bedroom and closed the door softly behind her. The couch in the sitting room was large enough to stretch out on and sleep.

Exhausted as she was, she could not fall asleep. The sofa was comfortable, but she was afraid Greg would wake up. Her eyes stayed focused on the bedroom door though no movement came from behind the door. It suddenly dawned on Sarah why Greg must have been so angry with her. The stranger was only an excuse he used. She had never given Greg any reason to be jealous. If anyone had the right to be jealous it would be her. When they were dating, he'd flirt with other girls, but Sarah never looked at another guy. No, there was a reason, and she believed money was the answer. He must have lost a lot of money and was taking his frustration out on her. That must be the reason. Tomorrow she would talk to him. The alcohol obviously had a bad effect on Greg and made him act the way he did. Otherwise he would have never treated her this way. This was not the Greg she knew and married.

Not that this revelation made her feel any better, but at least now she could try and understand. As her eyelids became heavy, she pulled the warm, soft comforter up around her neck and drifted into a restless sleep.

Morning sickness hovered over Sarah as she attempted to drink orange juice while soaking up the warm sun. Restful sleep had evaded her, causing her to wake numerous times throughout the early morning hours. By 7:00, Sarah got off the couch, took a hot shower and dressed in khaki shorts, a white tank top underneath a pale blue, unbuttoned, long sleeve, cotton shirt. The temperature was warm but her bruises needed to be covered. Her hair was pulled up in a pony tail which hung out the back of a khaki baseball cap.

The upper deck was almost vacant which she was thankful for, because she did not feel like talking to anyone. Sarah fought back the tears and laid her head against the cushioned chair and closed her eyes. The memory of last night was fresh in her mind along with the incessant pain in her arm. Soreness and stiffness had set in, which made certain tasks painful.

The morning sickness slowly began to pass, so Sarah decided to take a walk around the deck. The hour was still early and Greg probably would not be up for some time. The ocean was calm and the sky free of clouds making it a perfect day for stopping at St. Thomas. There was shopping and a variety of activities to choose from, though Sarah didn't feel much like being a part.

No telling what frame of mind Greg would be in when he did wake up. How much of last night would he remember and how much should she say. She would play it by ear after she saw him. No one had prepared her for marital problems of this nature.

By 9:00, the deck was starting to come alive with activity of organized games for children while parents, couples and lovers dove into the day with an eagerness of new adventures they would encounter.

Loneliness was a stranger to Sarah, but today it was her companion. A clear, blue sky floated above, but the heaviness in her heart was weighted down by a dark cloud. Troubled thoughts filled Sarah's mind. What if Greg's behavior was not a one time occurrence? How could you love somebody and treat them this way? Was he really like his mother? Sarah tried to push those thoughts from her mind.

She must not think this way. He loved her and the baby. No one forced him to marry her. Alcohol was to blame for his behavior last night and she'd just have to ask him not to drink anymore. Greg didn't want to hurt her or the baby.

Feeling a little better she decided to go back to their cabin and see if he was up. They were going to have a good day and put last night behind them.

As Sarah reached the cabin door she stopped suddenly and put her hand on her stomach. A grin broke out across her face as she felt the baby move. Forgetting her troubles for the moment, Sarah burst through the door and yelled "Greg, Greg!" The room was as she left it, and the bedroom door was still closed. She called Greg's name again and opened the door. The covers on the bed were in a mess and all she could see was Greg's foot hanging out the end of the bed.

Disappointed, Sarah sat down at the foot of the bed. The baby's first movement was an important event, and she had so wanted to share the experience with her husband. She wanted Greg to put his hand on her stomach and feel the life of their baby. For a split second she'd been able to forget about last night, but the smell of sweat and alcohol brought back the reality.

A little disheartened, Sarah left the bedroom and closed the door. She walked over to the porthole, and stood quietly while she gazed into the ocean. She thought of her family and wondered what they were doing. The urge to call them overwhelmed her, but she knew they would know something was wrong the instant they heard her voice. With a deep sigh she turned away from the ocean. She would begin this day with the past behind them. She loved Greg and forgave him. She would work hard to be a good wife and to help him with his weakness. For better or worse. Those were the vows she had taken only three days ago, though she did not expect the worst to show up this soon. With her head high and shoulders back, Sarah made a solemn promise to herself that their marriage was going to survive no matter what obstacles life might throw.

In better spirits, Sarah decided to go and eat breakfast. Now that morning sickness had passed, she was famished. If she saw anyone they had eaten dinner with she would just say Greg was still asleep for it had been a late night. There would be no reason for anyone to question her.

Sarah stepped in front of the antique mirror to check her appearance. With the ball cap and pony tail, and no makeup, she hardly looked old enough to be married. Quite a change from her attire last night. Probably no one would recognize her anyway. With a tug on the front of the cap she turned toward the door.

A thoughtful expression crossed Sarah's face as she cast another glance toward the bedroom. By the time she finished breakfast, Greg would most likely be up and about. She would bring him back a tray of food, a kind gesture to represent a peace offering. Josephine always told her the way to man's heart was through his stomach. Sarah smiled at the thought and left the cabin with a lighter heart.

Chapter Seven

Cold, blistering wind blew through Alex's thick hair as he stood on the large, stone balcony while he looked down below at the white, foaming waves crash into the rocks. His body was protected from the harsh weather because of his goose down jacket, unlike his cheeks and nose which were red and numb.

The door slid opened quietly and Catherine stepped outside to join her husband. "Darling, what are you doing out here? It must be twenty degrees." She shivered as she wrapped her arms around herself.

"I just wanted some fresh air." Alex turned and half way smiled at her. "Cath, you're freezing." He put his arm around her and walked her back into the den. A gust of wind blew into the room before he slid the door shut. "The wind is starting to pick up. The temperatures will drop by nightfall." With frozen fingers, Alex unzipped his jacket and removed it from his warm body.

The fire was homey as Catherine stood in front of the fireplace rubbing her arms. "I'd ask you what you were thinking about out there, but I think I know."

Alex walked up behind his wife and put his arms around her waist. "It's that obvious?" He kissed her long slender neck as she snuggled against him.

"Well, just a little." She laughed as Alex released her.

"How bout a brandy to warm us up." Alex walked over to the wet bar while Catherine moved over to the loveseat.

"Sounds good." He watched his wife and poured the brandy. The twins were at a friend's house for the day which made for a peaceful afternoon. The times were far and few between when they were alone. They didn't need to do anything special, just being together was enough.

As Alex sat down next to his wife, she laid her head on his shoulder. The only light in the room was from the fireplace and the glow made for a cozy, relaxed atmosphere. With his arm around Catherine's shoulders, Alex stroked her silky, auburn hair.

"You're awfully quiet. I'm sure they're having a wonderful time." She looked at him when he didn't speak. Wrinkles creased his forehead when he looked at her. "Alex, what's wrong? You seem troubled." She sat up and put her feet back down on the Persian rug.

Alex knew he couldn't hide anything from her. She knew him too well. "Do you remember Kyle Hewett? He works over at the high school." Alex kept his eyes focused on Catherine's face.

"Yes, I remember him. He's the head football coach." She looked intently at her husband and waited patiently.

"Yesterday I had lunch with him over at the country club. We haven't seen each other much since our twenty year reunion. We caught up on life, talked about the wife, kids, that sort of thing." He paused for a second and then continued. "Well, anyway, the subject of Sarah's wedding came up. Kyle saw the announcement and picture in the paper." Alex looked way and gazed into the fire.

"Alex, what did he say?" Catherine asked as she put her hand on his arm.

"Back in October there was an incident which involved Greg and a girl who works with Kyle. This girl wants to go into sports medicine and she works with the guys on the team when they get sprains, pulled muscles, that kind of thing. Anyway, this girl came to Kyle very upset. She told him she had been seeing a guy who was an assistant manager at the fitness center up the street from the high school."

"I assume this guy is Greg."

"Yes, it's Greg. The girl claims that she and Greg were intimately involved and hey were to be married after she graduated. When Greg told her of his forthcoming marriage to Sarah, the girl went into a fit of rage and threatened to tell Sarah of their relationship. The girl said Greg assaulted her." Alex was not surprised to see the shocked look on his wife's face.

"What kind of assault?" Catherine said slowly.

"Supposedly, Greg gave her a black eye and bruised her jaw with additional threats if she told Sarah or anyone else. Kyle said Greg denied everything including the relationship. Without enough proof or witnesses, the charge was dismissed and that was the end of the matter."

Catherine looked like a ton of bricks had hit her as she leaned back against loveseat.

Alex put her hands in his, trying to reassure her. "I only told you because I don't like to keep things from you. I'm not even sure if I believe the girl or not. I don't know what to believe."

"Wouldn't Sarah have said something if Greg was violent or not? She never once said a word except good things about the way he treated her," Catherine questioned.

Alex sat back against the loveseat and pulled his wife into his arms. "Let's not worry prematurely. I can't believe Sarah wouldn't tell us if Greg had ever hurt her. We'll wait and see how the kids seem when they come back from their honeymoon."

"You're right. We know our daughter and would know if something was wrong."

She smiled at her husband gratefully. "You always know how to make me feel better.

As his finger stroked her cheek, her skin reminded him of porcelain, hand-crafted to perfection. At times, Catherine seem so childlike and vulnerable, which made him want to protect her. He must not let her know how concerned he really was. Without saying another word, he bent his head and kissed her tenderly.

"But, Marina, we're only talking about dinner here. I'm not asking you to go on vacation with them. Our son did marry their daughter. We need to have a good solid relationship with them for the kid's sake." Sick of her as he was, Frank kept his cool, in hopes of changing her mind.

Marina looked up at Frank with hard eyes, then went back to reading her *Vogue* magazine. He ignored her rude gesture and continued on with a different approach. "Don't you care about your son? The Matthews are now his family too. Alex and Catherine are nice, decent people. They have raised a beautiful, kind daughter who Greg is fortunate to have for a wife."

Marina slammed her magazine down on the table which caused the cheap, yellowed lampshade to hang crooked. "My answer is still no! No! No! If you think I'll spend one minute, let alone another night with those people, you'd better think again." With her temper on the rise, Marina stood up and walked over to a large plate window. She fumed with every breath while her hand pushed against the cold window pane.

"What's your problem with the Matthews? They've never done anything to you. I think you're jealous of what they have and you don't."

Marina's words were hateful and full of venom as she lashed out. "They think they're so chic and sophisticated in their mansion up there on a cliff with their money and servants. I can't even read the morning paper without that woman's face gloating up at me. This charity, that bazaar, another fashion show. It makes me sick! Those people don't have a clue as to what a real life is. I bet her highness doesn't even know what it means to get her hands dirty."

With a jerk of her head, Marina turned around to face Frank. Frank was taken back at the hatred in her eyes. This woman, he called his wife, yet he didn't even know her anymore. Her voice was full of bitter sarcasm as she ranted and raved.

"And let's not forget the great Alex Matthews with his prestigious law firm and all his hot shot associates who are probably better at brown nosing than they are in the courtroom. I never met an attorney I liked or trusted, and he's no different. You like them so much, you have dinner with them, but you can count me out." Marina paused and then said in a bitter sweet tone, "Or I could go with you and have a a repeat dinner of last time."

Frank knew it was pointless to argue. There was no use to try and get her to change her mind. He shook his head in disgust at her and walked over to the phone. Marina grabbed her magazine and headed out of the living room. When she reached the door, she turned and watched Frank pick up the receiver.

The anger in her voice was gone, replaced with a nonchalant attitude. "Make up one of your stupid excuses or tell them the truth for all I care. Their opinion of me means nothing." She cast a final, haughty look at Frank and then stormed out of the room.

Completely frustrated and mad, Frank dialed the Matthews' phone number. He hated to lie, and his hands were clammy as he nervously listened to the phone ring. He was thinking about what to say when Catherine's pleasant voice came over the receiver. Just the sound of her voice relaxed him. Alex was a lucky man and he was envious of him.

"Hello."

"Catherine, this is Frank Winslow." He steadied his voice to sound as normal as possible.

"How are you, Frank?"

"Oh, I'm fine. You doing okay?" Frank inquired.

"Yes, I'm fine. I've already had a busy morning. There just doesn't seem to be enough hours in a day to accomplish all that needs to be done."

"Yeah, I know what you mean." The cord became tight around Frank's finger as he twisted it. "Listen, I hope this won't inconvenience you and Alex too much, but Marina has one of her migraine headaches. She went upstairs to lie down and I don't think she'll be up to dinner tonight. I hope you understand." God, he hated lying to her He was glad she couldn't see his face for his eyes would be a dead give away. Hopefully, his voice had sounded convincing.

"Of course we understand, Frank. Tell Marina I hope she gets to feeling better soon and we can get together some other time."

Frank thanked her and promised to pass on the message before he hung up the phone. Angrily, he stood there and looked down at the phone. One more victory for Marina. For her, this was a game played by her rules. People's feelings didn't matter as long as she won. He grabbed the receiver and banged it repeatedly against the cradle as he cursed her. Mad at himself because he lost control, Frank put the phone back in order and sat down on the couch. With his arms stretched out over the back of the couch and his head back, he took in deep breaths.

Not sure how to bring Marina to defeat, he vowed to himself the day would come when Marina would lose. Somehow he would find a way, even if it took him until the day he died.

One last look. It was hard to believe this was their last morning aboard the Royal Princess. But Sarah wasn't sad to return home. Ten days was a long time to be gone and she missed her family. No contact had been made since they had left after the wedding. The sunrise seemed even more spectacular today than all the other mornings she had stood leisurely on the deck.

Their honeymoon had been wonderful except for the first evening's nightmare she had survived. She shuddered as she tried to block out the tormenting memory. But unfortunately, she knew this was an experience she would never forget. Hopefully, though, with time, the memory would fade and become only a distant thought.

"I thought I'd find you here." Greg said, as he walked up and stood beside her. With his fingers curled around the rail, he looked at her intently. "Sarah, there's something I want to talk to you about, but I was waiting for the right time. The time never seemed right, but now that we're about to leave, we need to talk before we get home."

Sarah thought Greg seemed anxious, almost nervous. Sarah blinked back the tears and spoke in a soft voice, "You've already apologized and we worked it out. What's there to talk about?"

"I know we've worked this out between us." Greg stammered around like he was searching for the right words. "I think what happened needs to stay just between us. No one else needs to know, not even your parents. And of course, my parents, too."

Too ashamed of what happened, Sarah had no intention of ever telling anyone, let alone her parents. With tenderness, she reached out touched Greg's face and said, "Just between us."

With sweaty palms, Greg let go of the rail and put his arms around Sarah. She thought Greg almost seemed overly worried. Maybe he was afraid of her father. No, that was ridiculous. Her father and husband were not close, but they were cordial to each other. She had never even shared with Greg how her father felt about him, even though Greg had told her more than once how his mother felt about her. Her father was an influential figure in the community who owned a successful law firm. Possibly, Greg felt insecure and wanted to look good in front of her parents.

Sarah had to admit that if her father had found out what happened, he would be furious with her husband. This would only cause a division between the two men, and Sarah didn't want that to happen.

With one last look out over the ocean and the sunny, blue sky, they headed back to their cabin hand in hand. The ship would dock in Miami in two hours and they still had luggage to pack.

When Sarah had shut the last of her burgundy, leather suitcases, she walked over to Greg and said, "Would you mind terribly if we didn't spend the night in Miami and flew back to Maine tonight instead?" She was so homesick and anxious to see her family.

"That's fine with me. We can surprise them and call them from the airport when we arrive. But let's call your parents to pick us up. My mom doesn't like to be surprised."

Sarah threw her arms around Greg's neck and smothered his face with kisses. "Oh, thank you, thank you. I love you so much!"

Greg removed himself from her embrace to go and answer the door as a second knock came forth.

"Sir, I'm here to collect your bags if they're ready." Greg stepped back to allow the porter to enter the cabin. After all the luggage was loaded on the carrier, Greg tipped the young man generously.

"Thank you, Sir!" the porter said as a wide grin broke out across his face.

With one final look around the cabin, they made sure they had not left anything behind before they closed the door. Farewells were exchanged with passengers they'd become acquainted with on the cruise, as everyone made their way off the ship.

Sarah laid her head back on Greg's shoulder while the taxi sped its way through the traffic to the airport. The driver was competent and completely at ease zipping in and out of lanes at a fast pace. Palm trees passed by the window as Sarah tried to keep her heavy eyelids opened. As wonderful as their honeymoon had been with all the activities on the ship, the tours of the Islands and the time they spent in bed making love into the early hours of the morning, she was exhausted. Sleep had been a resource they'd rarely used.

The drive to the airport was peaceful and relaxing. Greg's arm went around her shoulders to allow her to recline against him even more.

As she drifted off to sleep she was somewhat hypnotized by the constant tranquil sound of the air conditioner as the vents blew cool air across her face and hair. Between subconscious and consciousness, faded images floated through her mind. Farther and farther she was pulled from the taxi cab back to the ship. The sun shined down on the Royal Princess. The nearer she came, the sky grew darker. Her vision was distorted and her ears were haunted by angry words which ran together.

Rough hands grabbed her arm as she tried to run, and her feet were heavy which kept her from moving. She tried to scream, but no sound would come as dark, sinister eyes broke through the blur and glared at her. The stranger's mouth laughed and mocked her with agonizing words. Without warning the darkness dissolved. Sarah screamed because the faceless stranger became the face of her husband's.

"Sarah, wake up." She sat up and gasped, looking at Greg who gently shook her by the shoulders. "That must have been some dream. You look like you've seen a ghost."

Sarah leaned forward and trembled. The dream seemed so real and she felt frightened.

"Hey, it was just a dream." Greg put a finger under her chin lifting her face toward his. "You're safe with me." He kissed her on the forehead as the taxi exited the ramp for departures. With a faint smile she looked back out the window. For some reason she didn't understand why she felt so uneasy. It was just a bad dream, but she didn't feel safe and more than anything she wanted to see her parents.

They boarded the plane and quickly found their seats in first class. With no persuasion, Greg gave up his window seat to Sarah. The fear of heights had plagued him since he was a small child. After lunch had been served, Greg asked for a pillow and fell fast asleep. Afraid to go back to sleep, Sarah chose one of the magazines the flight attendant offered. First class was comfortable with its extra wide leather seats and first rate service. Unable to concentrate on the People magazine, Sarah laid it on her lap and stared out the window into a clear empty sky.

Confused as to why she was so troubled by her dream, Sarah longed to talk with her mother, who would put her at ease. But if she told her mother about the dream, she then would be tempted to tell of her incident with Greg's violent behavior. As much as she loved her parents, they would never understand. Knowing her father as she did, he might try and convince her to have the marriage annulled. Anyway, how could she expect them to comprehend when she didn't understand herself?

With her head laid back against the seat, she shut her eyes and settled into the seat. Rest would do her good whether she slept or not. She needed to look refreshed and cheerful, not worried. Her parents knew her so well and they would be able to detect something wrong.

The voice of the pilot came over the intercom to inform the passengers their flight was on schedule and they would arrive in Seaside Cove shortly. He continued to report on the weather conditions. The temperature was a cold, twenty-three degrees, with a snow storm expected later that night. Their sun filled days were behind them and the captain's announcement was a reminder that the honeymoon was officially over.

The thought of the cold temperatures made Sarah smile. Not just because she enjoyed winter, but because she was home. When she had dressed that morning, she'd deliberately put on a long sleeve shirt for the return back to winter, but also for the fact, Sarah wanted to cover the bruises on her arm. The black and blue coloration had turned to shades of green, yellow, and purple. Determined to put the short lived past behind her, it was their secret which would stay buried.

The landing gear grinded when the wheels came down, ready to make contact with the salt rocked covered pavement. This was her least favorite part of flying. Greg had slept right through and she envied the fact that very little unnerved him. First class would be the first to exit, so they hurriedly gathered their carry on and stepped into the aisle.

"Sarah, you go to the lounge and call your folks, while I go to baggage claim and get our luggage." He said authoritatively and pushed the three bags at her.

Sarah quickly spoke as he turned to walk away. "But I'm not supposed to lift this much weight at one time. I have to be careful now that I'm pregnant." She stood there with a bag over each shoulder with the third on the floor by her feet.

With annoyance written all over his face, Greg just stood there and looked at her making no attempt to retrieve the third bag. "Don't tell me you're going to be like all other women and use your pregnancy as an excuse for not being able to do anything." His tone was short and rude. Before she had a chance to respond, he turned and walked up the aisle off the plane.

Embarrassed and hurt by his attitude and words, she bent over to pick up the third bag. A muscle in her back pulled as she lifted the bag onto her right shoulder. With difficulty, she slowly made her way down the aisle, fighting back the tears. Thoughts were scrambled in her mind and she tried to resist them. Right now she didn't want to think about anything. Soon she would see her parents and she didn't need to look troubled. Tomorrow would be a new day and Sarah could sort all this out after she rested.

At the end of the walkway Sarah stopped and looked for the sign to baggage claim. A black porter in a uniform and sky cap approached her with a friendly smile and a luggage cart. "Here let me take those for you. Those bags are almost as big as you, Miss."

With swift, capable hands, the bags were loaded on the chromed railed cart. She dug down into her shoulder bag grabbing the first bill her fingers touched. "Thank you so much. They were getting pretty heavy," she said, handing him the money.

A surprised look came over the porter's face when he looked down at the ten dollar bill. "Thank you, Miss and you have a good evening."

Sarah smiled at him as he tipped his hand to his hat and walked away. With determination, she lifted her shoulders back and pushed the cart toward baggage claim, with the promise of another tomorrow and a new beginning.

Chapter Eight

 The pilot had been true to his word. Sarah opened her eyes to fresh, white snow which glistened around the window frame. The snow storm must have arrived after she had fallen asleep last night. Sunshine filled the small bedroom, intensifying the pale yellow walls. Sarah stretched her arms above her head, and turned to look at Greg, who was still sound asleep.

 With her hand propped beneath her chin she watched his bare chest rise rhythmically with each steady breath. Sarah studied him and made a memory of the peaceful expression on his face. Only hours ago it had been tense and hostile. That moment seemed like a bad dream she just wanted to forget. Today they would put those episodes behind them to start a new life together in their own home.

 Rolling back over she glanced at the alarm clock on the night stand. The time was already 10:30. She must have been more tired than she realized last night.

 Today she would start her life as a full-time housewife. She had wanted to get a job but Greg did not want her to work. He didn't want someone else to raise his child, and wanted to come home from work to find a hot meal on the table. Sarah had not minded. If her staying home made him happy, then that is what she wanted, too.

 At eighteen she was already a pretty good cook. "You need to be independent," her mother would say. "Marry for love, not for someone to take care of you." On the other hand, her father had pampered her. But between her parents, she felt she had balanced out okay.

Sarah threw back the covers, and quietly got out of bed. Since Greg had to go back to work in a couple of days, she wanted to let him sleep in. Later on she would fix him breakfast or lunch, depending on what time he got up. There were wedding gifts that still needed to be opened, and thank you notes to be written, so she welcomed the time alone. Her mother had offered to come over and help, but Sarah declined her offer because she was uneasy about what kind of mood Greg might be in.

Last night when her parents had picked them up at the airport, Greg was charming and very talkative about their honeymoon. He was even friendlier with her father than usual. Sarah had remained quiet during the drive to their apartment. When her parents asked if anything was wrong, Greg had quickly answered, "Oh, she's just tired," and turned to her saying, "Aren't you, Honey?"

Without looking at him she answered, "Yes, I'm just tired." He then pulled her toward him and laid her against his shoulder.

His behavior perplexed Sarah and she wasn't quite sure what to think about it. During the entire time they had dated and throughout their engagement, he never showed any signs of anger toward her, only toward his parents, which she had tried to understand. More than anything she wanted to be a good wife to Greg and make him happy.

But after almost two weeks of marriage, she felt somewhat isolated from her husband in the sense she did not know what he thought or felt. Instead of talking with her about the two incidents, he shut her out and acted as if they had never happened.

Now that they were married, she knew things would be better, although it was going to take time for them to get used to being together on a regular basis. There was so much to learn about each other. Sarah was a little overwhelmed with the changes, but at the same time she looked forward to her new life with her husband.

She zipped her faded blue jeans and struggled to buttoned them. They were a little snug and she knew it would not be long until she would have to shop for maternity clothes. She was determined not to gain a lot of weight. With her petite frame she would have to watch her weight carefully. Greg made it very clear that he did not want a fat wife. He had told her his mother only gained fifteen pounds when she was pregnant with him and he did not see any reason why she could not do the same.

She assured him she would control her weight and continue to work out while she was pregnant. So far, she had only been to the doctor a couple of times and was doing well with her weight, and that was how she intended to keep it. Sarah pulled her hair up with a scrunchy, grabbed her dirty laundry out of an opened suitcase and quietly left the bedroom.

Last night she had been upset and tired and didn't feel much like talking with her parents. Later in the day she would call them and maybe invite them over for dinner that week. She laughed at the idea of fixing dinner for her parents and brothers in her and Greg's apartment. Everything seemed so strange, almost like she was in another person's life.

The telephone rang and broke into her thoughts. Our first phone call she thought as she picked up the cordless phone and pushed the talk button. "Hello," Sarah said cheerfully.

Marina's tone was cold and short. "Could you put Greg on the phone?" Caught off guard by her mother-in-law, Sarah sputtered. "How are you, Marina?" After what seemed like an eternity of silence, Sarah was about to say something further when her mother-in-law's voice responded curtly.

"If you don't mind, I'd like to speak with my son." The irritation in Marina's voice came across loud and clear. Any hope Sarah may have had of a relationship with Greg's mother was diminishing rapidly. On one hand, she wanted to cry and ask this woman what she had against her even though she already knew. But she also felt like telling her to get over it. She decided not to do either and wake up Greg instead. By now the time was 11:00 and hopefully he would be ready to wake up.

Sarah pushed the mute button and walked back into the bedroom where Greg was still asleep. With his head underneath the pillow she gently shook his shoulder and spoke softly, "Greg, wake up. Your mother is on the phone. She wants to talk to you." He mumbled something she could not hear, so she said again, "It's your mother. She wants to talk to you."

With his eyes shut, he pulled his head out from under the pillow and turned away from Sarah and grumbled sheepishly. "I don't want to talk to her. Tell her I'm asleep."

Greg was not making this easy for her. She did not want to talk to his mother either. Sarah persisted. "But she sounds mad. I don't think she'll take no for an answer. Can't you just talk to her for a minute?"

Sarah was frustrated. If Greg would not deal with his own mother, then how could he expect her to. "Your mother doesn't like being told no and she won't give up until she talks to you."

"All right, give me the phone." He was annoyed as he extended his left arm behind him and held out his hand for the phone. Sarah place the phone in his hand and sat down on the bed next to him.

"Hello." His voice was sluggish and he sounded half asleep. Greg held the phone away from his ear when Marina's voice yelled at him in an accusingly.

"Are you still in bed? It's after 11:00."

"Mom, don't start. Our flight got in late last night and we got to bed even later.

Besides I don't you an explanation anyway." He buried his face into the pillow unable to escape.

"If you want to sleep your life away that's your business, but—"

"Mom, why did you call? Tell me you wanted something more important than to talk about my sleeping habits?" Sarah could tell he was about to hang up on her.

"Yes, it's important. I didn't appreciate hearing about your early arrival from Sarah's mother. Why didn't you call me and your father last night to pick you up instead of the Matthews? We live a lot closer to the airport than they do." Marina was talking in such a loud voice that Sarah had not missed a word.

He ran his fingers through his hair and gripped the phone tightly. His words were loud and hateful as he yelled back. "You woke me up for that! Because you're jealous! What is your problem?" His tone was sarcastic. "Don't you have anything better to do?"

Sarah moved closer to Greg so she could still hear. Marina's loud tone increased to hostility as she lashed out. "Just because you're married, doesn't mean you can speak to me disrespectfully. I will not put up with this treatment. Do you hear me! There isn't one thing about that woman I'm jealous of! I wanted to talk with you. Is that asking for too much?"

Greg laid back down and put his arm across his forehead. Sarah knew Greg hated it when his mother played the victim. When you're a victim then you have feelings, and Marina was cold as ice. There was not a compassionate bone in her body. She was an aggressive, arrogant female who would stop at nothing to get what she wanted, no matter who she hurt.

"Mom, is this how it's going to be, now that I'm not at home? Yeah, you have a right to see me, but I'm married now. I was going to call you later today. It's not like I've been home for a week and haven't called you. Look, I'm really tired. I'll call you guys later."

"Okay, but don't forget," Marina scolded.

"I won't. Bye." When Greg clicked off the phone, Sarah could have sworn Marina sounded like she was going to cry. Not possible, she thought. His mother did a lot of things, but crying wasn't one of them. Sarah took the phone and started to say something, but Greg rolled onto his stomach and covered his head once more with his pillow.

She couldn't tell if he was still upset or if he just wanted to go back to sleep.

Probably both, she thought. It made her sad to think about the kind of relationship or the lack of relationship her husband had with his mother. Maybe somehow her family would be instrumental in helping the Winslow family to be restored. But Sarah knew in her heart that restoration would most likely never happen. The damage appeared to be beyond repair. They didn't get this way overnight and to hope her husband's family could be salvaged was not realistic.

Sarah felt sad for Frank and Marina. They obviously didn't care for each other and she couldn't imagine living in a marriage with someone she couldn't stand. Her parents only showed love for each other and Sarah wanted to share that kind of love with Greg, but she was starting to wonder how close he would allow her to get. So far she didn't feel close to him like she wanted to. Sarah wouldn't try to push anything with Greg. Everyday it became more clear to her how totally different they were.

She was more of an open book where he was a locked door. Patience was a virtue she possessed and she'd wait for him to open up to her. After all, he hadn't had a good example to follow to show him what a good and healthy marriage was. Fortunately, her parents were wonderful examples, but Greg wasn't anything like her father except for his good looks.

"I'm not going to let my mother-in-law affect my marriage." Sarah whispered closing the door. Already, she knew her work was cut out for her. Ready to tackle the wedding gift list, Sarah sat down at the kitchen table with a renewed confidence that she could conquer any obstacle life threw her way.

She tensed more as her head continued to pound with pulsating stabs. Her eyes stared hard at the phone while she sat stiffly on the couch. Sleep had evaded her last night after she'd received Catherine's phone call. And now, to have Greg treat her his way. Well, she had news for the Matthews family. Greg was her son, not theirs. Who do they think they're dealing with? A fool? Marina laughed out loud at a mental image of Catherine at one of her charities. She was no match against her.

Still deep in thought, she never heard Frank come through the front door. "How many times have I told you not to smoke in the house!" He walked angrily over to the window and raised it abruptly. "It's bad enough I have to work around smoke all day. I don't want to have to come home to yours, too!"

"I wasn't expecting you home so early. Besides I always have the room aired out before you get home. And don't act so stupid. You know I smoke in the house when you're not around."

Her words dared him and she knew he wasn't in the mood to challenge her. After Catherine's phone call last night, she was so mad she'd stayed up most of the night cleaning out cupboards in the kitchen. She had banged things around downstairs for hours.

"I don't want to fight. Thanks to your childish episode, I didn't sleep all night." Frank rubbed his red, glassy eyes overshadowed by heavy eyelids and dark circles.

Marina looked away from him and gazed out the opposite window. "You couldn't even began to understand." Her voice was somewhat dull and lifeless now.

"Understand what? That your hatred for the Matthews family increases with each day that passes. All she did was call to let us know the kids were coming home early and you were outraged because Greg didn't call us. You act as though Catherine has done something personally against you." Frank looked at Marina's back which still faced him, but she never said a word as she breathed deeply.

"Marina, I know you hear me whether you act like it or not. I'm warning you. You better snap out of this vendetta before you go to far. You'll push Greg even farther away than he already is. The Matthews are his family now, too. You're going to have to accept the fact that Sarah is his wife. I think you should consider getting professional help. Your anger and bitterness will destroy you and everyone around you." Frank spoke matter of fact, as he started to walk out of the room.

Marina stood up and whirled around toward Frank. Her voice was full of animosity. "You think you have the answer for everything, don't you? Professional help. Why don't you practice what you preach!" Sarcastically she continued. "Wife beating, or I believe it's now called domestic violence, is a good reason for getting—how did you say, professional help." Her voice was evil as she laughed with her head back. The laughter stopped abruptly as she looked hard at Frank with hatred swimming in her eyes. "Why don't you call Oprah and tell her about our dysfunctional family, you hypocrite!"

For a moment there was a disturbing silence that filled the room while Frank and Marina remained motionless. They were at a stand still to see who would make the next move. She knew this could go either way. He would walk away or fight this out till the bitter end. A place she had been many times over. Every word possible that could hurt each other had already been said through their miserable years together. All they ever did was stir up old wounds and keep the hate alive between them.

Once, a long time ago when they were both young and carefree, Marina had been drawn to Frank. He was like a magnet she couldn't resist, not that she really wanted to. He had a way of making her feel like she could do anything or be anyone she wanted to be. Marina had put Frank on a pedestal. And then he came crashing down with all her dreams and goals. Marina felt nothing now, except contempt. Her regret had turned into bitterness for all the years she had wasted with him. She knew her face, once full of laughter and joy, was now replaced with a rage so deep that the root penetrated into the depths of her soul. Any love for her husband was now only a faded memory, which was buried in the caverns of her mind.

They should have walked away from their marriage years ago when there would have been something left to salvage of their self-respect and dignity. But it was too late. They were now detestable monsters in each other's eyes. This was their self-inflicted punishment, living with each other.

Frank walked away and went up the stairs as Marina yelled after him. "Go ahead, walk away! You're a coward, Frank! Do you hear me! A coward!" By now she stood at the bottom of the stairs and gripped the wood banister, screaming out the words over and over, even after her husband had shut the door.

Her angry words turned into hot, burning tears as she slumped down on the bottom step. Her body shook violently with each uncontrollable sob. A face of perfection now marred with black smears and streaks. Marina was surprised at her display of emotional breakdown. She felt like she was locked in another person's body, unable to flee the torment. But with no one to comfort her, or offer solace for the agony which surfaced from her inner being, Marina sat there feeling lost and desolate, destined to be a prisoner within.

Chapter Nine

Days turned into weeks as four months passed while Sarah and Greg plodded through the daily routine of marriage. At first, the task of housework, cooking and getting the nursery ready was an enjoyable life Sarah settled into with ease. But now, eight months pregnant, she felt the discomfort that comes with preparation for child birth.

The baby was active, keeping her from restful sleep, but she didn't mind. Soon she would hold their child in her arms. Sarah only wished that Greg would share in her excitement about their baby's arrival. In the early stages of her pregnancy he had talked about the baby with enthusiasm and seemed genuinely concerned about how she was feeling. At times, he'd even cook dinner and clean the kitchen so she could put her feet up and rest.

Over the last two months, though, Greg had exhibited frequent mood swings. He had become depressed, distant and less attentive. Sarah tried to talk to him, but he'd only say there was nothing wrong, he just needed his space. The more space she gave him, the more he was gone from home. His excuses were always the same. He had to work late, or he was out with his friends and forgot about the time. Greg hadn't shown any more physical outbursts toward her since their honeymoon, but when he was upset she was cautious and kept her distance.

When he was at home, he constantly griped about her appearance. He made hurtful remarks about her weight even though she had only gained seventeen pounds. Going out in public together had stopped all together. She knew the reason was because he didn't want to be seen with her, although he denied her accusations.

Her parents weren't happy that her attendance in church had dropped. Greg refused to go and she didn't want to go without him. The excuses she made for him were becoming harder and less believable. Sarah hated lying to her parents, but just couldn't tell them the truth about what was going on in her marriage. She believed their problems could be worked out, and there was no reason for her mom and dad to worry needlessly.

Besides, whatever Greg was going through would surely pass sooner or later. Hopefully, sooner. Sarah wished she wasn't so sensitive. She tried not to let her feelings get hurt, but they did. She told herself to just be patient and love him.

Lower back pain had become her ever present unwanted companion. Sarah winced as she turned from her back onto her side hopping to bring some relief. The red digits on her alarm clock displayed eleven-thirty. Greg had called from the fitness center at five o'clock to say he was going out with friends and not to wait up for him because he would be late. He was nicer to her over the phone than when he was at home.

With sleep out of her reach, she decided to get out of bed to watch TV. Unable to resist a craving, Sarah fixed herself a bowl of ice cream topped with peanut butter. She sat in the recliner with her feet up finishing off the ice cream, when she heard Greg mumble something as his key turned in the deadbolt. Unsure of what kind of mood to expect she continued to watch TV when the door opened.

She didn't have to look at him to know he'd been drinking. The stench of alcohol filled the living room as he walked in. His promise not to drink after the honeymoon had obviously been a lie. Sarah looked away from the television to Greg, and her heart began to race. His eyes were wild and glazed over. He was drunk and she was apprehensive. The dreaded nightmare she fought so hard to forget and push from her mind was back. Sarah struggled to stay calm as Greg walked over to her.

The expression on his face told her what he was thinking when he looked down at the empty bowl of ice cream in her lap. A sneer came across his face. "This is how you keep off the weight," he said sarcastically. "What else have you lied to me about?" He towered over her waiting for an answer.

"I have kept off my weight. It was only a little bowl of ice cream." She dared not mention the peanut butter. "I hardly ate any dinner tonight." She was tired of his harassment. She reached for the lever on the side of the recliner to lower the foot rest, but Greg's leg blocked her. In a gentle, but nervous voice she said, "Greg, please move your leg. I want to go to bed."

He leaned over and gripped each arm rest bringing his face directly over hers. His breath suffocated her with its repulsive smell of alcohol. Sarah turned her head away and took in a deep breath as his hot, sticky mouth moved down her neck toward the open gap in her nightgown. He lifted his head and spoke in a foul whisper, "I'll come with you."

The thought of sex with him right now disgusted her. Sarah tried to keep her voice calm. She kept her head turned away from him and said, "No, you don't have to do that. You must be exhausted after a long day."

"I'm not that tired," he retorted. His hand grabbed her chin and jerked her face roughly toward his. "You're my wife and I want to have sex." His eyes grew dark as his mouth came down hard on hers forcing her lips open with his tongue.

She tried to push him away, but Greg held her arms down and lowered himself onto her. The pressure from his weight only increased the pain in her lower back. His tongue left a putrid taste in her mouth while she struggled to pull away. When Sarah gagged, Greg pulled back and glared at her with eyes cold as steel.

With trembling lips, Sarah spoke barely above a whisper. "Greg, please don't. The baby. I'm too far along. We shouldn't have sex, not now." She fought back the tears and pleaded.

Greg released her arms and stood up. Sarah cringed at the disgust she saw in his eyes as they moved slowly from her face to her stomach. "Always the baby. Look at you! You make me sick!" With words that taunted he said, "Don't worry about me. I won't be lonely." He stepped away from the chair, losing his balance and falling into the wall which knocked a picture to the floor shattering the glass. Slightly dazed, he hung onto the recliner as he attempted to pull himself to his feet.

Sarah sat still in the chair as she wrapped her arms protectively around her stomach. She was afraid he would fall on her and hurt the baby. She didn't want to upset him any further and tried to think of a way to calm the situation. "Let me get out of the chair and I'll help you to bed. It's late and you need your rest." Even though her voice appeared to be in control, she was shaking on the inside as she reached out to put her hand on his arm.

"Don't tell me what I need!" Angrily, he jerked away from her and made his way over to the TV and turned it off. "I'll tell you what you need! And you need to go to bed by yourself!" Unexpectedly, he lunged at her. Hard fingers grabbed her arm and pulled her roughly out of the recliner onto the floor.

Sarah cried out in pain when her leg scraped against the chipped metal bar that connected the foot rest to the chair. Salty tears streamed down her cheeks as warm blood ran down her leg. The cut on her leg ached and throbbed as her trembling fingers covered the wound. She bowed her head and wept silently as she could.

"Shut up! Do you hear me? Just shut up!" Greg staggered backwards and fell back onto the couch. "Get out of here. Just the sight of you makes me want to puke!"

Sarah clung to the arm of the chair, slowly pulling herself to her feet. The effort was painful, but she managed to make it to the bedroom with little disturbance. She quietly shut the door and lowered herself on the bed. The blood had seeped through her nightgown making an ugly red stain. Carefully she lay down keeping her leg away from the white comforter. With her face buried deep in her pillow, Sarah sobbed until there was nothing left.

She wasn't sure how long she lay there like that, but time didn't seem to matter. It was as though time had stopped, and she was caught somewhere in a dimension where nothing was real. She tried to think, but was unable to focus. Her thoughts were clouded and unclear. Sarah could hear Greg's heavy breathing coming from beyond the door. His very presence that once made her feel safe and secure, now caused her to feel threatened.

She needed her parents. Her father would know what to do. She could go back to the Pines where she would be loved and cared for. Her parents would take care of her and the baby. Her old life awaited her. All she had to do was call. Reluctantly, Sarah pushed that thought from her mind as she felt her heart being weighted down into a pool of despair. Her Daddy had tried to tell her and she wouldn't listen. They were both stubborn and she'd been in love. She couldn't stand the thought of hurting her parents again.

The decision to marry Greg had been hers, for better or worse. Isn't that what the vows said? Was she going to be a quitter? To quit on her marriage and Greg meant her child would grow up without a father. Even though Sarah didn't understand, she knew her husband was deeply troubled. Why hadn't she seen this before now? Maybe she did and chose to look away. Had Greg been right when he said she lived in a fantasy world?

He couldn't turn to his parents, and if she deserted him, who would be left to help him get through whatever demons tormented his soul? She believed in the sanctity of marriage and still wanted to believe in her husband. Her love for him was strong and she had to believe that it would pull him through his troubles.

Sarah sat up and wiped her face with the sleeve of her nightgown. The hour was late and she had to be up early in the morning to go the children's center with her mother, but first she wanted to take a hot shower. She knew she needed to clean her cut so infection wouldn't set in. The wood floor was cold beneath her feet as she quietly made her way into the bathroom. Sarah placed her nightgown in the sink filled with cold water in hopes of removing the blood stain, which had turned to a darker shade of red.

She wanted to wash away every reminder of tonight's atrocity, if only externally, for she knew her emotional wounds would remain fragile. The warm water ran over her slender shoulders and down her body. Sarah placed her hands on her stomach tenderly and said, "Don't you worry, little one. Your Daddy will love you as much as I do. Once you're here and he holds you, you'll have his heart forever. No one will ever hurt you. I promise."

The sunshine poured through the living room window with the promise of a splendid day. Springtime arrived unannounced like a welcome guest who appears on a doorstep. The flowers were in full bloom as a cool breeze carried the intoxicating fragrance of each blossom through the screen door.

The aroma of eggs and bacon filled the kitchen, along with the smell of coffee brewing. The music of the Beach Boys blared from the stereo with an upbeat tempo, but Sarah was far from an upbeat mood. Greg had been quiet when he woke up and seemed to avoid her. She had said good morning, but he went into the bathroom without acknowledging her. She was on edge and felt the need to walk on eggshells around him, even though she shouldn't have to.

With the orange juice poured and food on the table, Sarah sat down as Greg came out of the bedroom. He sat down without saying a word. They ate in silence, for there was an awkwardness between the two of them. With a feeble attempt to act normal, Sarah asked, "How's your food?"

"Fine." He never looked up and continued to eat in the resumed silence.

Not able to stand the quietness any longer, Sarah raised her shoulders back with courage and said boldly, "Greg, could we please talk? I'm no good at games. I don't want us to be like this." She looked over at him. "I love you. Do you still love me?

He put his fork down, pushed his chair from the table and stood up. "I'm going to be late for work. We'll talk later." Greg turned and walked toward the front door.

Sarah got out of her chair and followed after him. "Please, don't walk away from me. This is important. You still have a few minutes before you have to leave. I have to go soon too, but we need to talk first." Sarah pleaded with him.

"Where are you going today? I thought you were going to clean the apartment and do the laundry." Greg stood by the door and held onto the door knob, ready to leave.

"You know on Tuesdays and Thursdays I work at the Dale Evans Center." Sarah tried not to sound aggravated, although she was, because she felt like Greg was avoiding the issue.

"I don't want you to go to that place anymore. Go in today and tell them you're not coming back." Greg's words were an order, not a request.

"What!" Sarah exclaimed with disturbed surprise. "Not go back? But why? I've been working with those children since I was fifteen. I have to go back. They're part of my life. I love them."

Greg stood there annoyed. "I don't want you around those retards. What will my friends think? It's embarrassing."

"Are you telling me you're ashamed of me?" Sarah's tear moistened eyes stared at Greg in disbelief. "How can you be embarrassed because I try to help mentally handicapped children. They are not retards as you so coldly put. They're Downs syndrome children and they're the most wonderful children I've ever known." Sarah felt like she was having to defend a part of her life, to explain something that was so natural for her. "Where is your compassion? Who will help these kids?"

His words were insensitive and harsh. "Let someone else do it. Besides, our baby will be here soon and you won't have time to take care of those kids. I told you before, I want you home with my child."

She was speechless as he turned and opened the door. With a heavy heart, she cried after the door banged shut behind him. The pain in her leg couldn't compare to the hurt she felt in her heart right now. Those kids meant everything to her. There must be a way she could change his mind. There had to be. But the more she pondered her dilemma she knew there was no hope. His mind was made up and he'd only be angry with her if she went against his wishes.

She was not going to give up this easily. Somehow she'd find a way to make him come around and see things differently. Greg came from a family who hadn't shown him how to love or be compassionate toward others. Except maybe for Frank. In her heart Sarah felt Frank was different. She believed he loved his son, but Marina had kept him from being the father he should have been to Greg.

Sarah wiped away her tears. Her mother would be here in about ten minutes to pick her up and she didn't want to give the impression that anything was wrong. It was times like this when she wished her parents didn't know her so well. She was like an opened book to them.

Back in the kitchen she loaded the dishwasher and wiped off the counter top. Greg liked a clean apartment and she didn't intend to give him a reason to be angry with her. She was going to be a good wife and make a happy home for him. When he saw how hard she tried to please him, surely he would want to do the same for her. Tonight she would make his favorite meal of lasagna and cherry cheesecake. After dinner they could sit down and talk about last night. For their marriage to survive, they'd have to to be able to communicate, even when it was painful.

Sarah had just finished up when there came a knock at the front door. "Coming," she yelled, turning off the stereo. Her mother's face smiled at her through the screen door. "Mom, come on in. The door's unlocked. I'll be ready in a minute." Sarah fluffed the pillows on the couch before her mother walked in.

"Can I help you with anything?"

"No, I'm almost finished." Sarah straightened the magazines on top of the coffee table.

"Sweetie, what's all the fuss? Everything looks great."

"Greg just likes everything so, so." Sarah gave one final look around the room.

"You're doing a good job, Sarah. How could Greg be anything but proud of you."

Sarah looked away for she felt her eyes water. "I'll be just a minute." She hurried into the bedroom. "If you were my shoes, where would you be?" Sarah was frustrated as she rummaged through the bedroom closet. "I seem to always be misplacing them."

"Unless your organizational skills have changed, try under the bed."

In a few moments, Sarah came into the living room with shoe in hand which caused Catherine to laugh. "I guess some things never change." Sarah laughed back and sat down to put on her shoe. When Sarah stood up she winced and instinctively reached down to grab her leg.

"Sarah, what's wrong?" Her mother's eyebrows bowed together in a worried expression.

"Oh nothing, really. Last night I tripped over the chair and cut my leg. It was awfully clumsy of me. My leg is still a little sore." Sarah looked quickly away for she feared her mother would see that she was lying.

"Let me look at the cut. Sometimes nothing can turn into something." Catherine stood up to walk toward Sarah, but the young woman moved away.

"Honest, Mom. I cleaned the wound and put on a Band-Aide. It wasn't very deep at all." Sarah picked up her jacket and headed for the door.

With a loving gesture her mother put her hand on Sarah's arm. "Are you okay? You seem a little on edge."

"Mom, quit worrying. I'm fine. With my back hurting, I haven't been able to sleep much lately."

"Unfortunately, those are the unwanted benefits of being pregnant. But they'll pass, and then you'll acquire new ones like the baby waking up in the middle of the night." Catherine looked at her in a motherly way and said, "But you know, it's worth it. Every part. Being a mother has brought the greatest joy to my life."

"I just hope I'll be as good as a mom as you've been." Sarah admired her mother and wished to be like her in every way.

"That's the nicest compliment I think anyone could ever give me." Catherine's eyes misted as she looked warmly at Sarah.

"Mom, there is something I need to tell you. When I get to the center today I'm going to resign for awhile." Sarah spoke slowly, for she wanted to be careful of what she said.

"I'm not sure I understand." Catherine sounded confused. "You mean resign for good or take a leave of absence when you have the baby?"

Sarah felt guilty for what she must tell her mother. She felt guilty for all the children she would let down. They would miss her when they didn't see her anymore. Those children had been part of her world for three years and now they were being taken from her. Her heart ached as if she had lost her unborn child.

"I mean for good." Sarah paused to see her mother's reaction, but when she gave none she spoke further. "Greg is concerned about my time away from the baby after it's born. He is very much against me leaving our child with a baby-sitter. That's why he didn't want me to work. He feels this volunteer position will interfere with my responsibilities here at home." Sarah knew her voice quivered, but she would rather die than tell her mother the truth about what Greg had called the kids.

Her mother had a big heart and she would have never been able to comprehend how anyone couldn't care for less fortunate children.

Sarah felt her mother's eyes search deep into hers. "I don't mean to pry, but is everything okay between you and Greg? All you've said was about what Greg wants. But what about you? Do you really want to quit the center, or is this honestly just his wishes?" Catherine spoke kindly as she walked over to the sofa, sat down and patted the cushion next to her indicating for Sarah to come and sit by her.

She felt like a little girl again sitting next to her mother. Here she was talking about her marriage when she didn't feel old enough to be married. "There has been some tension between us lately. Mom, I know this sounds stupid, but I think Greg feels threatened as a husband even though I haven't done anything to make him feel that way."

"Have you tried to talk with Greg about what he is feeling?"

"That's easier said than done. I know daddy is not this way, but Greg is like a clam. We haven't talked much lately. He won't open up to me."

"What do you think is going on with him?" Catherine asked.

"His whole life he watched his mom control and manipulate his father. And maybe he feels that will happen to him if he doesn't take control now. I don't know what to do. I'm trying to be a good wife, but I don't want to give up my volunteer job. I love those kids so much. Just the thought of not seeing them anymore is tearing my heart out. Oh, Mom, what should I do?" With tears in her eyes, Sarah took her mother's hand.

"I can't tell you what decision to make. All I can do is offer my advice and listen to you. Marriage can be hard at times, especially the first year. It's difficult enough going through the normal changes of being married, but you're also adding a baby to your list. Maybe Greg's a little jealous of the baby although he probably wouldn't admit it. So there could be some issues he's had to deal with and doesn't feel comfortable sharing with you." Catherine squeezed Sarah's hand to reassure her. "But give him time. He'll open up.

"I just feel so helpless when he shuts me out. I'm his wife and should be able to reach him." Sarah blinked back her tears.

"Not that it makes this any easier, but you've got to remember his parents' marriage is anything but desirable. There's been no one to be an example to

Greg. But you've come from a family where your father and I love each other. If anyone can help him, it's you. You're not a quitter and the love you have for Greg can truly heal a wounded heart."

Sarah squeezed her mother's hand and kissed her on the cheek. "Mom, I always feel so much better after we've talked. I know you're right. I will have to be the one to compromise right now. Maybe I'll resign temporarily and hopefully Greg will come around later. You said he may be jealous of the baby. Well maybe he's also jealous of these kids and this is just his way of coping."

A more relaxed expression settled across Sarah's face. Her mother stood up and glanced at her wrist watch. "We'd better get going if we don't want to be late," Catherine said, walking toward the door.

Sarah picked up her shoulder bag, grabbed her keys off the coffee table and briefly looked around at their small apartment. This was her home now and their life together could go either direction. They had come from two totally different environments, one which consisted of love, the other hate.

Sarah believed that everyone had good in them. Sometimes you just have to dig deep enough to find it. Greg had built a wall around himself to protect his heart, which was badly bruised and torn. With her devotion and love, she knew he could be reached and changed. No matter how long it took, she wouldn't give up on him. She needed him and so did their child. Whether he realized it or not, Greg needed them, too.

She hated the fact she was having to abandon the Down Syndrome children, even though she knew the other volunteers loved them too. Her presence would be missed, but the children wouldn't be neglected. Maybe this decision was for the best right now. She could devote more time to Greg. With the baby coming soon she'd have to divide her time between husband and child. The adjustment of having an infant in the house might be hard for Greg and it was probably for the best not to have any outside distractions.

Time had a way of working things out. Change was the only tangible element which was consistent, good or bad. All she could do was take one day at a time and hope for the best.

As she closed the door and locked the deadbolt, Sarah felt like a balance. One side was light with resolution, the other heavy weighted with sadness. She was unprepared for her farewell today and thought of the special children who held a key to her heart. A tear ran slowly down her cheek as her lips silently mouthed, "One day at a time."

Chapter Ten

Sarah placed the last cherry on the cheesecake, then stood back and surveyed the table. She had spent most of the afternoon carefully setting the table for this intimate dinner for just her and Greg. She wanted tonight to be extra special from the appetizer to the dessert. A breakthrough in their relationship was overdue and a good dinner would be the icebreaker she needed.

She quickly wiped her hands on the dish towel for the doorbell rang. Sarah was surprised when she opened the front door to see her husband standing there with a smile on his face, while one hand held a brown paper sack and the other yellow roses.

"You gonna just stand there or are you going to let me in? I would have used my key, but as you can see I'm loaded down," said Greg.

Embarrassed that her reaction must have been so obvious, Sarah blushed and pushed open the screen door. "Of course, silly." She stepped aside so he could enter the apartment. Greg whistled and went into the kitchen with the sack and roses. Sarah followed him and watched as he put the flowers in a vase and took a loaf of French bread and a bottle of wine from the sack.

"The flowers are for you and the wine is non-alcoholic." He turned and looked at her. Only hours before his eyes were cold and angry, but now they were filled with a tenderness she had almost forgotten.

"They're beautiful. Thank you." She felt like a school girl again, when she and Greg had first gone out. She didn't move for she wanted to savor the moment.

"Dinner smells great. I'm starved. I'll go wash and leave the bread to you." He patted her stomach as he passed her on the way toward the bedroom.

Sarah hummed to herself and sliced the French bread, buttered it and sprinkled garlic salt across each slice. So far, so good, she thought, pulling the steaming lasagna out of the oven. The evening was off to a good start and she would wait for the right time to talk to Greg. Sarah placed the yellow roses at the end of the table so they wouldn't block the view between her and Greg.

The conversation throughout dinner was kept to simple conversation about Greg's job, their families, and the baby. Sarah was anxious to get to the heart of tonight's discussion, but she was happy Greg was showing interest again in their baby.

"This cherry cheesecake is the best I've ever eaten." Greg spoke between mouthfuls.

"You say that every time I fix it, but thanks." Sarah laughed and took another sip of wine. Well, this is as good as time as any, she thought, and sat her glass down. "I'm glad you enjoyed the dinner." Sarah took in a deep breath and placed her hands in her lap.

"Greg, I would like to talk to you about something." She looked at him as he finished off the last bite of his cheesecake. "I'm not sure where to start, so please bear with me."

He pushed his chair away from the table, and leaned the chair back, balancing on the legs. "Sarah, I think I know what you want to talk about. If you'll let me talk first, I can save us a lot of time."

This was the second time tonight her husband had caught her by surprise. "Sure, you go ahead."

Greg placed his hand on the table and tapped his fingers. Sarah knew this was hard for him. Hopefully, his talking about their problems would begin the process of healing their marriage. Even after all the hurt and pain he'd caused her, she loved him and her heart went out to him.

"Saying I'm sorry is not my specialty, so I won't pretend I'm any good at it. The way I acted last night and well, I guess the past few months have been awful for you. I've treated you badly. If you can forgive me, I'll do my best to change and treat you better."

Sarah got out of her chair and stood next to Greg with her arms around his neck. Her tears flowed freely as he stood up and held her. "I love you, Sarah.

Please don't cry." With gentleness, he lifted her chin and kissed her. Sarah surrendered herself to him and parted her lips willingly, allowing his tongue to caress her inner mouth.

Emotions that had laid dormant for so long were now aroused. Greg lifted Sarah in his strong arms, carried her into the bedroom and lowered her onto the bed.

Experienced fingers unbuttoned her shirt while his mouth moved from her lips down her neck. "I've missed you." He whispered passionately. His hand touched the soft, creamy flesh of her breast.

Sarah went weak under his fingers, longing for more of him. As his hands explored her body, awakening forgotten sensations, Sarah responded to his needs as well. Even though they couldn't make love, the pleasure they brought each other throughout the night left her fulfilled and loved.

It seemed liked hours passed as she watched Greg sleep. Her finger traced the form of his face, taking in every feature. This was the man she married, the one who had charmed her so. He had been gone somewhere and now he was back. All she knew was that she was ecstatically happy. Sarah wished they could lie there all night like this, for as long as forever could be.

"Cath, have you talked to Sarah today? Wasn't her doctor's appointment this morning?" Alex sat his briefcase down on his desk and opened it. "Now where did I put that file?"

Catherine laughed, for the file her husband wanted lay next to his briefcase. "If you would slow down for two minutes and give me your undivided attention, I'd be happy to tell you about your daughter's appointment." She crossed her arms and waited patiently.

"Honest, I'm all ears." Alex looked up briefly and then back down at the open file next to his briefcase.

With an amused look on her face, she laughed to herself and blurted out. "It's the most wonderful news. Sarah's going to have triplets!"

Alex turned over some papers and calmly said, "Triplets, that's nice."

Catherine began to count down under her breath, "One, two, three, four—"

"Triplets! Did you say triplets?" Alex almost turned his swivel chair over as he abruptly stood up.

"I knew I could get your undivided attention. One way or another." At this point she burst out with laughter. "I would feel terrible if I caused you to have a coronary at your age. No. I lied. But it was fun proving a point."

Alex stepped out from behind his desk and walked over to his wife. "I guess I deserved it." He kissed her and took her by the hand, making his way toward the den. "I could use a drink after that one."

"You sit down and I'll fix them. Then I'll tell you about Sarah's appointment. The truth this time." Again she laughed as she pictured her husband's face at the news of triplets.

They settled together on the sofa, then Catherine proceeded to tell Alex about Sarah. "The doctor said Sarah and the baby are fine. He thinks the baby will come on schedule. In about two weeks we will be grandparents." Catherine nestled against her husband's shoulder.

"Grandparents. Sounds kind of old, doesn't it?" Alex gazed down at his drink.

"It's harder to believe that our daughter is going to be a mother than us being grandparents. But now that the baby is almost here, I'm so excited." Catherine smiled and thought about the baby and what Sarah had said about her being a good mother.

"Cath, did Greg go with you and Sarah to the doctor?" Alex looked intently at his wife.

"No, he didn't. Sarah said he didn't want to miss work right now since he would have to be off when the baby came."

"How convenient for him." Alex's tone was sarcastic, and Catherine knew with he way he felt about their son-in-law, that anytime Greg did something negative, it was another mark against him in her husband's eyes.

"Alex, do you think that is really fair? Greg has gone to some of the appointments with Sarah." Catherine once again played the mediator, trying to calm a volcanic situation she one day felt would erupt.

"Has he been fair to Sarah? Has he been a good husband to our daughter?" Before she had a chance to comment he talked on. "It's not a particular incident I can isolate, but it's what I see in Sarah's eyes." Alex paused as if he were trying to remember something.

"What do you mean, it was what you see in her eyes?" Catherine wasn't sure what he could be talking about, because she felt sure Sarah would confide in her if anything was wrong.

"There were a couple of times when I went to visit Sarah at her apartment. Everything seemed to be okay, but I could see in her eyes she was troubled. When I asked Sarah how she and Greg were, she said all the right things, but it's the way she looked. There was a sadness she tried to cover up with words." Alex finished off his drink and lay back against the couch.

Catherine knew Alex didn't miss a thing about people, especially his own daughter. The times Sarah had talked with her when she had been upset about Greg, they were always minor problems. And Sarah always said she had felt better after Catherine encouraged her with motherly advice. Could it be possible there was something more that even she as Sarah's mother couldn't detect?

"I don't know what could be wrong. The times I talked with Sarah when she and Greg were going through adjustments, she always seemed to be truthful about what was wrong. The problems weren't anything to really worry about. Don't you think if there were major difficulties we would know?" Catherine laid her head on Alex's shoulder and sighed.

"I want to believe that more than anything. Sarah means the world to me. Even with her married, I still want to protect her. She's always going to be my little girl. Nothing will ever change that." Alex gave Catherine a kiss on the cheek before he rose.

Catherine stood up and took Alex by the hand. "I know you don't think a lot of Greg, but shouldn't we give him the benefit of the doubt? He is our daughter's husband and she loves him." Catherine looked at her husband with admiration, touching his cheek. "You're a good man whose heart holds so much love for this family. Can you try to make a little room in there for Greg, who is now part of this family? If not for Greg, then for Sarah and our grandchild?" Her words were tender and gentle.

Alex looked lovingly at Catherine. "I'll try. I promise. I love you, Cath." With a tenderness that touched her heart, Alex kissed her, relieving her of all cares for this moment in time.

She heard her husband come in the living room, though she pretended not to. Marina lay on the couch propped up with plush pillows, reading Cosmopolitan. Her appearance was impeccable, enhanced today by freshly painted crimson toenails. Even though Frank never complimented her any more, she knew he still thought her beautiful.

Marina turned the page as Frank walked in and sat down in the recliner. "Don't you have anything better to do than sit here watching me? Or is your life so dismal that this is the best thing you have to do?" Marina gloated behind her magazine. She loved reminding Frank of his worthless existence. She flexed her toes and stretched, settling deeper into the pillows.

"Why do we always have to be like this? Can't we try to be civil to each other?" Frank looked at her with frustration.

"And spoil this perfectly good marriage?" Her tone was thick with sarcasm. She raised her eyebrows and peered over the top of the magazine. Pushing Frank's buttons was the only satisfaction she got from of this marriage.

"Look, I don't want to fight. I came in here to talk to you about Sarah's baby shower tomorrow. Catherine wanted to know if we would like to come over early before the shower and have dinner with them, and Greg and Sarah."

"Why would I go have dinner over at the Matthews when I'm not going to the baby shower? You just don't give up, do you. I told you from the start I won't associate with those people. I don't care if our son married their daughter or not!" Her temper was on the rise. The mention of the Matthews made her blood boil. Marina made an attempt to get off the couch, but Frank quickly got out of the recliner and blocked her.

"I'm sick and tired of your attitude toward Alex and Catherine. You've never had a reason for the way you feel. It's jealousy, pure and simple, and it's eating you from the inside out. They are good people who've tried to be our friends, but you won't allow them to. I'm putting a stop to this right now." Frank's neck turned red as his jaw tightened.

Marina put her legs back up on the couch and looked out the window.

"You can ignore me all you want, but you're going tomorrow, both to the dinner and to the shower. You will be civil and polite. And if you don't, you will regret the day you ever met me, more so than you do now. You know I don't make idle threats, so I suggest you take heed."

She didn't have to see his eyes to know her husband meant what he said. But his threats didn't phase her. The few times he had hit her only increased her hatred for him and made her more determined to make his life as miserable as possible. Frank would tell her he didn't want to hit her, but she drove him to it.

Her blood began to boil as her thoughts went back to the Matthews. Somehow she would get him for this. Frank was a fool to think this was over. He would be the one with the regrets. Marina turned from the window to look at Frank. Her temple pulsated above her smoldering eyes.

"Whatever you say, Frank. I won't disappoint you." Her words were coated with honey, but underneath they were as deadly as venom.

"You don't fool me, Marina. I meant what I said." Frank started to leave the room, but he stopped, then turned to face her. "You talk about my worthless existence. You should take a good look at yourself. You're an empty shell with no heart, no love. You don't care who you hurt or what you do to people. I pity you. You've no purpose in life but to destroy everyone around you."

Marina's expression never changed while Frank spoke. He just looked at her before e turned and left the room. Her face remained hardened and cold. The contempt she felt for him was stronger than ever as she stared at the empty doorway. Frank was weak and spineless. His words meant nothing to her. Any regrets she had were only those of the wasted years she had spent with him.

Tomorrow night was the only thing on her mind right now. Her eyes narrowed when she thought of the Matthews. You will be sorry, Frank, she thought to herself, a smug expression darkening her face. She looked back out the window into a world that held only emptiness for her.

Chapter Eleven

The soft breeze from the silky night floated through the kitchen when Alex came in the back door. "Mmm, that smells good." He walked up behind Josephine, the faithful cook and house keeper of twenty years, leaned over her shoulder and looked down at the stove. "Need some help?" Alex liked to kid her because he knew she didn't like anyone in the kitchen when she cooked.

"You do your job and let me do mine," Josephine snorted as she continued to stir the Irish stew, with a twinkle in her eye.

"Oh, Josie, don't ever change." He laughed as he left the kitchen. The sound of Mozart drew him to the den where he found Catherine asleep on the couch. Softly he walked over to the couch and sat next to her. Gentle fingers caressed her porcelain cheek.

Her eyelids fluttered open as he continued to admire her. "Alex, I must have dozed off. How long have you been sitting there? Why didn't you wake me?"

"Not long. You looked so beautiful lying here. I didn't want to disturb you."

Catherine smiled at him as he leaned down and kissed her. He lingered for a moment before he stood up. "I assume from the peace and quiet that Will and Carter are gone."

"You must have had a busy day. Remember, this is the weekend the boys went on the basketball camping trip. They won't be back until Sunday night."

"What did we do to deserve this added blessing? The whole weekend to ourselves to do whatever we want." Alex laughed and took off his suit coat.

"Well, since Josie is preparing dinner, why don't we just rent a movie tonight and relax." Catherine stretched as she sat up.

"Sounds great." The day had been busy and stressful, and this would be a good way to unwind. "I'll go change and run to Blockbuster to get the movie. Any preference?"

"How bout a romantic comedy?"

"A chick flick." Alex rubbed his fingers against his chin as though he was in deep thought. "Tell you what. We'll compromise. Some romance with a lot of violence." He laughed whole heartedly and turned to leave the den.

"All right, you win. But don't take too long in making a selection. Dinner will be ready soon." Catherine got up and followed him out of the den.

Alex was half way up the stairs when Josephine came out of the kitchen with the cordless phone in her hand. "Mr. Matthews, it's Sarah."

Quickly he descended the steps and took the phone from Josephine. "How's my favorite girl?" Deep set wrinkles embedded his forehead. "Where is Greg? Honey, you hold tight. Just sit there and stay still. We're on our way. Yes, I'll hurry. I love you, Sarah." Alex handed the phone back to Josephine and put his jacket back on.

The anxiety written all over his face caused his wife's light hearted expression to change.

"Is Sarah okay? What's wrong?" Catherine put her hand around his arm.

"Sarah's water has broke, and she's gone into labor." His tone of concern turned to anger when he spoke of Greg. "And Greg is nowhere to be found. Sarah said he'd gone out with friends, but didn't leave a number where he could be reached. What is wrong with him! A man's wife is due any day and he goes out with friends." Alex's jaw tightened as he grabbed his keys off the foyer table.

"Alex, not now. Sarah needs us and we can't upset her. Please don't let her see you like this. What's important right now is her and the baby."

"You're right. We must be there for her. I'll get to the bottom of this later." Alex opened the front door and hurriedly went down the walkway, but Catherine stopped and turned around.

"Josie, please call the Winslows. Let them know that Sarah has gone into labor and we're taking her to the hospital. See if they can find Greg and let him know."

"I will. Please call me."

"Of course," Catherine said, casting a troubled look at Josephine before she shut the door.

Alex drove swiftly down the cliff as he thought of Sarah. She deserved better than this. The doubts he'd had about his son-in-law were no longer doubts. How could he make Sarah see the truth? If he tried to convince her again there would only be conflict between them. He had tried to be supportive for Sarah's sake, but now after this, Alex didn't know how he'd be able to contain his feelings any longer. Somehow, Sarah's eyes would have to be opened, without his help. Maybe she already knew the truth and hadn't said anything to him or Catherine.

His hands gripped the steering wheel harder when he thought of Greg. Alex had been fair and given him the benefit of the doubt, even against his better judgment. From now on his son-in-law had better watch his step. Sarah meant everything to Alex, and he wasn't going to let Greg hurt her in any way.

The features in his face softened as he remembered his daughter. Right now he had to think of her and the grandchild she was about to give him. Nothing else mattered. His heart pounded harder as he applied more pressure to the accelerator. "I'm coming, Sarah. I'm coming," he muttered under his breath.

The maternity waiting room was empty except for Alex. Sarah had been in labor for almost three hours. He'd tried to stay in the labor room with her and Catherine, but he couldn't stand to see his daughter in pain. Perspiration had soaked her hair, and her face was a pale ash. The agony in her eyes was more than he could bear. Now Alex paced back and forth across the taupe carpet and waited.

"Any news yet?"

Alex stopped in his tracks and turned toward the familiar voice to see Frank Winslow standing there. "No. She's still in labor." Conversation was the last thing he wanted, but he didn't want to be rude to Frank. Greg's behavior wasn't his father's fault. If anyone was to blame, it was Marina. Yes, Greg made his own choices, but his mother planted the bad seeds in him. Frank had been loving and supportive to Sarah from the beginning. He was an attentive father-in-law and Alex appreciated the kindness he'd shown his daughter.

"I got over here as soon as I heard. Listen, I don't know what to say about my son. There aren't any acceptable excuses so I won't try to make any for him." Frank was obviously uncomfortable and Alex felt sorry for him.

"Marina would have come with me, but she's waiting at the apartment for Greg to come in."

"Frank, there's no need for you to try and apologize. Greg is a grown man who makes his own choices. I don't hold you responsible for your son's actions. If you don't mind, I'd rather not talk about him and focus on Sarah and the baby." Alex put his hand on Frank's shoulder and looked at him kindly.

"I never quite understood why these things take so long. I guess the baby will come when it's good and ready," Frank said, more relaxed.

"It's probably going to be a girl because they don't do anything until they're ready." Both men laughed together as they sat down on the couch to continue to wait.

Three more hours passed before Catherine entered the waiting room with a broad grin on her tired face. "Frank, Alex, you're the grandfathers of a healthy baby girl!"

Both men jumped up at the same time. Elated Alex put his arms around Catherine to hug her, while Frank put an arm around both of their shoulders.

Alex was relieved the ordeal was over, for the memory was still fresh in his mind of how Sarah looked when he last saw her. "How's Sarah?" he asked his wife.

"She's fine. Happy, but tired. Even though the labor only lasted six hours, it was hard labor. You better go see her now because she'll be asleep soon." Catherine smiled wearily as Alex put his arm around his wife.

"You look exhausted. Frank, would you mind taking this tired grandmother to the cafeteria to get a cup of coffee? I'll stay with Sarah until you get back."

"I'd be happy to. She can tell me all about the baby." Frank said proudly, as he and Catherine walked toward the elevator.

Alex smiled at them before the elevator door closed and was about to go back to Sarah's room when he saw Greg at the nurses' station. He didn't need a rocket scientist to tell him that he'd been drinking. He slumped as he questioned the nurse in an attempt to find Sarah. His voice was overly loud, with slightly slurred words.

With slow steps, Alex approached Greg with the intent to stay calm, although the tone in his voice was cold and sarcastic when he addressed his son-in-law. "How good of you to show up."

Greg swayed when he turned around. For a brief moment he just looked at Alex before he spoke hesitantly. "Alex, I didn't recognize you for a second."

"Really. I hear that alcohol dulls the senses." Alex's face hardened before he took a step closer. Causing a scene was the last thing he wanted, for Sarah's room was only a few feet away.

With narrowed eyes, Greg wiped his mouth with the back of his hand. "I want to see my wife." He tried to step away, but Alex blocked him.

"Your wife just happened to have your child while you were out drinking with your buddies. What's the matter with you?" Alex's temple began to throb as he glared at his son-in-law. "Sarah needed you and you weren't there."

"I want to see Sarah, now get out of my way!" A feeble attempt was made to push his way past, but Alex grabbed him by the front of his shirt and pulled him roughly into the waiting room, forcing him down into a chair.

"Look at you. You're a mess! Is this how you want your wife to see you? Drunk. You're not going to go in there and upset her. She's been through a lot and she doesn't need this. You have a beautiful daughter who needs a decent father, not a drunk." With disgust, Alex stepped back and looked at Greg.

Slouched down in the chair, Greg remained motionless, looking off into space.

"I'm not going to let you ruin my daughter's or granddaughter's life. You either get your act together or get out of their lives. Sarah deserves better than this. If you want to drag yourself down in the gutter that is your choice, but you're not taking them with you." Alex continued to stare at his son-in-law. By nature, he wasn't a violent person, but in Greg's case he could easily make an exception.

Awkwardly, Greg pulled himself to his feet. His eyes were glazed over as he faced Alex. "The great Alex Matthews has spoken." Thick words lashed out with malice, as he swore profusely. "You never wanted Sarah to marry me. I wasn't good enough for your precious little princess. But she is mine now, and that drives you crazy. I've taken your place, and you can't stand not being in control. Get used to it, Bud, because Sarah does what I want her to. She belongs to me and so does my daughter. And there is nothing you or anyone can do to change that." Greg sneered and laughed mockingly.

Everything he'd suspected about Greg was true. All this time had been a front to cover what he really was. A lying womanizer, who didn't care who he hurt to get what he wanted. Alex knew now that the incident with the high school girl was fact. Alex uncrossed his arms and put his index finger in Greg's chest. "You better watch your step because I am. You ever do anything to hurt Sarah or the baby, there won't be a hole deep enough for you to hide in that I won't find you."

Greg shoved Alex's finger away from his chest and stepped forward. "Don't think you can threaten me. I may not be a hot shot lawyer but I hold the dice. I can take Sarah and the baby and move so far away you'll never see them. If I were you, Alex, I'd watch your step. You're a smart man and you know that life is a game where chances are taken. It's a pretty safe bet to say that this is one chance you're not going to take." With his shoulders raised back, he arrogantly cocked his head, and started walking out of the waiting room.

Human behavior never surprised Alex, because he was usually a good judge of character. With Greg, he was only surprised that it didn't take longer for his pretentious, charming, outward character to be diminished by his dark alter ego. If only Alex had been wrong about Greg. After this confrontation, Alex was convinced Greg didn't care anything about Sarah. No matter how much he despised his son-in-law, he wasn't going to let his daughter get caught in the middle. Alex had age, wisdom and experience on his side. All Greg had was his ego and pride.

"I won't let our dislike of each other destroy Sarah. And if you honestly care anything about her you'll do the same," Alex said calmly.

Greg stopped and turned halfway toward Alex only revealing his profile. "Is that fatherly advice? Should I thank you now or later?" The bitterness in his voice was undeniable. And with those final words, he turned and left.

Difficult situations had challenged him before, but had seldom left Alex this angry. This time though, it was different, because the stakes were personal. A daughter, for whom he'd done everything to protect, had become a prized possession just to prove a point. The thought of a troubled relationship with his daughter is what would keep him from telling her about tonight. The only thing Alex could do for the time being was stay involved with Sarah and get along with Greg the best he could.

A large part of him wanted his daughter to see Greg for what he was, but he knew that would only bring hurt to her and his grandchild. Deep in his heart, Alex knew the best thing for Sarah would be if Greg would become a good husband and father. More than anything he wanted Sarah to be happy. Somewhat calmer, Alex left the waiting room. The hour was late and he wanted to say goodnight to Sarah, but didn't. After this exhausting ordeal of childbirth, she would need rest to regain her strength. Not only for the sake of taking care of a baby, but to face a marriage with harsh tremors.

Chapter Twelve

The baby brought more joy to Sarah's life than she ever thought possible. Though the days were filled with feedings, diaper changes and all her other responsibilities, she had never been happier and so completely fulfilled. Yes, motherhood suited her well, and she couldn't imagine her life now without her daughter.

Their baby girl had been christened Katelan Nicole Winslow. Picking a name for their child hadn't been an easy task. Over all the family names, she and Greg never could come to an agreement. Eventually, they decided not to go the traditional way and came up with something on their own.

Where had the last six months gone? Sarah looked at Katelan napping in her crib. It was plain to see her daughter was going to be a beauty with her dark brown hair and emerald green eyes like her own. Her lips, which offset her ivory complexion reminded Sarah of pink rosebuds. Changes in her daughter seemed to take place every day. Not only with her appearance, but the things she could do. Life had a funny way of sneaking up on a person. Tears formed in Sarah's eyes as she gently touched her baby's soft cheek. Everything in her life was perfect except for Greg.

When they first came home from the hospital with Katelan he was wonderful. The late nights out with his friends stopped. He liked being home with her and the baby. Even though Sarah was nursing, she sometimes put her milk into a bottle so Greg could feed Katelan. But when she turned four months old, the new had worn off. Once again, Greg became distant and withdrawn. The apartment was never clean enough, or the baby cried too much. His complaints never seemed to stop. The harder Sarah tried to do what he wanted, the more he pushed her away.

At least three times a week she took Katelan to spend the day at her parents' house.

With her father working so much and her brothers at school, her mother welcomed the company. Her mother adored her granddaughter and enjoyed the time together.

Occasionally, Sarah felt slightly guilty for not visiting Marina more often than she did. But those visits were tense and unpleasant. And besides, Marina didn't really act interested in Katelan at all, though Frank was crazy about her.

The knock at the front door came in three swift taps. The only one who knocked that way was her father. Sarah wondered why he was here in the middle of the day. Quietly, she closed the nursery door and went to the front door. The wind had picked up, and cold air rushed through the room when she opened the door and stepped aside for her father to enter. "Daddy, what are you doing here? Not that I'm not glad to see you, but it's still early afternoon," she said, kissing him on the cheek.

"I didn't know I had to have a reason to stop by and see my daughter and grandchild. Should I have my secretary call next time and make an appointment?" Alex tweaked her nose as he walked over to stand in front of the fireplace to warm himself.

"Oh, Daddy. Always the teaser. I guess I should feel honored that you left the office to come see me." Sarah smiled at her father. Any unexpected visits were always welcomed. Even with the baby, loneliness was with her more than she wanted to admit.

"With the cold weather and only two weeks till Thanksgiving, the office has slowed down. I'm going home early today and thought I would stop by and see you first."

"Well, I'm glad you did. I miss you." Sarah's voice quivered a little as her eyes locked with her father's.

"I miss you, too," he said, holding his hand out to her. Though he'd never told Sarah what had happened that night at the hospital when Katelan was born, he had distanced himself somewhat. Not sure if Greg's threat to move away was legitimate, Alex decided not to rock the boat for the meantime. He knew Catherine saw Sarah frequently and hoped she would be able to tell if something was wrong.

Tears flowed down her cheeks as she rushed into her father's arms. Just the feel of his strong, loving arms around her was all it took for her to break down. She clung to him desperately. Time seemed to pause while her father held her and stroked her hair. It was as though she was a little girl again and her father could make everything better. All his words of encouragement and reassurance had driven away her hurt and fears. She wasn't his little girl anymore, but a married woman with problems even her father couldn't make go away.

Reluctantly, she withdrew herself from his embrace. "I don't know what's come over me. I guess I've missed you more than I realized." She took the handkerchief her father offered and blew her nose.

"Are you sure that's all it is?" His voice was gentle, yet inquisitive. Alex lifted her chin to meet his eyes.

"Daddy, I'm just going through some adjustments. Marriage, a new baby, growing up." She wanted to look away from her father, but she dared not, for that would be a dead give away that she wasn't telling all. "Really, I'm fine."

"I don't mean to pry. It's just that I know you, and I feel like you're not telling me something. I'm here for you." He wanted to be careful not to push too hard. That might only make her clam up tighter. "If you ever want to talk, day or night."

"You've always been there for me, Daddy. And I know you'll always be. That means a lot to me. But honest, I'm fine." She forced a smile as she returned the dampened handkerchief. Quickly wanting to change the subject, Sarah knew one way to divert her father. "Would you like to see your granddaughter? I think I hear her stirring from her nap."

The worried lines across his forehead diminished at the mention of Katelan. "You must have been reading my thoughts." Alex winked at her and followed her toward the nursery.

Sarah wasn't sure if she had convinced her father that everything was okay. With a lawyer's sense about him, he had a way of not exposing what he thought. Right now, all she could deal with was Greg. Things would only get worse if her parents knew the truth. Still determined that she could work out the problems with her husband, there was no need to involve her parents. She wanted them to be proud of her and to see how mature she was.

Things would get better. She had to believe that. Everyone had told her the first year of marriage was the hardest. Their one year anniversary was next month, and she would make it special for Greg. Her parents were going to baby sit so she and Greg could be alone. This would be the first time she'd spend the night away from her baby and she wasn't real crazy about the idea, but she wanted to devote her full attention to Greg.

Most of her time was consumed with her daughter, and she realized that she needed to give her husband equal time. Sarah was going to go that extra mile to try and make their marriage better. When Greg saw how hard she was trying, he would probably try a lot harder. One thing was for sure. Something needed to change soon. She was wearing her feelings on her sleeve, and it didn't take much for emotions to overtake her.

Alex's face lit up as Katelan smiled when she saw her grandfather. Sarah stood back and watched her father and her daughter. The sight of them together made her happy, for she knew they would be close. But she also worried about Greg's lack of interest in his daughter. Don't ever give up, she told herself. Hard times can either make or break a person. She wasn't one to be broken.

Dinner was just about ready when she heard Greg come through the front door. Her father had stayed longer than planned, which caused her to get a late start on the evening meal. Greg had made it very clear to her that he wanted his supper on the table when he got home from work. As she spooned up the last of the spaghetti, Greg came into the kitchen and plopped down into a chair.

"Why isn't dinner on the table?" His tone was short and almost angry.

"It's coming right now." Sarah set the spaghetti and meatballs on the table and reached for the bread from the stove as she sat down.

"Aren't you forgetting something?" he asked impatiently.

With a quick survey of the table, Sarah was at a loss. "I don't think so."

"The parmesan cheese. How am I supposed to eat spaghetti without parmesan?"

Sarah did her best to keep her voice calm, but she was irritated with him. He either had a bad day at work or he was just in a bad mood, and she was tired of him taking it out on her. Without a word, Sarah got up to get the cheese and sat back down.

Silently, Greg ate, never even looking up at Sarah. Another fun evening at the Winslow house, she thought, as she picked at her food. "I thought we could rent a video and just have a quiet night and relax." She glanced over at him to find him already staring at her.

The expression in his eyes was cold and distant. "I'm going out with friends."

"I could get my parents to baby sit and I'll go with you. It's been a long time since we've been out together, " she said enthusiastically.

He ran his hand through his hair and leaned back in his chair. "Only guys are going."

"Couldn't you stay home with me tonight?" Her eyes became sad as she looked down at her unfinished food. "I get lonely when you're gone."

Her request left Greg untouched, uncompassionate. "You've got Katelan. Go to your parents. You're over there all the time anyway." Greg set his chair back down on the floor with a hard thud and stood up.

"Katelan is wonderful and I love her, but I love you too. We're supposed to be a family. Families spend time together, not apart from each other." Sarah stood up and walked around the table to her husband. Her eyes watered, but she was determined not to cry. "I'm not always at my parents, but what if I were? You wouldn't notice, anyway. You're never here."

"Don't get smart with me, Sarah. I'm the man of the house. I do what I want, when I want. No woman is going to tell me what to do. My mom has done that to my dad for years. You're my wife, not my mother." Angrily, he left the kitchen and went into the bedroom.

The fact that he would even compare her to Marina was unbelievable. She wasn't anything like her mother-in-law. Couldn't Greg see that she wasn't mad, just hurt that he obviously didn't want to be around her. He just couldn't walk away again. This would have to get resolved for their marriage to survive. Sarah followed after him. "We have to talk, Greg. You constantly walk away from me instead of dealing with whatever is wrong. Greg, please." Her eyes pleaded with him, but to no avail.

"It's never enough for you. You wouldn't have an abortion, so I married you. But that still wasn't good enough. You don't want me to spend time with friends. I work all day at a dead end job only to come home to a wife that is consumed with a baby. This is the life I'm supposed to be content with! You're suffocating me!"

Sarah was in total shock as she slowly sat down on the bed. Hot tears ran down her cheeks. He might as well have taken a dagger and put it through her heart, for how brutally his words ripped through her heart. She couldn't believe what she was hearing. Greg didn't have to marry her, she had told him that. She loved him so much she had been willing to let go. He told her he loved her.

Nonchalantly, Greg changed his clothes as if nothing had taken place. The bathroom door remained opened while he combed his hair and put on fresh cologne. Sarah wiped the smeared mascara from her eyes and watched her husband prepare to go out. Did he care nothing for her, or their daughter? Were their marriage vows a farce? Hurt was still a high emotion, but anger had taken its place as well, as Sarah stood up.

"I never made you marry me. My parents didn't even want me to marry you. I was willing to raise our child without you, but you said you wanted to marry me." Her voice climbed to a higher volume as she walked toward the bathroom. Sarah felt lost as though she were grasping for something to hang on to ."What has happened between us? Do you even love me?" A part of her wanted to know the truth, but the other part was afraid to hear what he had to say.

With a final look in the mirror, Greg turned to face her. Sarah's heart sank. There was no remorse on his face, no regret, only resentment toward her. For a brief moment their eyes locked, but then Sarah looked away. She felt weak and alone, intimidated by her husband. Why was this happening? Her world was falling apart and she felt helpless.

"Move, I'm late." He took a step forward, but stopped when Sarah didn't budge.

"Please, stay home so we can work this out. I've been a good wife to you. I've done everything you've asked of me. Can't you do this one thing for me?" Desperation was evident in her voice, but Sarah didn't care. As fast as she felt she was losing him, she was trying just as hard to hold on.

"There's nothing to talk about. Don't push me. Now move!" he yelled and shoved her roughly out of the way.

Maybe it was because he hadn't been drinking or that she was angry herself, but she walked quickly after him into the living room, with no thought of his previous violent outbreaks. "Stop. This isn't solving anything," she begged as she clutched his arm.

Unexpectedly, Greg whirled around and grabbed her by the throat. His face was only inches from hers as his eyes blazed with fury. "Leave me alone!" he yelled.

Her fear increased as his grip tightened around her throat. She gasped for air, Greg seemed to grow stronger. She struggled to speak, but the words made no sound. A tingling sensation overtook her as her body went limp and lifeless. Though she could hear Greg's hostile words, they had become faint and vague like she was being pulled somewhere far away. Jumbled thoughts swirled through her mind when a dull pain shot up the side of her face and head. The discomfort to her head subsided as she fell backwards into darkness.

Chapter Thirteen

Faint sounds of muffled cries could be heard, though Sarah thought she was in a dream where nothing was tangible. Her surroundings were unclear like fog. Images came and went as her eyelids fluttered opened to darkness. The cries grew louder, and Sarah's eyes adjusted to a dim light from a distance as she became keenly aware of sharp pain in her face and throat. As the setting became clearer, her first thought was for the baby, and she made a feeble attempt to get up from the floor. "Katelan,'" she whispered. Upon standing, her head began to spin, followed by a wave of nausea. "Please, God, help me."

With slow, unsteady steps, Sarah made her way to the nursery. The door was slightly ajar, and she could see the glow of the night light coming from behind the rocking chair. Katelan's little body shook as she cried. "Sh, sh," Sarah repeated softly as she picked up her baby and held her close. Sarah sat down in the chair, raised her shirt and nursed a very hungry infant. All was quiet except for the content sucking sounds as she laid her head back against the rocker. Sarah placed herself far away from the apartment in sanctuary where comfort and peace awaited her.

A place to run away to where there was no fear, no hatred, and no sadness. What had she done to make Greg hate her so? The answer was always the same, nothing. She had tried so hard to make him happy, but his anger never stopped. Hot tears filled her eyes, and she bit her lip to keep from crying out loud. She didn't want to upset her baby any further.

Doing her best to put aside hurtful feelings, Sarah burped Katelan and rocked her to sleep. Sarah moaned softly as she stood to put the baby back to bed, for a rush of pain shot through her head. Being a little lightheaded, she carefully laid her daughter in the crib and quietly left the room.

The duplex seemed cold and threatening as though an intruder lurked near by. Sarah turned on a light in the living room, but there was still a darkness which wouldn't go away. Not that she could see it, but the blackness was there. The antique clock on the entertainment center showed the time to be 10:45. It was later than she thought. Sitting down on the sofa, Sarah picked up a throw pillow and held it close to her body. The side of her head began to throb again, but her emotional pain was far heavier to bear than the physical suffering.

With her face buried deep into the pillow, she began to sob from the deepest part of her soul. She was all alone and empty inside. Her face had been transformed to that of a tragedy mask which only displayed its misery and grief. A life which should have been full of joy and happiness was crumbling beneath her. Mixed emotions of hurt, anger and despair stirred within. The worst part was realizing Greg couldn't possibly love her and probably never did. Over and over, Sarah tormented herself with the same question, what have I done to deserve this? But no answer ever came to bring relief.

Sarah removed the wet pillow and wiped her face with her shirt. Was this marriage really over? If so, she had to get away from here. But where could she go? Not to her parents or any of her friends. Shame and humiliation hung over her like a dark cloud. Everyone thought she had a wonderful life with a loving husband, only because she had led them to believe that. Sarah had been so sure she and Greg could work through their difficulties. All they needed was some time to adjust to each other. Maybe the truth was always in front of her and she refused to recognize it. If only she had dropped hints now and then to her parents, but she kept covering for Greg.

Sarah was afraid to stay for fear of what might happen when her husband returned home, but she couldn't bring herself to call her mother and father either. Reluctantly she headed toward her bedroom, but first she stopped at the nursery door to check on Katelan. When Sarah saw that her daughter was peacefully sleeping she went into her bedroom to put on her nightgown. She longed to take a hot shower, but she wanted to be in bed asleep before Greg came home, that is, if he ever came home.

The warmth from the flannel sheets would normally have felt good against her body, but now they served as a shield which hid her briefly from a reality that had become a hellish nightmare. A dull throb pulsated in the side of her head as she lay on the pillow. Physically and emotionally drained, Sarah shut her eyes in an effort to block everything out. All she wanted to do was to sleep and escape her life. Tomorrow she knew she'd have to think about what to do, but for right now she couldn't. With a heavy heart and troubled spirit, Sarah rolled over and thankfully drifted to sleep.

Sarah woke abruptly when the phone rang. Half asleep she reached over and picked up. "Hello."

Barely awake, she was surprised when Greg's voice said, "Sarah, it's me."

She hadn't had time to realize before the phone rang that he wasn't home. Not sure what to say, Sarah just sat there.

"Sarah, are you there?" His tone was soft spoken and gentle.

Just the sound of his voice was like throwing salt on an open wound. Her stomach tightened up in knots and tears formed in her eyes, but she fought hard not to cry. She trembled as she sat up in the bed and moved her hair away from her face. "Yes, I'm here."

Again, there was a brief silence which only caused more anxiety for Sarah.

"I wanted you to know where I was so you wouldn't worry. I stayed over at Ryan's last night." There was a slight hesitation as if he were thinking about what to say next. "Sarah, I—I don't know what to say. You must hate me. I never meant to hurt you."

Sarah wiped the tears from her eyes with the sleeve from her nightgown. But he had hurt her, and not just physically. She was afraid of him. How would she be able to trust him. Would he hit her every time they had a disagreement? If he was in a bad mood, would he take his frustration out on her? God, she wanted to believe him more than anything. Just to have his arm around her again, and love her. She longed for the way he used to look at her. But the memory of last night was too fresh in her mind.

"You don't have to say anything right now, just listen," he said. "I'm sorry. That may not mean anything to you, but I'm sorry. I do love you, Sarah, and Katelan, too. We can make this work. I know we can. Please, don't make any rash decisions about us. Let's talk when I get home from work."

The urgency in Greg's voice surprised Sarah. Did he really mean what he said? Was he truly sorry? She so wanted to believe him, but she was confused and afraid to trust him.

"I've got to get going, but I'll see you later. Please, think about what I said. I love you," he pleaded.

The words that she'd longed to hear for so long echoed in her ear as he hung up. It was almost 7:30 and she knew Katelan wouldn't wake up for another hour or so. She still felt tired, as though she hadn't slept at all and thought about going back to sleep, but now that she was awake her mind was racing. Greg's words were played over and over like a tape recorder as she thought about what he'd said.

A part of her wanted to run into his arms and believe everything he said. The way his touch made her feel. It would be so easy to let him charm his way back into her heart and make her forget, if this had only been a bad dream. But it wasn't. Sarah shuddered at remembering last night. The fear she'd experienced and the hatred in Greg's eyes was frightening. It was a horrible feeling not being able to breathe, to know you were going to die.

No, she could never forget. Greg's presence would always be a reminder of what had happened. Maybe she could forgive him, but now she would fear him. How could she live like that? He would see the fear in her eyes and that would only make him even more angry.

Sarah so needed someone to confide in. Her parents were out of the question. The only way she could go to her mother and father was if her marriage was over. Once her dad found out the truth, he wouldn't allow her to stay with Greg. She had lost contact with most of her friends. Occasionally she saw them at the mall or when she and her mom went out to eat, but it wasn't the same. Marriage and motherhood kept her busy at home, which didn't leave much time left for socializing.

The only other person she would even consider talking to was Father O'Connor. But she hadn't been to church in ages, not since Katelan's christening. Even though a priest was sworn to secrecy by his vows, Sarah wasn't quite sure he might not say something to her father. They were good friends and he thought a lot of the Matthews family. He had christened Sarah and her brothers when they were infants. If Greg ever found out she'd talked to anyone about their marriage, he would be outraged. On their honeymoon, he'd made it clear that they keep their problems between themselves.

Left with no solution, Sarah got out of bed to take a shower. She wasn't prepared for what she saw when she turned on the bathroom light and looked in the mirror. Instinctively, she took a step backwards as her hand went to her mouth. White finger impressions were on her neck surrounded by hideous bruises. Now she could understand why her head kept throbbing when she saw the side of her face. Greg must have hit her even though she didn't remember, for her cheek was swollen two times the normal size. Her skin was puffy and red, laden with dark blue and purple bruises. There was a lump to the right of her cheek bone.

The only words that came out of her mouth were, "My God, my God." Once more she began to cry as she leaned back against the bathroom door and slid to the floor. The sight of what Greg had done was more than she could take. It was like she'd been branded with his anger, his hostility and hatred for her. Marked for the world to see what her husband thought of his beloved wife. How could he say he loved her and yet do this to her?

Sarah had never been one to feel sorry for herself or to question God as to why things happen. But now she couldn't help it. She didn't deserve this. Why was her life turning out this way? All her life she'd been a good person, done things to help people. Maybe God was punishing her because of getting pregnant outside of marriage. Fornication was a sin, and she'd betrayed her parents' trust. Questions continued to invade her thoughts, but no answer ever came to ease the pain.

Time was slipping away as she tried to pull herself together. Katelan would be awake soon and Sarah was supposed to have lunch with her mom today. Another phone call to lie and cover the truth. This luncheon was important to her mom. Josephine was going to baby sit so she could go. Catherine was heading up the annual charity luncheon to raise money for the Dale Evans Center for Down Syndrome children. And now she'd be the reason for her mother's disappointment.

With a heavy heart, Sarah stood up and avoided looking back into the mirror. Carefully, she slipped her nightgown over her head and turned on the shower. As the warm water ran down her back, she wondered what she could tell her mother. The lies she used in the past had varied and her parents always seemed to believe them. But her real worry was what to do when Greg came home tonight. The truth was she feared her husband and was afraid of what he might do next. If she said something he might not like, would he hurt her? She didn't want her daughter to grow up in this kind of environment.

So many issues to think about and so little time. No matter what, she had to put Katelan first. A child needed a secure and stable foundation to grow on. Not one of turmoil and distress. Her child's welfare must always come first. At the thought of her baby, Sarah hurried through her shower, knowing she would awaken soon. As for tonight, she'd stay busy around the apartment today in an effort to keep her mind occupied. This was something you couldn't really plan for. Her grandfather's philosophy of life was let the chips fall where they may. Until now she had never really understood what he meant.

Sarah had made her decisions and now she had to live with them, but situations changed and so did people. A marriage built on trust and love could survive hardships that life brought its way, but without love there were no solid walls to hold the marriage together. Everything really depended on Greg and what his intentions were. Her heart wanted to make the marriage work, but the way it should be. Deep in her heart, Sarah longed for Greg to make the right choice. To want to be with her and Katelan more than anything else in the world.

As she combed her wet hair, Sarah reluctantly looked in the mirror. Just the sight of her face brought tears to her eyes. Maybe she should cover the bruises with makeup before Greg came home. But she decided not to. He needed to face the reality of what he had done. Why should she make this situation any easier for him. A heavy sigh escaped her lips as she left the bathroom. Though she wanted to believe for the best, Sarah couldn't shake the cold feeling that a stranger lived inside the man she married. A stranger that was dark and dangerous to her, and maybe even their daughter.

Anxiety gripped Sarah with every minute that passed. Greg would be home shortly and she was on edge, though she tried not to be. The apartment was clean and dinner was cooking on the stove. She had deliberately kept Katelan from her nap so she would go to bed earlier. The less interruptions the better, though her expectations were low of what was to come. Soft music flowed from the stereo, no words, just music. The smell of chicken parmesan filled her nostrils, letting her know dinner was almost done.

The meal had been kept simple, along with the plain table setting, even down to the way Sarah had dressed in blue jeans and a long sleeve tee shirt. She didn't want Greg to think he was coming home to such a forgiving wife as all the other times when she had fixed a special dinner and fixed her self up. Purposely she didn't light a fire in the fireplace, for that indicated a cozy atmosphere.

A cold gust of wind swept through the apartment when the front door opened. Immediately, Sarah's stomach tightened as she set down the dish towel and breathed deeply. What she'd been dreading all day had arrived and though she'd tried to prepare herself, she knew she wasn't ready. She didn't know what to say or how to act. Should she turn around or just stand there and wait for Greg to say something. Before she could make a decision, his voice broke the barrier.

"Sarah, I'm home." He said the words like he always said them, as if nothing was different this time. As though this evening were like all the rest.

Nervous fingers put her hair behind her ear as she turned around slowly to face the unknown. The hurt in her eyes couldn't compare to her bruised and battered face. At first, Greg's eyes widened in shock as his mouth slightly dropped open. Did he actually expect her to look better after what he had done? Could it be possible that when he was in a fit of rage he didn't realize what he was doing? Was Greg really two people sharing the same body and mind? Like Dr. Jekyll and Mr. Hyde.

"I don't know what to say." He spoke slowly as if choosing each word carefully. "I can't believe I did that to you. You must hate me and I wouldn't blame you." Instead of going to her, he sat down in a chair at the kitchen table. The silence seemed endless between them as they looked at each other. "Please, say something."

Tears filled her eyes as her chin quivered. "What do you want me to say? That it's okay and I forgive you?" Her words were filtered through hurt. "How could you do this to me and say you love me?" She trembled as tears fell down her cheeks. "Greg, why? I've been a good wife to you, have done everything you've asked of me. How can you say you care about me and then hurt me the way you have?" Sarah leaned back against the kitchen counter and wept.

In her weakest moment of vulnerability, she couldn't pull herself away from Greg when he came over and held her against his masculine chest. He never said anything, just held her and stroked her hair while she cried. Why did she have to love him so? He didn't deserve her love, yet she couldn't free her heart of him. Sarah relaxed in his arms as she wiped her puffy eyes and nose. They would have to talk right now before another minute passed. Slowly, she pulled gently away and walked into the living room toward the couch.

Greg followed quietly behind her and sat down beside her. Though he slouched down and leaned back against the sofa, Sarah sat sideways to face him.

With a little bit more confidence, she sat tall as she began. "I've had a lot of time to think about us today. My emotions were all mixed up of hurt, anger and even what I thought was hatred for you." Sarah paused for a moment to watch Greg's face, but his expression never changed as he stared off into space. "At first I was going to call my parents to come get me and Katelan. I wanted to get as far away from you as possible. Up until the time you walked through the door I was still thinking that way. But I love you, Greg, and I want our marriage to work. And it can if you want that, too."

She looked down as Greg's fingers took hold of her hand. "I want our marriage to work. I'm just not sure I can measure up to your expectations of what I should be as a husband. Sometimes I think you compare me to your father. That's not me. I have to be who I am."

"Hitting me, is that who you are? I've never expected you to be like my Daddy. Never. All I ever wanted was for you to love me and be a good father to our child. I love you Greg, but I can't live like this anymore. Never knowing what kind of mood you're going to be in or if saying or doing the wrong thing may make you mad enough to hurt me."

She could feel him stiffen slightly as his hand tightened around hers. He leaned forward and touched her swollen cheek with the back of his hand. "I never meant to hurt you. It all seems like a bad dream I just want to forget. Could you give me another chance to make things right between us? I swear I'll never touch you that way again. Please believe me."

"I want to believe you. I do. But there is a part of me that is afraid of you now. How can I be sure. This sort of thing has happened before. You said you would be different then too, and you were for awhile. There's a side of you I don't even know, Greg. And it scares me." As Sarah looked into his eyes he almost seemed like a little boy who got caught doing something he wasn't supposed to, and now he was trying to make amends the best way he could.

"You can believe me. You'll see, I'll be different. I'll stay home more and spend time with you and Katelan. We'll do things together. Just the three of us." He smiled reassuringly as he drew her into his arms and kissed her gently. Gently releasing her, he stood up and stretched. "I'm starved. Would you mind heating up the food while I go see Katelan?"

"No, not at all." Sarah watched as he walked into the nursery and leaned over the baby bed. This was how life was suppose to be. A loving husband and doting father. If only she could believe her husband was sincere and would change. More than anything she wanted to believe him. He had asked for another chance, and she felt obligated to grant him his request. Maybe the horror of what he did made him realize there was another side to him he didn't like. Time would tell if he meant what he said or not. She would do her best to help and encourage him.

In her mind she felt as though she'd come to some closure with this situation, that they'd taken a step in the right direction. But there was a heaviness in her heart she couldn't shake, which seemed to beckon to her like a lighthouse warning ships of dangerous rocks ahead. Sarah tried to clear her thoughts as she went into the kitchen to warm up the food. Another chance is what he'd asked for and if she was going to give it to him, then the past would have to be put behind them. Love was supposed to conquer all, and if love failed, then what was left?

As her fingers moved across her injured face, Sarah knew tomorrow was another day for fresh start, a time for physical wounds to heal. The days to come would even allow her to eventually forgive Greg, but the emotional scars would never allow her to forget.

Chapter Fourteen

Three weeks had passed since the night Sarah thought her life was at the lowest point ever. The bruises and swelling took longer to vanish than she thought they would. This kept her close to the duplex. As she brushed her silky auburn mane, she examined her face. There was no trace of evidence that anything had happened to her.

Since Greg had been true to his word, not a day had gone by he wasn't charming, loving and affectionate toward her and Katelan. Occasionally he went out with friends, but never came home late. Their lovemaking was passionate and sometimes very intense, whereas before he rarely wanted to be with her, let alone kiss her. And now she was frequently in demand. The change in him was everything Sarah deeply had hoped for, but she felt as though she was holding her breath. Like if she breathed she'd wake up and find she were dreaming.

"Sarah, are you ready? They're expecting us at 6:30." Greg's tone was a little on edge, but she knew it did not have anything to do with her. After weeks of making up excuses as to why Greg could not go to his parents for dinner, Sarah had finally convinced him they couldn't avoid his mother forever. Not thrilled at the idea of spending an entire evening in the presence of Marina, she didn't want to deprive Frank of his granddaughter. In the back of her mind she still had hopes of some kind of restoration between Greg and his father. As for her mother-in-law, Sarah saw the situation as a lost cause.

"I'm ready." She had taken extra time on her appearance tonight, for she wanted Greg to be proud of her. Marina never missed an opportunity to find fault with Sarah, especially in front of her son.

Greg smiled at Sarah when she walked into the living room. "You look beautiful." It had been forever since her husband had called her beautiful. Except for recently, he hadn't seem to notice her at all. She smiled back at him, not just for the compliment, but also because he had packed the diaper bag and had Katelan ready. Mentally she made a picture in her mind of this moment; she always wanted to remember how things were between them right now.

The drive to her in-laws was quiet and peaceful. Soft music filled the car while Katelan chewed contentedly on a stuffed animal as she sat in her car seat. Greg's face was a little tense, and Sarah knew he wished this night was already over. Marina had a way of transforming a pleasant atmosphere into drudgery. Yet, no matter what her mother-in-law did tonight, Sarah vowed not to let Marina ruin the evening.

"You get the diaper bag and I'll get Katelan," Greg said as the car pulled carefully into the driveway. The driveway had been cleared of ice except for a few patches here and there. Katelan cooed and looked up at the multi colored Christmas lights which twinkled on and off to the sound of Christmas carols. Because of Frank, this holiday would be celebrated at the Winslow house this year. According to the stories Greg had shared, his memories of Christmas were filled with sadness and resentment.

Christmas at home with her family had been a wonderful part of her life. She cherished those memories, and Greg's loss saddened her heart. This would be their first Christmas together as a family, and she was going to make the season extra special.

When Greg pressed the doorbell the front door flew opened. There stood Frank, who was obviously very glad to see them.

"Merry Christmas," Sarah said cheerfully.

"Come in, come in. It's freezing out here." He kissed Sarah on the cheek and shook Greg's hand. "Good to see you, son." Frank held out his hands to take Katelan who went willingly. "She changes every time I see her. She'll be walking before we know it." He beamed as he kissed her forehead.

After removing their coats, they followed Frank into the living room. The room was warm from the embers that crackled in the fireplace. Lit candles gave off the aroma of spice and cinnamon along with hot apple cider which sat on a colonial tea cart. Sarah was amazed at what she saw. A fully decorated tree of tiny white lights accented by mauve, gold and white Victorian ornaments stood by the fireplace. Christmas music from the stereo filled the room with a spirit she was not expecting to experience in this house. Briefly she wondered if Greg had exaggerated his story. Then she realized from the hurt expression on his face that he was just as surprised as her. Her heart went out to him, but she didn't know what to say or do.

After all the years of hardly acknowledging Christmas why the change now? Sarah wished the reason was because Marina had a change of heart, but she knew that couldn't be the truth. This was all probably Frank's doing. He must have done all this for Katelan, or maybe for all of them.

Before she could ponder the thought any further, Marina entered the room. The smile and hello she extended Sarah's way might have seemed friendly enough to anyone who didn't know any better, but the coldness was there. With a sincere effort, Sarah returned the smile along with a comment on how lovely the tree was. Katelan was the recipient of a meaningless pat on the head as if she were a cute puppy. Marina's affection was directed toward Greg as she wrapped her arms around his neck and planted a kiss on his cheek, leaving a smear of red.

"Mom, you know I hate that crap on my face," he snarled and jerked her arms away from his neck and walked over to a mirror on the wall. With his fingers he rubbed hard until the red lipstick came off.

"Just what is your problem? A little lipstick and you go ballistic." Marina crossed her arms and stood behind him.

"You know how much that irritates me, yet you continue to do it." Greg turned around and caught Sarah's, please don't do this tonight look. "Let's stop before we start. I just want to get through this evening peacefully."

"Get through this evening. Is that what you're doing? I didn't realize coming here was such a chore." Marina's eyebrows bowed together as her almond shaped eyes narrowed.

With Katelan still in his arms, Frank approached the battle ground. "Now, Marina, don't get all upset. I'm sure that's not what Greg meant at all. You've spent all afternoon preparing a terrific meal. Let's not ruin everything by fighting over a misunderstanding."

"This is far from a misunderstanding. I think our son knows exactly what he meant." Marina's eyes never left Greg's face.

Unsure of what to do, Sarah stood there bewildered at her mother-in-law's behavior. An opportunity never passed her by that she didn't make the worst of it. Tonight had held a glimmer of hope for a tolerable evening, but Marina's claws were sharp and fully extended. Sarah's heart sank as she looked at Greg. His eyes darkened as he squared his shoulders back. What Marina had started, Greg was going to finish.

"This is exactly why I didn't want to come. We can't even come under the same roof without a fight. I only came because Sarah insisted. She said we needed to make an effort for Katelan's sake. So she could grow up close to all her grandparents." Greg sneered as he glared at his mother. Sarah knew there was no turning back now for he had drawn first blood, and Marina was not one to back down. At Greg's words, Sarah's face turned red and hot as her mother-in-law looked over at her with such hatred it caused her to step back.

For what seemed liked an eternity, Marina finally withdrew her cold stare from Sarah and reverted her eyes back to Greg. "This is all her fault! Ever since you married that, things haven't been the same between us. You've changed because of miss uppity over there. You're too good for us now." Marina looked harder at Greg. "That's it, isn't it! You never come over, or call. We don't even get to see our granddaughter. I know for a fact that Sarah goes over to her parents all the time." Marina calmed down some, only to play the part of the victim. This always amazed Sarah. How she could go from one role to another so smoothly.

"Don't play me for a fool and try to make me feel guilty," Greg said. "I don't come over because we end up like this. And you don't make any attempt to come over and see Katelan. From the day she was born you haven't shown much interest. Dad's the one who stops by to see us, not you." Greg stepped away and walk over to the tree. "Ever since I got here, I've been trying to figure out. Why a tree after all these years? When did you ever start making hot apple cider? And then I realized. Dad did this, didn't he? Tell me that I'm wrong?" Greg's eyes misted as he turned to look at his mother.

Until now, Sarah had never seen Marina look embarrassed. But she had been found out and she knew it. The obvious was apparent and there was no way out. For the first time, she was at a loss for words. But she would recover and make sure she came out on top even if only in her own mind, for Marina couldn't live with defeat.

"No you're not wrong. Your father did every bit of this except for the dinner which I might add is splendid. I admit I've never been one much for the holidays. Ask your father if you don't believe me, but this was my idea to invite you over tonight." Marina was giving her best performance, but Sarah didn't know where this was going. For her to admit she was wrong wasn't like her. "I don't mean to cause trouble, but I have never felt welcome in your home. Now, I'm not blaming all this on Sarah. We never got off to a good start and we just didn't seem to click."

Her mother-in-law looked at her as though she were hurt. What lay behind her eyes sent a chill down Sarah's back. Sarah cast a glance over at Frank, whose expression told her he saw through his wife just as she did. Marina had turned this whole thing around to make Sarah out to be the bad guy. She wasn't going to let her get away with this. Marina was trying to cause trouble between her and Greg.

"I apologize if I have done anything to make you feel that way. You and Frank both are more than welcome in our home at any time. I want Katelan to be close to both of you." Sarah smiled sweetly, regretting they had come over tonight.

"Oh, Sarah, I'm so glad to know you feel this way. Why this means everything to me and Frank. Doesn't it, honey?" Sarah saw Frank out of the corner of her eye, and he looked as though he could slap his wife. He started to speak, but Marina carried on quickly not giving him a chance. "I have so wanted to spend time with my granddaughter, and I do appreciate your gracious invitation, but I was hoping to have Katelan come over here to our house with just me and Frank. Not that I don't want you here, dear. But this way we could spend time with her by ourselves and develop that close relationship you mentioned." The sarcasm was an obvious and intentional message directed at Sarah.

Panic struck Sarah. Her horrified expression was a dead give away of what she was thinking, and it was too late to take it back. Marina set her up and she fell right into the woman's trap. The thought of Katelan with Marina was unthinkable. Sarah knew Frank truly loved his granddaughter, but she knew Marina was only doing this to spite her.

"I can tell by your face you're not pleased with my request. I can assure you, Katelan will be fine and have a wonderful time." Marina said insincerely, as she stepped over to Sarah and patted her shoulder.

"There's nothing wrong with what you're asking," said Sarah, "but Katelan is at the age where she's very attached to me. At seven months she is clingy and tends to cry when I'm out of her sight for too long. I hope you'll understand and maybe we'll try visits without me when she's closer to a year old."

She'd done her best to sound convincing as possible without revealing the truth. If Marina persisted, hopefully Frank or Greg would speak up on her behalf. After all, she was a young mother, and this was completely normal for her to feel this way. No one had to know her reason was not the complete truth.

"Of course, we understand," said Frank "And Sarah can also come by here as often as she likes with Katelan. We wouldn't want to upset this little precious by keeping her from her mother." Frank grinned as Katelan hit his nose playfully. The harsh look Marina threw at Frank wasn't missed by anyone.

"Sarah and I don't get much time by ourselves since the baby, and she's always saying she wishes we could go out more." Greg's words were a complete surprise to Sarah. Every time she had mentioned they go out, he always had an excuse. Until lately he hadn't shown much interest in his daughter, and she hated to admit what she felt, but maybe Greg liked the idea of their baby out of the house more.

"For once we agree upon something." Marina looked at Greg and smiled as if she had just won a gold medal before turning her attention back to Sarah. "I'll call you tomorrow and set up a time when you can bring her over." Before she could reply, Marina announced dinner was ready and led the way to the dining room.

This is not over yet, Sarah said under her breath as she followed. Tonight when she and Greg got home, she'd make him understand why Katelan shouldn't come over here without her. Things were going so well between them, surely he'd be agreeable to support her on this.

Marina would just have to accept what they wanted, and that would be the end of an unpleasant predicament. More self-assured, Sarah sat down at the table and pretended to ignore her mother-in-law's haughty stare. You may have won the battle, but the war's far from over she thought, as she looked at the woman with a confident smile.

The hour was still early when they arrived back at their apartment. Greg had said he had to be at work early the next day, though she knew he just wanted to leave which was fine with her. Now they could have time to talk before they went to bed, and she wanted to get this issue resolved before Marina called tomorrow. Thankful that Katelan went down without much of a fuss, Sarah tucked her in and left the nursery. She found Greg in the kitchen drinking a glass of scotch and looking out the window.

She came to a dead halt. There had never been any alcohol in the apartment. When Greg drank, he went out with his friends. But to her knowledge he hadn't taken a drink in three weeks. And here he was drinking in their apartment as if he were having a Coke. How long had the alcohol been here? Where had he kept the bottle? Sarah was angry, but managed to maintain her cool. "Where did that come from?"

He looked surprised when he turned to face her. "How long have you been there?"

"Long enough, and you didn't answer my question." She tried to appear calm even though she was upset that Greg had lied to her, again.

The tone in her voice must have been apparent, for he became slightly defensive. "I don't have to answer to you, but since it's no big deal, I bought the scotch." He poured himself another drink as he watched her. "When was there a law passed that a man couldn't have a drink in his own house?"

"Why are you being this way? You have been so wonderful lately. Please don't do this to us." Sarah hated to plead, but she couldn't help herself. The thought of things going back as they were was more than she cared to think about.

"Do what? Have a drink?" He looked at her with a blank expression. But she knew this was just a game with him. Reality became clearer all the time. Greg was a lot like his mother.

"You know what I mean, Greg. You and alcohol don't mix well. Have you forgotten our honeymoon and the other incidents? Especially the last one." The thought of what happened reopened a wound she tried hard to forget everyday. Hot tears filled her eyes as she crossed her arms. "You promised me, no more drinking. What was the cause this time? Me? Katelan? Or was tonight with your mother the only reason you needed to drink?" Sarah jumped as Greg slammed his glass down on the counter top.

"Shut up! Do you hear me? Just shut up!" Angrily, he pushed his way past her and went into the living room and turned on the television.

Sarah turned toward him, but she didn't move. Somehow she had to reach him. The last few weeks had been incredible, and she couldn't sit by and watch their progress be destroyed. Greg had really tried to be a better husband and father. She couldn't let it end like this. Their relationship was worth fighting for.

"I didn't mean anything against your mother. She seems to upset you a lot and I thought—"

"You know nothing about my mother! You have never liked her, so don't pretend to understand anything about us!" Greg dropped the remote control as he stepped toward her. By the way his eyes were glazed over, she decided he'd had more to drink than she realized. Sarah felt like a mouse trapped in a maze; that no matter what corridor she chose would be a dead end.

Fear seized her, for he was close enough that she could smell the odor she'd come to despise. She felt nauseated and wanted to step backwards, but dared not. "Please, calm down. Can't we talk quietly and not wake the baby?"

"Tomorrow I'm going to take Katelan over to my mother's for a visit." He blurted out his words no differently than if he'd asked her to take out the trash. The same panic she'd experienced earlier was back. And now with Greg against her, there was no one to side with her.

"You can't mean that. How can you send your own daughter over there when you don't even like to be there?" A strong person is what she wanted to be, but she felt weak and helpless. "Please, don't do this. You're not thinking straight. This is not a good situation for our baby. You know how your mother is." The harder Sarah pleaded and begged, the angrier he got.

"She is going and that is final. Now shut up for the last time!" As he started to walk away, out of desperation Sarah took hold of his arm to stop him.

"Greg, you're only doing this to spite me just like your mother, and I won't let you take her." Sarah yelled back.

"Like I need your permission to do anything." Greg sneered as he grabbed her arm yanking it behind her back.

Salty tears flowed down her face as she cried. "Stop! You're going to break my arm. Please, stop!" Her knees were wobbly, but she knew if she buckled under, the pain would be unbearable. Greg relaxed a little, but held tightly onto her.

"Now what was it you weren't going to let me do?" He laughed maliciously as she trembled with fear.

All she could think of was survival. Before she could answer him, Greg grabbed her hair with his free hand and jerked her head back. "I didn't hear you, Sarah," he mocked as he yanked her hair harder until she thought her neck would snap.

"Nothing," she whimpered as Greg threw her roughly to the floor. Too afraid to move, she lay still.

When he bent over and touched her hair, Sarah cringed as he whispered sadistically in her ear, "Don't ever go against me again or you'll regret it till the day you die." As he stood up, she lowered her eyes. The only way to get away from him was to try and block him out mentally. Sarah's shoulder and neck ached as she focused on the carpet, praying that he would leave her alone. Tormented by his heavy breathing, she just wanted him to go.

Greg's boot kicked her rib cage with such force and rage the impact was like she'd been hit with a sledge hammer.

"This is to make sure you took my threat serious." His sinister words burned in her brain as if someone had seared her with a hot iron. The pain was excruciating and she gasped for air while her insides were on fire. The sound of Greg storming out the front door and slamming it rang through her ears.

Sarah wanted to die. Her spirit and soul were already dead. "God, please just let me die." There was nothing left to live for. She lay there motionless, waiting. Maybe death was close by. Not friend, nor foe, only a servant bound to his calling. Death would be the easy way out. But what about her precious daughter. How could Sarah even think about leaving her behind? Katelan needed her. Tears streamed down her face. Life was a precious gift and she'd been so willing to throw it away. "I'm so sorry, God. Please show me what to do." With humiliation and shame for her solace, Sarah wept bitterly into the carpet.

Chapter Fifteen

The noise was constant and dull, yet close by. Each knock grew louder, impatiently demanding a response. Her eyelids fluttered opened to the morning sunlight that shone through the bedroom window. "Sarah, are you in there? Sarah!" Catherine's voice called from beyond the front door.

Time hung in the balance as a vagueness hovered over Sarah. Inside she felt dead and lifeless like a zombie. She slowly sat up unable to escape the pain that wrenched through her chest. "God, oh God, please help me," she begged, barely above a whisper. With all the strength she had, Sarah stood and walked tentatively toward the living room, but first stopped at the nursery. The sight of Katelan's empty baby bed sickened her stomach. The thought of her baby with that woman brought tears to already swollen eyes.

"Sarah, Sarah." The knocks became rapid and persistent along with the familiar voice.

What would she tell her mom? She didn't need to look at her reflection to confirm the results from the previous night's horror. Sarah's afflicted body couldn't compare to her battered heart.

No words were needed, for when the door opened, her mom's mouth dropped opened in shock. "Sarah, what's wrong?" Catherine quickly came through the door and immediately went to her daughter's side. "You're white as a sheet. You're sick."

How she longed to tell her mother everything, the whole ugly truth. To go back home where it was safe. But words wouldn't come, only hot, shameful tears.

"You come over and lie down on the sofa. I'm here now." Her mother's presence was a comfort, but couldn't relieve the agony, for when Catherine put her arm around Sarah's waist, she cried out. "You're in pain, what's wrong?" Deep concern settled on the woman's face as Sarah gently laid down.

With short breaths, she explained in a low, dull voice. "I fell down the porch steps last night. I went to get something out of my car and slipped on the ice." She closed her eyes to find relief, yet to no avail.

"Where do you hurt? You may have broken something."

"I'll be fine. I just need to rest. Greg took Katelan over to his mother's so I could stay in bed." One lie after another. But the truth was unthinkable. Catherine's surprised look was expected because her mother knew how Sarah felt about her mother-in-law.

"You're not fine. You're suffering and I'm taking you to the emergency room.

"She stood up to use the phone. "I'll call your father and let him know what's happened."

"Please, Mom. Not the hospital. I'm only a little banged up. In a couple of days I'll be back to normal. Really. When Greg gets home, he'll take care of me and Katelan." Sarah bit the inside of her mouth to keep from moaning. But Catherine wasn't convinced and dialed Alex's office number.

This nightmare grew worse by the minute. By what was said, Sarah knew her father was going to meet them at the hospital, and there was no changing his mind. Catherine got Sarah's coat out of the closet and helped her to stand. Tears moistened her eyes when a sharp pain shot through her side. Carefully her mother put the coat around Sarah's shoulders and buttoned up the front.

"Now I'll hold onto you gently as possible. You just rest your weight against me." The time it took to get to the car seem like an eternity, for with every step, Sarah suffered. The roads were icy which forced the car to progress cautiously. With closed eyes and her head laid back, Sarah was filled with regrets. If only the hands of time could be turned back before Greg had entered her world. For her desired life of love and happiness had turned to hopelessness. How she longed to be carefree again. But she couldn't live in the past except in her dreams.

Good advice had been offered from her parents out of love and concern, yet she'd refused to listen. Sarah willingly went down the wrong path and now it was time to pay the piper. A situation created from blind faith could only be escaped by her alone.

The car eased its way up the drive to the emergency entrance. Sarah saw Alex with a wheelchair. How easy it would be to let her father fix everything. But no. She was an adult now. A mother. She had to take responsibility for her own life. The success of her marriage was in her own hands. Whatever happened would be the outcome of her decision. A decision she would have to live with, no matter what.

The car had barely come to a complete stop before the car door was quickly opened. Her father's face, normally confident and secure, seemed frightened and unsure. With strong arms, he gently lifted her from the car and held her close. In spite of the pain, she felt safe as she buried her face in his broad chest, clinging to him desperately. The inner strength he possessed made her feel like the small child she'd been a long time ago.

Their eyes met when Alex set her down carefully in the wheelchair. The anguish she saw caused her to look away. Alex pushed the wheelchair into the emergency room where an attendant stepped forward to lead them to an examining room. "A nurse will be right with you." The female attendant smiled and closed the curtain behind her as she left.

No one had a chance to break the morose silence before a middle age woman with a brisk step entered the room. "Hi, my name is Maggie, and I'll be your nurse here in the ER. Now, I'm assuming this young lady here is the patient."

Sarah looked at her and smiled weakly. "Yes, that's me, Sarah."

"And you two are?" Maggie raised her eyebrows over the brim of oval shaped glasses.

"We're her parents, Alex and Catherine Matthews." The tense urgency was apparent in his tone.

"I'll need you both to wait in the waiting room right through the double glass doors." Maggie pulled back the curtain, but Alex didn't move.

"We want to wait with our daughter and speak to the doctor." Alex's words were cordial enough, yet final.

"Mr. Matthews, I assure you, Sarah will be in good hands. The doctor will need to examine her. When he is finished, an attendant will come to bring you and your wife back here." Maggie spoke reassured and smiled warmly at them.

"Mom, Daddy, I'll be okay. Go get some coffee. You'll be back before you know it." The lies she would have to tell the physician would be easier if her parents weren't there.

Catherine bent over and kissed Sarah on top of the head. "We won't be long. We're right down the hall if you need us."

With the back of his hand, Alex touched her cheek affectionately. Misty eyed, he turned and left the room.

"Darling, it's only been twenty minutes. Why don't you stop pacing and come sit by me. I'm worried about her, too." Catherine grabbed his hand when he walked by the couch.

His steps came to a halt, but he remained standing. "It's not just Sarah I'm thinking about. If this happened last night, why didn't Greg take her to the emergency room then? You'd have to be blind not to see she was hurt! Something's not right."

"Does everything have to be analyzed? Why would Sarah lie to us? Maybe she wasn't honest with Greg in telling him how bad the fall was. Our daughter has never been one to complain." Catherine released his hand and sat back. "Is it so hard to believe she really did slip on ice? Why must we always assume Greg has done something? They've had their ups and downs just like any other married couple. Alex, if there was a serious problem between them, don't you think she'd tell us?"

Alex locked his eyes with Catherine's. "All I want is for Sarah to be happy. I long to believe she has a marriage made in heaven with a husband who loves her." He looked up and sighed, as though a heavy burden weighted him down. "But I don't believe it." Alex remembered the night Katelan was born all too well. Greg had exposed his true character, which was dark and disturbing. Catherine had been so excited about the baby he couldn't bring himself to tell her of the hellish encounter with their son-in-law.

Before their conversation could continue, a male attendant called them back to Sarah's room. The curtain was opened, and Maggie was adjusting the drip control of the IV which was in Sarah's left hand.

"Are you okay?" Catherine inquired, looking at the bag of liquid.

Alex made his way to the other side of the hospital bed Sarah had been placed in. "What did the doctor say?"

"They took some x-rays. Dr. Rheinhart will be in shortly with the results. Sarah was a little dehydrated and we're giving her some fluids. If she needs to get up for anything, please call me. I'm right outside at the desk." Maggie picked up the chart and pulled the curtain behind her.

Alex's strong fingers gently stroked Sarah's forehead. Her silky auburn hair seemed darker next to her ashen colored complexion. "How's my girl? Is there anything I can get for you?" Alex would have taken her pain if he could.

"What time is it? Greg will be home soon and he won't know what's happened." Sarah tried not to appear anxious.

"Don't worry. I called the Winslows and explained everything to them. They said not to worry about Katelan. She was doing fine."

Even though Sarah hated the idea of her baby over at Marina's, her main concern was Greg. What would his reaction be when he found out? There wouldn't be a chance to talk to him before he got to the hospital. If her parents knew the truth, no telling what her father would do. But what terrified her more was what Greg would do when they got home. The impact of his boot in her ribs would remain embedded in her mind forever. Marriage had become a dangerous place to be, a place where fear and dread had taken up residence.

Greg had crossed a line, and things could never be the same between them. The one who was her lover, husband and once a friend, was now an enemy she couldn't run from. He'd told her she belonged to him and he would never let her go. If she ever left him, he'd find her no matter where she went. And when he did find her, he'd make her wish she was dead. The thought of being alone with him terrified Sarah. But if she stayed with him she could also be dead, for after last night she was convinced her life was in grave danger.

"I just didn't want him to worry," Sarah said, turning away from the IV and shutting her eyes.

The softness of Catherine's fingers glided back and forth across her forehead. "You just rest. We'll take care of everything."

Sleep had barely touched her before Dr. Rheinhart entered the room. "Hello, I'm Dr. Rheinhart." He shook hands warmly with Catherine and Alex. "Your daughter's going to be fine, but she'll need to stay in bed for a few days. She's sustained two broken ribs and a sprained arm. The fall was nasty though it could have been worse. There were no injuries to the head or back. Sarah will need to follow up with her primary care physician in a week."

Silently, a sigh of relief escaped Sarah's lips. The doctor obviously believed her story or he would have questioned her further.

"The nurse will be back in to put a sling on her arm and give you a copy of the discharge instructions. I've written a prescription for some pain medicine." The physician patted Sarah on the shoulder and spoke in a concerned tone. "You take care of yourself. Those ribs will take about four to six weeks to totally heal."

"I will, and thank you," said Sarah weakly.

"Thank you, Dr. Rheinhart." Alex extended his hand with gratitude. "We'll make sure she has the proper care."

Catherine offered her sincere thanks before he left the room.

"Thank God, you're going to be okay." Alex's face relaxed a little more.

"Now, I don't want to hear any argument, but you're going home with us. With Greg at work all day and the baby to care for, this is the best solution. Cath and Josie can both help with you and Katelan during the day while the boys and I will be home at night."

"Daddy, but Greg—"

"Don't you worry about Greg. I'll talk to him. He'll be glad you're okay and won't have to take off from work." A smile of reassurance forced its way across Alex's lips. "We'll get you settled in at The Pines and then your mother will go by the Winslows and pick up the baby. In the morning I'll run over to your duplex and pack some of yours and Katelan's things."

There was no point to argue, not that she honestly wanted to. A wave of relief swept over her. She would be back in the safety and love of the home she grew up in. This would give her some time to think about what to do. Greg likely wouldn't go against Alex's wishes, for fear the truth might be revealed.

I'll go bring the car up to the entrance while your mother helps you get dressed. If Greg doesn't arrive by the time we go, I'll leave a message for him at the check in desk."

Alex put on his coat and kissed Sarah on the forehead before he left.

Maggie returned with a sling and the discharge papers. "Let me get the IV out of your hand, put your sling on, and you can get dressed and be on your way." With expert fingers, she removed the tape and needle. After placing the sling on Sarah's arm, she went over the discharge instructions. "Sarah, if I can get you to sign here. It basically says you understand everything I've explained to you."

Sarah signed the form and thanked Maggie before she left the room.

"Let's get you out of that hospital gown." Catherine untied the gown and slid it off Sarah's arms. "I'll be as careful as I can, " she said as she helped Sarah put her clothes back on. "You'll feel better once we get you home back into your old bed."

The thought of being back at The Pines made Sarah warm inside even though she knew her stay would only be temporary. Feeling safe, loved and appreciated were things she had always taken for granted, until now. Now she would cherish them like the precious gifts they truly were.

Catherine helped Sarah sit down in the wheelchair that had been left right outside the curtain. "Well, were ready to go."

As soon as he stepped out into the frigid air, Alex spotted Greg. With gloved fingers he buttoned up his coat and pretended to search for car keys in the pockets. He wanted to speak to his son-in-law before he saw Sarah. Greg's face was tense and his body rigid as he approached Alex.

Without a cordial hello, Greg spoke in an irritated manner. "Where's my wife? Is she ready to go yet?"

"Don't you even want to know if she's okay or not?" Alex's voice was full of animosity; no attempt was made to conceal it.

Eyes blazing, Greg stiffened and shoved his hands deep into the bomber jacket pockets. "I assume if she wasn't okay my parents would have told me. If you've got a beef with me spit it out, otherwise get out of my way. I'm taking my wife home."

Alex didn't move and continued to look Greg in the eyes. "I can't understand how you went to work today and left Sarah alone. You had to have known she was hurt and in pain. What were you thinking! The truth is you flat out don't care, do you? I saw through you from the beginning, but I wanted to give you the benefit of the doubt for my daughter's sake."

"I'm always the suspect. I've never been good enough for your little girl. I'm crushed I don't measure up to the expectations of the great Alex Matthews." Greg's words were soaked with sarcasm. "I don't have to answer to you, and I don't have to explain myself either."

Alex noticed two paramedics by an ambulance watching them. His and Greg's voices were pretty heated and he didn't want to cause a scene. "Sarah is going home with us. She has two broken ribs and a sprained arm. The doctor said she'll need to stay in bed for at least a week, and you can't take care of her and Katelan while you're at work."

"We'll see about that. You don't make Sarah's decisions anymore. I'm her husband and she'll do what I tell her to." With a smirk on his face Greg stepped around Alex and went into the emergency room.

A chill went up Sarah's back when she saw Greg. His lips were parted revealing clenched teeth and his eyes were narrowed. The menacing way he looked at her was frightening. "Mom, why don't you go wait at the entrance for me so I can talk to Greg. I'll have him bring me along." She tried to appear as normal as possible under the circumstances.

"You take all the time you need. I'll go call Marina and let her know we'll be by to ick up Katelan." Catherine left the wheelchair in place and walked toward Greg. She gave him a friendly hello and patted him briefly on the arm before she went outside.

Everything seemed to be in slow motion as Sarah watch Greg moved closer to her. She felt like prey being stalked. This was the first time she had seen him since he'd left her on the floor last night. Sarah's body began to tremble followed by a wave of panic. If Greg hadn't pressed his mouth hard against hers, a scream might have erupted. Greg rested his hands on the arms of the wheelchair. His breath was hot against her face.

"You don't seem happy to see me." His face darkened with malice.

This was a chess game to him and it was her move. The stakes were high and the wrong move could be costly. Just breathe and stay calm she told herself. There were people all around. She was safe for now. "It's not that. They gave me some pain medicine and I'm starting to feel the effects."

Greg's hand moved from the chair to her wrist and squeezed tightly. "What did you tell them?" Hard, cold eyes bore deep into her own.

A stranger in a dark alley would have frightened her less than her own husband. For what she saw was a monster. The slightest hope she may have had for Greg to be remorseful, to beg for forgiveness and a promise to get help had vanished. The man she thought she knew was gone. "Only that I fell outside on the ice." Sarah looked away with tear filled eyes.

Greg's grip tightened. "You'd better be telling the truth." His threatening words rang through her ears.

"Do you think you would be here with me if my parents knew the truth?" Sarah looked up and for a brief second felt bold. "My daddy would kill you."

The sneer on his face made her shudder. "Don't you know that I own you? Have you forgotten why you're in this emergency room? I don't make idle threats. No one is going to help you because if you ever say anything to anyone, you'll never see your daughter again. Never. I'm taking you home." Greg stepped behind the wheelchair and began to push.

Fear and nausea seized Sarah. The urge to vomit grew stronger as she bent over. urse Maggie quickly approached with a basin in hand. "You're white as a sheet. The pain medicine can make you sick to your stomach."

Sarah knew the drug wasn't the culprit. She couldn't go home with Greg, but there was no way out. "I'll be fine. I feel better already. Thank you." With a faint smile she motioned Greg to push. Her distraught expression was still evident, for as her mother walked down the hall and saw Sarah, tiny, worried lines imprinted on Catherine's forehead.

"What's wrong?" Catherine pressed the back of her hand to Sarah's cheek. "You don't seem to have a fever."

"Mom, I'm okay. I just got a little sick to my stomach. The nurse said the pain medicine can do that." Sarah bit her lip hard to keep back more tears. "Greg wants me to go home with him."

Catherine cast a quick glance from her daughter to Greg and spoke in a firmer tone than usual. "Now Greg, how will you be able to care for the baby and Sarah while you're at work? After a hard day you'll have to come home and cook, clean, and do whatever else needs to be done. Sarah will need help to get up and down. Katelan is a handful at this age." With a serious look, Catherine gazed off into space as though deep in thought. "But if you're set on this, the only thing left to do is for me to stay with you until she's better."

By the way Greg responded, Sarah knew he didn't like this idea. "Catherine, I really appreciate your thoughtfulness, but than isn't—"

"No, I insist. I'll run home and pack a few things and meet you there. Well, then, it's all settled." Catherine kissed Sarah on the forehead and turned to leave.

"You know I think the original plan would probably work better after all. I might not be able to take off work, and besides the couch isn't very comfortable." Greg flashed a most captivating smile at Catherine.

A heavy weight temporarily lifted from Sarah. Her mom's reverse psychology worked perfectly. Someday Sarah would have to truly thank her.

"Well, let's be on our way. Alex is waiting at the entrance with the car." Catherine led the way while Greg pushed the wheelchair slow enough to be out of earshot.

His voice was low and dangerous. "Remember what I said. If you say anything to anyone, you'll live to regret it. I promise."

Her heart pounded in her chest as she rung her hands together. Oxygen slipped away as Sarah began to drown in a pool of desperation. He'd never let her go. There would never be a way out. Every door of resolution only disclosed another dead end. But behind one door was the inevitable journey Sarah feared. The ultimate escape which would end her life.

Chapter Sixteen

The past two weeks Sarah had spent with her parents and brothers were wonderful. She had slept in every day, relaxed and just enjoyed her family. But now the day arrived for Sarah to return home. The physical wounds were on the mend though her heart remained torn apart. A phone call from Greg stating he would be by in the afternoon to pick her and Katelan up only resurrected fears that temporarily laid dormant. The morning flew by with Sarah's best attempt to keep her distance from the family. To maintain a smile was difficult, and she didn't want them to see her dread.

While she was at The Pines, Greg had come by or called everyday. Not out of concern, but to check upon her. He was sociable and friendly enough in front of her parents, but when they were alone, Greg was arrogant and hostile. He constantly reminded her of what would happen if she said anything. Sarah was afraid for herself, but more fearful of his threats to take Katelan away. The idea of contacting a lawyer for legal advice played heavily upon her mind. Her father knew all the attorneys and he might get word of the visit even though what was said would be kept confidential. Because of the shame that clothed her, Sarah couldn't bare the thought of her parents knowing the truth.

Only a few personal items were left to pack in the bathroom and then she would have to go downstairs to wait for Greg. The reflection that looked back at her in the mirror was a stranger. A face which once glowed and eyes that sparkled were now sad and troubled. The energy and life she used to feel were replaced with despair and regrets. If it weren't for her daughter, Sarah wouldn't have the will to go on. She felt like she was dying a slow death on the inside. It was all she could to do to get out of bed each day. But for Katelan, and even herself, Sarah had to find a way to get her life back.

Back at their duplex, Sarah would have to walk on eggshells around her husband to avoid confrontation. She needed a plan and that could take time. Survival had taken on a new meaning to Sarah. Alex had taught her that real strength came from the inner self and could overcome anything. It had been a long time since she had thought about those words. For the first time she understood what they meant.

This situation was not going to beat her. She would use her brain and figure out a solution. The life she shared with Greg had become a living nightmare and time was of the essence. Her heart ached at the thought of going home with her husband. She was afraid of him and what could happen. "God, please watch over me and my baby," she pleaded, wiping a tear from her face. "Give me the strength to go on." With one final look around Sarah shut the cosmetic bag and sighed deeply.

The living room was warm, though a coldness was present. A home Sarah and Greg made together based on love had become a prison sheltering dark secrets. Sarah sat down on the couch and watched Greg carry Katelan in. The silent treatment was deliberate, but she didn't mind. There was nothing to say and this way they wouldn't fight. A slight tinge of jealousy swept over Sarah as Greg gently laid the baby in the crib and covered her with a quilt. Why couldn't he love her anymore? What did she do to make Greg hate her so? Tears of sorrow filled her eyes, spilling down onto her cheeks.

No matter how insane and stupid, there was a small part of her which still loved him. If he would come and throw himself at her feet begging for forgiveness with the promise to never hurt her again, Sarah would forgive him. But Greg was not remorseful, and the reality of that truth birthed pain she would live with for the rest of her life.

Sarah wiped away the tears and stood up slowly. Sleep was a way to escape, but any hopes of a nap faded when Greg blocked the bedroom doorway.

"Where do you think you're going?" he demanded with crossed arms.

"I'm tired and my side hurts." Sarah wanted to step aside, but was apprehensive.

"You're not going anywhere except to the kitchen. My parents are coming to dinner." A smirk parted Greg's lips when Sarah's mouth dropped opened.

"I'm not up to dinner guests, Greg," she gasped. "I can't move without hurting. The doctor said I need to take it easy so my ribs will heal properly."

"You're milking this for all it's worth. You stayed at your parents for two weeks and never lifted a finger while you were there. They waited on you hand and foot, for God's sake. Well, here's a news flash for you. The vacation is over and you'll cook for my parents." Greg advanced with narrowed eyes. "Do I need remind you of what happens when you go against me?" Brutally, he dug his fingers deep into her rib cage.

Sarah cried out in agony and fell sideways against the wall. "Please, don't," she begged between sobs. "I'll fix dinner. I'll be a good wife."

Placing his mouth next to her ear he whispered sadistically, "I know you will."

Sarah clung to the wall and wept like a frightened child while Greg watched in disgust.

"You're a pathetic, worthless piece of crap!" he hissed. Only adding to her humiliation, Greg spit on her before he plopped himself down on the sofa to watch T.V.

Saliva dripped down her forehead and united with a tear soaked face. Overcome by anguish, she felt her will to survive diminish. Life had regressed to existence. She had always believed there was hell after death, but Sarah now knew hell was here on earth because she was living in it.

Sounds of Katelan stirring in her crib flickered a light inside of Sarah's dark world. She had to hang onto hope for her child's sake. The grim thought of what could become of Katelan helped her to gather strength. She breathed in slow, shallow breaths. A way out eventually would reveal itself to her. If time presented itself as a friend and not an enemy, Sarah would make a plan for safe separation. This dream of freedom empowered her to go on.

The Winslows were right on schedule which surprised Sarah because Marina was never on time. Frank must have put his foot down. Exhaustion had set in and Sarah felt like she would collapse. Dull, throbbing pain throughout the afternoon had forced her to take a pain pill. In no time, Sarah felt light headed and fuzzy. Tonight couldn't be over soon enough. All she wanted to do was go to bed and sleep. Hopefully, Greg's parents would eat and leave shortly after. Sarah loved Frank, and she tolerated Marina, but Greg had done this on purpose. To know he cared nothing about her was hard to admit. She mustn't think about that right now. Their guests were here, and she had to play the part of the happy, obedient wife. If she didn't perform to Greg's specifications, the price to pay would be costly.

"Something smells great. You've really outdone yourself, Sarah," Frank said, looking at the food on the table. With a big smile he hugged her affectionately.

"Thank you. I'm glad you were able to come over." Even though Greg was in conversation with his mother, Sarah knew his eyes were on her.

"I was amazed when Greg called and said you wanted to have us over for dinner. But he said you were just fine and back to your normal self. I guess when you're younger you recover faster."

"Well, that's what I've heard." Sarah smiled sweetly at Frank and announced dinner was ready.

"Now, Frank, it's apparent Sarah is not as well as she's letting on. Dear, you're so pale. Are you sure you feel okay? We could always come back another night." Marina's eyes were icy and her insincerity annoyed Sarah.

Sarah couldn't believe her ears, come back another night. Sarah wanted to slap her. This meal had been prepared under dire circumstances of which she believed Marina was fully aware.

"Really, I'm fine. I grow stronger every day. But I appreciate your concern." The room began to spin slightly and Sarah desperately needed to sit down, but Marina wasn't finished.

"I noticed when I came in you haven't had time to clean. If you'd like, I'd be happy to send over the woman who cleans for me. After all, it's the least I can do after what you've been through." Perfectly lined red lips parted and bared Marina's fangs.

Sarah could usually camouflage her feelings regarding Marina, but the urge to pull out her mother-in-law's hair was intense. "Thanks for the offer, but I'll tackle that job tomorrow. I would've cleaned house today except I didn't get home till this afternoon, and as you can see my time was spent in the kitchen." Sarah didn't bother to return a smile.

"Yes, we can see that you prepared a feast for a king, which I greatly appreciate." Frank winked at Sarah and put an arm around her shoulders. "Now, why don't we sit down and enjoy the meal before the food gets cold."

There was no need for Sarah to turn around and see Marina's eyes afire, she felt them burn into her flesh. But she didn't care what that woman thought, only what Greg would say or do after his parents left.

The dishes were just about finished when Sarah turned to find Greg watching her from the doorway. A chill ran down her spine at the contempt in his eyes. Throughout dinner, he'd spoken only with his parents. But she felt as if she'd been placed under a microscope with her every move observed. Sarah locked her knees before they buckled. A combination of fatigue and fear depleted her energy.

"You thoroughly enjoyed yourself tonight, didn't you?" His tone was hostile.

Sarah turn to wash the remainder of dishes. "It was a nice evening and I'm glad you invited them over." Perspiration beads dampened her forehead and she hoped Greg didn't notice her uneasiness.

"Did it make you feel good to put my mother in her place?" To embarrass and take her down a notch or two?" The sound of his heavy breathing only increased her anxiety.

Her hands shook and she pinched herself under the water. If she accused Marina of being the one to lash out, Greg would take his mother's side and only be angrier. "I'm sorry if that's how it seemed. That was not my intention. Tomorrow morning I'll call and apologize to your mother."

Not sure what to expect, Sarah turned around to face Greg. The response she gave to his accusations must have caught him off guard because he looked puzzled.

The corners of Greg's mouth turned up and he looked at her in the strangest way. "Don't count on her to be nice to you. You'll get what you deserve. You always do, don't you?"

Sarah shuddered at his unmistakable threat. The unknown was terrifying, and what lurked behind Greg's eyes frightened her. Was it possible that whatever her husband had become was the way he'd always been, and she'd been to blind too see the truth? A day never passed that Sarah didn't live with remorse. Why couldn't she have listened to her parents, especially her father, who had been so against the marriage? Stop doing this, Sarah scolded herself. You can't change the past. But she could do something about the present and the future.

"Yes, I get what I deserve," she trembled as she spoke. Sarah was afraid of what would happen if she said the wrong thing or made a wrong move.

As if he could read her thoughts, Greg stepped toward Sarah and left only a couple of inches between them. Dark eyes peered deep into hers. His chest rose and fell with each hot breath. The urgency to run grew stronger as each second passed. But she couldn't get away from him.

"Sarah, " he whispered eerily. "You'll never leave me, never. I own you now." Greg wrapped his fingers around her delicate throat and applied pressure. "Remember our sacred wedding vows, till death do us part. The only way you'll leave this marriage is dead." He pressed his mouth hard against hers. "Sealed with a kiss," he taunted as he released her. "I'm going out. Don't bother to wait up for me." Greg laughed sarcastically before he left the kitchen.

The instant the front door closed, Sarah dropped to the floor and began to cry unrestrained. Her body rocked back and forth while she sobbed and gasped for air. All her emotions were released through tears of fear and sorrow. Her crying eventually subsided when there was nothing left but emptiness. Sarah pulled a tea towel down from the cabinet to wipe her face. The calm had come after the storm, and she remained on the floor completely drained.

Terror took on a new form. Before, Sarah feared her life could be in danger. But now, there was no doubt. Greg implied he would kill her and she believed him. There was a thin line that he had crossed. He was deranged and capable of doing anything without remorse. Greg was past rationality. It was only a matter of time before he'd snap. So much to think about, but right now she needed to sleep. Hopefully, Greg would stay out all night. Just the thought of lying next to him turned her blood cold.

Sarah raised herself from the floor and walked to the nursery. Thankful that Katelan's slumber had been undisturbed, Sarah went into the bathroom and undressed quietly. Too weary to shower or perform any other hygiene rituals, she pulled on a flannel nightgown and crawled into bed. Even though she was physically and mentally exhausted, and her eyelids were weighted down, Sarah knew peaceful sleep was out of reach. For when she'd drift into a state of subconscious, fear would be there. It was everywhere.

Chapter Seventeen

Two months passed and her broken ribs had healed, but Sarah's heart remained ripped open for Greg to trample whenever he chose. Though there had been no further physical attacks against her, the verbal and emotional abuse was just as bad, if not worse. When she thought she'd never be able to shed another tear, Sarah would break down at any given moment. Greg was gone from home more and more, but she no longer cared. Their marriage was long past the point of salvation. One night he came home late smelling of perfume and liquor. Up until that point Sarah had been suspicious, but now she was sure Greg had committed adultery and for that she would never forgive him. In Sarah's heart she believed the marriage bed was sacred and he'd defiled their union.

The March weather was bitter cold and Sarah stayed inside, consumed with thoughts of escape. When he was home she stayed away from him the best she could. Even his attention to Katelan had dwindled to almost nothing. Their daughter, who used to adore Greg, was now distant with him and clung more to her. For their child's sake, Sarah pretended to be happy when the child was awake. Some days this burden took every ounce of energy she had. Often, Sarah put off her parent's countless invitations for dinner. The lies were easy to tell now because she had repeated them over and over. If they didn't believe her, they never said anything.

This weekend Greg was going to the lake with friends to ice fish, or so he said. With him gone, there wasn't any excuse to refuse her parents' invitation while he was away. They were thrilled when she told them she and Katelan would visit. Maybe Sarah could find the courage to tell them the dark and shameful truth. This could be fate, her one chance to be free from the prison which held her captive. If only it could be so easy, but it wasn't. Greg would kill her. That knowledge haunted her daily.

Yes, her father was a powerful, influential man, but even he couldn't protect her from what her deranged husband might do. No one could watch her twenty four hours a day. The only plan she could think of was to run away with Katelan to another state. Even then Sarah knew she'd always be looking over her shoulder in fear. Not to live close to her family would be unbearable. This wasn't fair, and she hadn't done anything to deserve this. For this she hated Greg. He'd made her life a continuing nightmare.

The crimson and burnt orange embers flickered and glowed in the fireplace, radiating a cozy atmosphere. Alex and Catherine sat nestled together on the sofa, enjoying each other's company. "I'd give you a penny for your thoughts, but I think I know what they are." Alex said with a half grin.

"It's going to be wonderful to have Sarah and Katelan here for the weekend. Even Will and Carter are excited," said Catherine. "I've missed them so much. We live in the same town, but we hardly see our daughter anymore," she commented sadly.

Alex slid an arm around his wife's shoulder and pulled her closer. "Something has changed Sarah, we both know that. The reasons vary as to why they don't come over, and that's not like our daughter. I want this weekend to be comfortable for her, but I've got to find a way for her to open up to me."

Catherine leaned forward and turned toward Alex with a concerned look. "Oh, sweetheart, please don't push Sarah. I've tried numerous times to find out what was wrong between Greg and her. The story stays the same. Everything is fine, she's just tired or has a lot on her mind. I don't know what's going on, but Sarah obviously doesn't want to tell us. We can't force her."

"Don't worry. I won't upset her," he reassured his wife. "But I just can't sit by and watch Sarah drift farther away from us." Alex rose and walked over to the fireplace. His shoulders tightened as he looked down at the cinders. "I'm sure all this has to do with Greg. I can't pin point the problem, but it's there. And I do intend to find out what's going on."

Catherine sighed deeply and sank back against the leather cushion. "I'm just as worried as you are. She's put a wall up around herself. If we persist, she might pull back even more. Whatever the trouble is, she'll have to come to us when she's ready."

"Cath, I don't know if I can wait." Alex turned to face his wife. "I felt like I lost Sarah when she got married, and I'm losing her again." Alex looked away as his mind drifted back to the night his granddaughter was born. Greg had threatened to keep Sarah away from them if Alex didn't back off. Is that what he was doing?

"I know this is hard, darling, but we'll just have to be patient and give Sarah some space. If anything is truly wrong, I have to believe she would have told us by now. Let's have a nice time with her and the baby and see what happens," Catherine said hopefully. "Maybe with Greg away she'll open up."

"I hope you're right because I can't go on forever acting like everything is okay when we know it's not. I will get to the bottom of this, one way or another." Alex wanted to tell his wife he'd go to Greg if he had to, but decided against it. There was no need to cause his wife to worry. He would do what he had to do.

A black duffel bag lay on the bed half packed. Greg's friends were picking him up by 12:00 and Sarah couldn't wait for him to leave. The past few days they had barely exchanged words and the tension was thick. Sarah had learned her best defense was to avoid him and only speak if the need arose. She decided not to disclose her weekend plans, to avoid any strife. He wasn't due home until late Sunday night and she would just make sure she'd be home first. There was no risk he'd call home. Greg and his friends would probably stay plastered the whole time they were gone.

The pipes squeaked as the water in the shower was turned off. Greg came out of the bathroom with a towel wrapped around his waist. "Why aren't the rest of my things packed?" he demanded. "The guys will be here any minute." He flung his towel across the room and grabbed a pair of neatly folded jeans off the bed.

"I had to wait for the rest of your laundry to dry. I was just going to get them out of the dryer." Sarah proceeded to walk out of the bedroom, but Greg blocked her.

"You have an answer for everything, don't you? But it's never the right answer. If you weren't so lazy the clothes would have already been done." Greg stood there naked looking down at her.

"How can you call me lazy? I get up before you and I'm up late at night. I cook, clean, do laundry, run your errands and take care of Katelan." Sarah spoke with a calm voice, but underneath she was fuming.

"Why is it you stupid women always think you deserve a pat on the back just for doing what is expected of you? Housework is all you're good for and you can't even get that right." His words were like a slap in the face.

Any self-esteem she had left was being sucked out of her body as if she were covered with leeches. The hatred Greg had for her was like drinking his poison every day. Sarah was dying a slow and painful death from the inside out, with no hope for recovery. Bitter tears slid down her face falling onto her shirt. "I have loved and honored you from the start of our marriage. I've been supportive of you in whatever you wanted. More than anything in this world, I wanted to be a good wife to you, a good mother to our child. What have I done to make you hate me so much?" Sarah continued to cry as she stood there before her husband, who only glared at her with absolute contempt.

"Yea, I hate you like I've never hated anyone. Because of you I'm trapped in this miserable life, confined in these walls. My mother was right about you. You got pregnant so I'd have to marry you! Greg's eyes were afire with venom. "I wished Katelan would have never been born. I should have forced you to get an abortion!"

Sarah took a step backwards in shock. "You blame our daughter? Oh my God, Greg. You would have had me kill her, to end her life. You really are a monster! I thought as long as we had Katelan there might be hope for us." A wave of panic came over her when she realized what she had said out loud. All she could think about was running to the nursery, grabbing Katelan out of her crib and run.

"A monster!" Greg gritted his teeth. "You think I'm a monster!" He threw the jeans against the wall and began to breathe heavily. "You have no idea what I'm capable of," he said and began to laugh like a madman. His voice sounded cold and murderous. "But you're about to find out."

Terror seized her as she tried to run past him, but the first blow struck Sarah on the right cheek shattering the bone beneath her flawless complexion. An agonized scream erupted from her throat. If Greg had not grabbed her around the neck she would have collapsed to the floor. Her feeble attempt to block herself from a second vicious strike, failed, for his fist slammed into the left side of her skull. Sarah's legs gave way as she lapsed into a state of semi-consciousness. Her eyelids fluttered open and shut to blurred images of rage, while excruciating pain ripped through parts of her battered body. Darkness engulfed Sarah, leaving her paralyzed and disoriented. There were no sounds, just a quietness which was almost serene. She was not alone though, for he was here. Sarah wasn't afraid, but at peace with his presence. Death had come for her.

"Once more our den looks like a daycare center." Alex said jokingly. "There are more toys in this room than in a toy store. No wonder Katelan likes to come over here."

"That's what grandparents are for. To spoil the grandchildren." Catherine was happy because Sarah and the baby would arrive shortly. "I've so been looking forward to this weekend. All of us together again."

"I don't want to put a damper on your mood, but remember, I really want to talk to Sarah about what's going on. Before you give me that look, I won't pressure her. I'll give her the opportunity to open up a little and see what happens from there." Alex winked at his wife. "I promise."

"If there is a problem between them, maybe with him away she'll be more apt to talk. I just want Sarah to know that we're here for her, no matter what." Catherine became quiet and looked at Alex. "Do you think that something serious is going on?"

"Cath, I don't know. I use to think I knew our daughter better than anyone, but the way she has changed, I can't read her anymore. One thing I do know, though. The problem is not with Sarah. I would bet my law firm that Greg is not the husband and father he appears to be." Alex felt a little guilty for not telling Catherine about his run in with their son-in-law. He just didn't want to worry her. Not until he had to.

"Sweetheart, I know you've never cared for Greg. And your perception of him could be better than mine, but for Sarah's, sake just take things slow and easy with her. I want her to be able to rest and enjoy herself. No worries, no cares, a vacation away from the stresses and responsibilities of being a wife and mother." Catherine smiled and began to put the toys in some order.

"So being a wife and mother is stressful. Maybe after this weekend I should take you on a vacation." Alex laughed whole heartedly. He definitely didn't want there to be a solemn atmosphere when Sarah arrived.

Catherine playfully threw a stuffed bear across the room at Alex, who ducked. Josephine stood in the double doorway with an amused look on her round, plump face. "Mr. Alex, there's a phone call for you. The caller is a woman who says she's from Mercy Hospital."

"Mercy Hospital? I wonder who it is. I'll take the call in here, Josie, thanks." Alex reached out his hand to take the cordless phone from Josephine, who retreated back to the kitchen to fix dinner.

"This is Alex Matthews, how can I help you?" Alex inquired in his professional voice. Unprepared for what the faceless woman told him, he stood there in shock as the color drained from his skin. "Yes, I heard you. What happened? Where is my granddaughter? Well, why don't you know?" He demanded in a harsh tone. "Yes, you have my verbal permission. We're on our way." The phone dropped from his hand to the floor as he turned to look at Catherine who was already by his side. The look in his eyes was all she needed to see something was terribly wrong.

Her fingers shook when she took hold of his arm. "What's wrong? Tell me what it is." Features normally soft and relaxed were now strained.

Alex gently moved his arm around his wife's waist and held her close. There was no easy way to break the news. In all of his courtroom battles he was a master with words, but now there were no right words. For what he had to say would only bring hopelessness and agony beyond belief. He could barely speak above a whisper. "Sarah's in surgery. She's bleeding internally. A neighbor found her and called an ambulance. That's all they told me."

Catherine went limp beneath his arms and began to cry. "Oh, my God, my God, what's happened?" she uttered.

"We've got to go to the hospital right now." Alex gently pulled her toward the front door and called for Josephine, who came out of the kitchen. He tried to gather some strength. "There's an emergency and we have to go. Don't say anything to Will or Carter. I'll call you later."

With a worried expression, Josephine wrung her hands together and prayed silently as she watched Catherine follow Alex out the front door into the cold, blistering wind.

Chapter Eighteen

The drive to the hospital was a complete blur to Alex. Catherine sat in the passenger's seat staring out the window, crying softly and praying. All he could think was, God, please don't let my little girl die. Please, God, don't let her die. The hospital came into view and Alex's heart began to beat faster. The unknown tore at him. If he ever needed to be strong it was now, because his wife needed him. Alex pulled into the emergency parking lot and parked the car. They got out of the car and walked rapidly to the automatic glass double doors. Alex approached the check in desk and spoke with urgency. "My daughter, Sarah Winslow was brought in. She's in surgery."

"Wait here and I'll get a doctor." The young woman went through another set of glass doors to a nurses station. The ER was full of white coats, and blue and green scrubs. Faces and voices blended together as Alex waited for what seemed an infinity. The doors slid open, and a man who appeared to be in his early forties emerged, wearing a white coat with a stethoscope draped around his neck.

The man, obviously a doctor, stuck out his hand and managed a slight smile, though his eyes were serious. "I'm Dr. Leiberman."

"Alex Matthews, and this is my wife, Catherine." He grasped his hand briefly. "How's our daughter and where is my granddaughter?"

"Why don't we sit over there where it's more private." The physician led the way to a waiting room in an area partly secluded by a partition.

Alex sat down next to Catherine and waited for the bomb to drop. The doctor's grave countenance only added to his fears. His palms began to sweat and his mouth went dry.

"Mr. and Mrs. Matthews, your granddaughter is fine. The paramedics brought her in and she's being looked after in pediatrics. You can go get her anytime you want. There is no easy way to break this kind of news, so I'll be straightforward. Your daughter is in critical condition. She has suffered multiple injuries with extensive damage." Dr. Leiberman paused as Catherine leaned forward and began to sob heavily. Alex, though numb and in a state of shock, took her in his arms.

A couple of minutes passed by before the doctor continued. "If you need a few moments—"

"No, I want to know everything now, and then I want to see my daughter." Alex swallowed hard to keep his voice from breaking.

The doctor shifted in his chair. "Sarah is in surgery to stop the internal bleeding. We won't know the extent of her injuries until the surgeon is finished. We know she has a left skull fracture and her right cheek has been shattered that will require additional surgery at a later date. There are lacerations to her face and neck. Two bones in her right arm are broken, and over fifty percent of her body is badly bruised."

A deathlike silence descended as Alex sat stunned, with Catherine still clinging to him. "What in God's name happened? We just talked to her last night. She and the baby were going to spend the weekend with us."

"The lady next door told the police that she kept hearing a baby crying. Eventually, she went over and knocked on the door. When there was no answer she tried the doorknob, found it unlocked and went in. Sarah was unconscious on the bedroom floor."

The impact of this news suffocated Alex to the point he felt as though his lungs would burst in his chest. He tried to speak but couldn't.

Dr. Leiberman cleared his throat and continued. "Your daughter was brutally beaten. She must be very strong to have survived an attack as severe as this. The fact she's alive is a good sign."

Beaten. Beaten. The word echoed through his mind. Who would do this to Sarah? She didn't have an enemy in the world? "Greg. Where is he?" Alex asked in a hostile tone.

"Who is Greg?" Dr. Leiberman inquired.

"My daughter's husband." The words spewed out like venom.

"I don't know. There was no mention of him when she was brought in. Do you have a number where I could try to reach him for you?" Alex ignored the doctor's offer to help.

"Doctor, are the police here?" Alex's thoughts began to race.

"I believe they went to your daughter's home to investigate. The sheriff did say he would have to talk with Sarah as soon as possible. The brain is a very complex organ. Memory loss is common in cases regarding head injuries." Dr. Leiberman looked at Catherine, who lay back against the couch. Her tears had subsided, and she appeared to be catatonic.

"Is there a place more private where we could go? I need to make a few phone calls." Alex stood up and looked down at his wife sadly. Their world was falling apart, and there was nothing he could do to reverse the damage. The initial shock had settled in, and though he felt numb physically, his senses were alert.

The doctor stood as his pager went off. "Yes, there's a room off the waiting area with a couch and telephone."

"Please, let us know the minute Sarah is out of surgery. I need to see her." Just her name touching his lips made Alex's heart ache.

"I'll check on the status." Dr. Leiberman shook Alex's hand before he walked away.

"Darling, let's go," he said softly, pulling Catherine to her feet. Her eyes were filled with despair, the distraught look on her face broke his heart. Alex lifted back his shoulders, then gently touched her tear stained cheek. "Sarah will pull through this. You've got to believe that."

She nodded her head and put her arm around Alex's waist. They walked in silence through the waiting area toward the private room. Next to the couch was an end table with two glasses and a water pitcher that sat next to a telephone.

They both sat down on the couch, holding each other. The room was quite except for the faint sound of their breathing. Neither one moved or said anything, and Alex stroked her hair in a calming manner. "Cath, she is going to be okay. I promise."

She nestled closer to him and let out a sigh, but remained silent. The main phone call he wanted to make was to the Winslows, though he should phone Josephine and the boys. But that call would have to wait. He didn't want to believe what he was thinking, but he couldn't get away from it. How could he have been so blind, so stupid! He clenched his fist. The warning signs had been there. Everything was so clear now.

At the realization of what became truth to him, Alex stood up and began to pace back and forth across the carpet. His hands pressed hard against both sides of his skull while the beat of his heart pounded profusely. Even the sight of Catherine's distraught appearance couldn't alter the rage which possessed him. "I'll kill him. So help me God, I swear I'll kill him!" Had it not been for his wife's presence he would have exploded.

His outburst startled Catherine. "Alex, what is it?" She looked at him with concern.

There was no use in trying to keep his suspicions from her. She could read him like a book. He walked over to her and sat back down. "Just listen to what I have to say before you say anything. This is not an easy situation and it's going to get a lot more difficult. This has been a great shock for both of us and we haven't had time to think clearly, until now." He wanted to be careful not to add any more shock on top of what she was already dealing with.

She put her hands around his. "I'll be okay. Just tell me. It couldn't be any worse."

"Remember all the times we felt there was something going on with Sarah. All the excuses she made as to why she couldn't come over. The way she's become more withdrawn and moody." Alex took a deep breath. "I think Greg is the one who did this to her."

"You can't be serious." Catherine couldn't even begin to believe this. "Your dislike of him doesn't make him a wife beater."

"I've never been more serious. Sarah has no enemies. She wouldn't have let a stranger in. I never quite believed that whole story about her falling on ice." Alex paused and then continued. "I should have told you this a long time ago, but I've had more than one run in with our son-in-law. The night that Katelan was born and at the emergency room." He watched his wife's expression change from one of unbelief to uncertainty as he relayed the details of both incidents.

"My God, Alex, could he have really done something like this? This couldn't have been the first time. There must have been previous assaults. I should have listened to you instead of discouraging you from trying to find out what was going on." Catherine buried her face in her hands. "If I hadn't been so worried about upsetting Sarah she wouldn't be in surgery fighting for her life." Tears ran through her fingers.

Alex put his arms around her and held her. "It wasn't your fault. Do you hear me? Greg is the one to blame. I don't know why Sarah protected him or why she didn't tell us the truth. That doesn't even matter right now. What matters is Sarah and making sure Greg pays for what he's done." Before they could talk further, a knock rapped on the door, followed by a nurse entering.

"Your daughter is in the recovery room. Dr. Andrison, the surgeon, is waiting to meet with you and your wife. I'll take you over to the family waiting room in the surgery unit."

They followed the nurse down long corridors which were illuminated with bright lights. Upon approaching two aluminum doors labeled Surgery Unit, Alex felt nauseous and cold inside. The doors slid opened and he proceeded like a puppet. They walked into a room similar to the one they had just left. The surgeon stood by the couch wearing green scrubs.

"I'm Dr. Andrison. Please have a seat." The nurse left as Alex and Catherine sat down, both looking very grim. "Let me first say, your daughter is a fighter and she's holding her own. She's not out of the woods. The first twenty four hours are critical."

"When can we see her?" Alex leaned forward, looking intently at the surgeon.

"After she leaves recovery, she'll be taken to the Intensive Care Unit where you can go to be with her. I must tell you though, you need to prepare yourselves. Your daughter's appearance has been altered. There is swelling and discoloration from the bruises."

"I understand. Is there anything else I need to know?" Alex felt like he was watching someone else's life. This is how the accused must feel in the courtroom when a judge is about to deliver the sentence; dead and empty.

"I was able to stop the bleeding, and Sarah was given two pints of blood. The damage inside was repairable to some degree. The right kidney had been ruptured allowing blood to seep in. We were able to flush it out. The spleen had to be removed, and a broken rib punctured her left lung." Dr. Andrison sat back in his chair and waited. "Mr. Matthews, do you have any questions?"

"Will my daughter live?" His voice cracked, and he fought to keep his emotions under control.

"As I said before, the next twenty-four hours are the most crucial. Your daughter is young and strong. That will work to her benefit. I'm very hopeful at this point. She will be in recovery for at least another hour. A nurse will come for you when Sarah goes up to ICU." Dr. Andrison stood to leave. "I have another surgery, so if you'll excuse me."

"Thanks for everything you've done for our daughter." Alex pulled himself to his feet and shook the surgeon's hand.

"I'll be checking in on Sarah later, and be back in the morning for rounds." With a nod of his head, he left the room.

The Matthews walked back to the other waiting room hand in hand. "Would you mind going to get us some coffee while I call Josie and then Frank?" Alex stretched and sat down in a chair opposite the couch.

"You're not going to tell Frank what you suspect, are you? Please, don't say anything over the phone. He deserves better than that." Catherine had a soft spot in her heart for Frank because of the way Marina treated him.

"No, I won't say anything. I'm only going to try and find out where Greg is. I won't say too much to Josie either. I think we need to tell her and the boys in person."

"All right then. I'll be back shortly." She looked tired, and the coffee would do them both some good.

After she closed the door behind her, Alex called home to break the news. He only told the housekeeper that Sarah had been in an accident, but she was going to be fine. Alex could detect from Josephine's voice that she knew there was more than he was telling. After speaking to his sons briefly, he hung up and prepared to call the Winslows.

His fingers tapped on the telephone while he stared at the receiver. The anger inside of him elevated with each thought of Greg and what he'd done to Sarah. His knuckles turned white as he grabbed the telephone cord and twisted the coil between his fingers. What was he supposed to say to Frank? My daughter's in the hospital fighting for her life because your son almost beat her to death. Frank was a good man and his son's actions weren't his fault. If anyone was to blame, it was Marina. She was a vicious, vindictive woman who would stop at nothing to get what she wanted. Greg was a product of her hatred and hostility. Frank had only been loving and kind to Sarah, a wonderful grandfather to Katelan and a good friend to him and Catherine.

Alex tried to calm down before he made the call. They might not give him any information about Greg if he threw accusations at them. Releasing the cord, he rolled his neck from side to side, took a deep breath and dialed the number. After two rings, Frank's voice came through the receiver.

"Hello." The sound of his cheerful voice made Alex slump down into the chair. Their world had been shattered today and now he was about to destroy Frank's.

"Frank, this is Alex. I'm afraid I've got some bad news." He could hardly bring himself to repeat what he had been told earlier. "Sarah's in the hospital. She was almost beaten to death." The agony and grief overwhelmed him as an unnatural silence fell.

All Frank could say was, "My God, My God." His voice was thick with emotion.

A part of Alex felt sorry for him. At least he had Catherine to share this tragedy with, but Frank had no one. Marina was cold and empty, incapable of love. "Frank, listen to me. Do you know where Greg is?"

"You mean he's not there?" The shock in Frank's voice was genuine. "I don't understand. Where is he?"

"There are many unanswered questions right now. The police are over at the kids' place investigating." This was not going to be easy. Soon enough the Winslows would know of Alex's suspicions about their son. Before he could continue, a nurse knocked on the door, then walked in the room.

"Mr. Matthews, your daughter's been moved to ICU. If you'll come with me, I'll take you to her."

"Frank, I've got to go. Please try to find Greg." He hung up the phone without saying goodbye. Catherine stepped off the elevator carrying two cups of coffee as Alex came out of the waiting room. "Sarah's out of recovery." He took one of the cups of coffee from her as they followed the nurse. When he walked into the Intensive Care Unit, the same nausea he felt earlier came back. There was a nurses station in the center of the area occupied by nurses and beeping monitors. A woman in white approached them and introduced herself as Mrs. Rankin, the ICU nursing supervisor. She told them she was sorry for their ordeal, and that their daughter was in the best possible care.

"Sarah is in room number four whenever you're ready to go in." She said, as she pointed toward a room. "If you need anything I'll be at the nurses station."

His hands were clammy and the nausea increased when he looked over at the door. "Cath, I want to go in first, alone. I just need some time. Please try to understand." He said, as he handed her his untouched coffee.

"I do understand. I'll wait here for you." Catherine wrapped her arms around his waist and held on to him briefly. "She'll be okay, just like you promised."

As Alex walked toward room number four, Catherine became teary eyed.

The pain she saw in his eyes was a reflection of what was in her own. She would have preferred they had gone in together, but knew her husband needed to see Sarah alone. She admired him for wanting to be strong, yet she knew his heart was broken as was hers. "Oh, Sarah," she whispered. A part of her felt as though she had died. They were close, shared many special times together. How could she not have seen what was going on with her daughter? A mother should have intuition about their children. There was no answer which brought relief from her inner torment.

With a trembling hand, Alex took told of the handle and hesitantly opened the door. His heart began to beat faster and his knees became weak when the hospital bed came into view. A curtain was pulled halfway, only revealing the end of the bed. Alex shut the door behind himself and walked slowly toward the drawn curtain. He had to force his feet to move forward. With closed eyes, he tried to envision how Sarah looked the last time he saw her. What was she wearing? How had her hair been fixed? Had she been smiling and joking with him? He tried so hard to remember, but couldn't. The images he longed for wouldn't appear. Alex opened his eyes to a reality he was afraid to face. His hand shook as he reached out and took hold of the drape, slowly pulling it back.

Chapter Nineteen

"God, no, no!" Alex cried out and dropped to his knees, sobbing uncontrollably. Burying his face in the bed covers, he clutched at the sheets while his body shook in agony as the grief he'd been able to restrain was released. Alex wept till the covers were wet against his skin. Gradually, his groaning began to subside as his body relaxed. He wasn't sure how long he remained on his knees with his head down, but he couldn't bear the thought of looking at Sarah again. The shock of this horror needed to sink in so that he could deal with his fears. Yet, guilt is what plagued him.

Sarah hadn't been herself for a long time. Alex should have found a way to make her tell him what was wrong. Signs of trouble had been there, but he never dreamed Greg was abusing her. Maybe he hadn't wanted to believe what stared him in the face. But now, it was too late. He was supposed to protect her, no matter what. As a father, he had failed her. The way Sarah looked would haunt him the rest of his life because he could never forgive himself.

Alex pulled a handkerchief out of his pocket and wiped his face. Taking in deep breaths, he slowly pulled himself to his feet. He forced himself to look at his daughter, his child who was everything to him. Tears filled his eyes once more, though Alex remained in control. This time, sorrow took a backseat to anger. His hatred of Greg consumed his entire existence. Alex reached out and wrapped his fingers around Sarah's cold and clammy hand. "I promise you, he'll pay for this." His voice cracked, but he kept his composure.

The surgeon's description of Sarah's physical condition didn't even come close to what Alex was seeing. This frail, battered form that lay nearly lifeless didn't resemble his daughter at all. Her auburn hair, which always shined, was dull and matted together with dried blood. Cuts and bruises covered her swollen face and neck. A deep cut over her left eye had been stitched together. Her bottom lip was sliced open and was two times its normal size. Alex desperately wanted to reach down and hold her. He needed Sarah to know how much he loved her. Carefully he bent over and kissed his daughter's forehead.

A light knock on the door brought Alex back to the world outside Sarah's room. "Mr. Matthews, your wife would like to come in." Nurse Rankin said.

Alex turned to face her. He realized he must have looked awful and didn't want Catherine to see him like this. She was going to need him. Somehow he had to prepare her for Sarah's appearance. "I'll be out in a minute." Nurse Rankin left the room as Alex walked over to where a sink and mirror were. He turned on the cold water and washed his tear stained, red and blotchy face. He was totally drained and felt physically weak. Everyone in the family would need to lean on him for mental and emotional support. More than anything, Alex wanted to be there for all of them, but an inner force was driving him toward his mission of vengeance. Finding Greg had taken precedence above even his commitment as a father and husband.

He patted his face dry with a towel and turned around to look at Sarah, who remained motionless. Alex began to twist the towel with his hands. His knuckles turned white as he twisted the cloth tighter and tighter. Wrinkles lined his forehead while his teeth clamped together. Responsibility to the judicial system he had upheld his entire life and his role as a father battled against each other inside him. But as far as he was concerned, Greg was a dead man. From either perspective his son-in-law deserved to rot in hell.

Alex remembered his wife and calmed back down for her sake. This wasn't going to be easy and he still had to break the news to Josie and the boys. A long night lay ahead and calls still needed to be made. Quietly, he walked out of the room toward the nurses station where Catherine was holding a cup of coffee. She looked apprehensive when she saw Alex. She put down the coffee as he took her by the hand and led her over to Sarah's room.

"It's bad isn't it?" Catherine's heart sank.

"Yes, she looks bad." Alex put his arm around her shoulders and spoke soothingly as possible under the circumstances. "I've been thinking of how to prepare you for when you see Sarah, but there is no way to lessen the shock. You need to brace yourself, Cath. She doesn't look like herself at all."

"I just want to see her." Catherine's voice trembled as she put her arm around his waist.

"Okay, I'll take you in." Alex said reluctantly and guided her into Sarah's room.

A shriek escaped her lips before she collapsed into his arms and cried in agony.

Alex held her like a child, trying to comfort her while she wept against his chest. "Sh, sh, everything will be okay. Sarah is going to make it. I promise," he whispered as he rested his head next to hers, tears streaming silently down his cheeks.

Twenty minutes later when Alex and Catherine emerged from Sarah's room, a nurse informed them that the sheriff and a Frank Winslow were waiting in the ICU family waiting room. Alex was all too eager to meet with Sheriff Parkerson, but not so anxious to see Frank at the moment. The expressions on his and Catherine's face must have said it all as they entered the waiting room, because both men seemed to be momentarily at a loss for words.

Frank spoke with a shaky voice, "How is she?" His eyes searched back and forth from Alex to Catherine's face.

Alex took a deep sigh and said, "Sarah's in critical condition. She's not out of the woods yet, but the doctors are hopeful. The first twenty-four hours are the most crucial."

Frank's legs became weak as he sat down on the couch. "I can't believe this. Ever since you called, I kept telling myself this was just a bad dream, a cruel joke. Why in God's name would anyone want to hurt Sarah?" Frank looked at Alex with tear filled eyes.

Alex knew Frank loved Sarah as if she were his own daughter. What would this do to him when he found out about Alex's suspicions of Greg? In a way, his grief could be far greater than what the Matthews were experiencing.

Jeff Parkerson stepped forward and put a hand on Alex's shoulder. "Alex, I'm so sorry. I wish I could make this easier on you and Catherine. I know this isn't a good time, but I need to speak to you in private."

Jeff and Sharon Parkerson had been friends of the Matthews family for years. Their kids had gone to school together, played the same sports, even taken family vacations together. When Jeff had decided to leave his job and run for sheriff, Alex had been a main supporter for his campaign. They shared a common bond for justice and Alex felt like he was betraying Jeff by what he was thinking of doing to Greg.

"Frank, could I ask a favor of you? Would you take Catherine home for me? This has been a long night and she's exhausted" Alex put his finger to his wife's lips as she started to protest. "Cath, please. Go to pediatrics and pick up Katelan and take her home. I'll be home as soon as I'm finished here with Jeff. You need to rest. I promise I'll call if there's any change in Sarah's condition."

Frank stood up and walked over to Catherine, gently putting his arm around her shoulders. "Come on. Your other kids need you too," he said, as he nudged her toward the door.

Alex knew she probably hadn't thought of Will and Carter and would start to feel guilty. The boys loved their sister and grief would consume them when they found out the truth. They would need their mother to console them in their hour of need.

"You're right, they'll need me." Catherine briefly looked at Jeff in acknowledgment and then faced Alex. "Promise you'll call me."

"I will. I'll be home as soon as I can." Alex kissed her goodbye and put his hand on Frank's arm. "Thanks."

"Anything I can do to help, just let me know." He started to walk out with Catherine but then stopped. "Before I left the house to come here, Marina got hold of Greg's best friend's roommate. The roommate told her as far as he knew, Greg, Ryan and some other guys had gone to the lake for the weekend. They were supposed to leave by noon. I've already called the lake ranger and he's going to send some men out to find their campsite and get word to him. I've tried to reach Greg on his cell phone, but I keep getting a message that says all circuits are busy."

The taste of blood rested on his tongue when Alex bit down into the side of his mouth. His heart was beating so loud he was sure the others would hear it. Greg beat Sarah into unconsciousness and then left her to die, while their child screamed and cried in the next room. All he could manage to say was, "Let me know when you find him."

Alex watched Frank and Catherine walk down the hall out of sight before he turned to Jeff. He wanted to know what Jeff had found out before he revealed his assumptions. "What did you find at the duplex?"

Jeff was of a slender build and almost six feet tall. He had an honest face and though he was only forty-one, his receding and thinning hair made him appear older. He was known for his straight forwardness in his business and personal life. "We've been friends a long time and have always been up front with each other even when we had our differences. I'm here as a sheriff, but more as your friend."

Adrenaline pumped through Alex's veins and he felt as though he would burst. "I appreciate that, Jeff. Now tell me, what did you find?" He felt he already knew the answer.

"My men and I went through every inch of that duplex, and there was no forced entry anywhere. I've been doing this for awhile and have seen it all, as you know. I have to tell you honestly, from what we didn't find, the perpetrator had to be someone Sarah knew and trusted. The way she was beaten is not the MO of a burglar who gets surprised by the victim. This type of crime fits the profile of someone who was sexually assaulted, though the doctor said Sarah wasn't. That only leaves a crime of passion, someone who was enraged by hatred or the need to control." Jeff gazed at Alex who stared steadfast at him.

"I didn't want to believe it, but I knew I was right." Alex turned away and slammed his fist against the wall. "I swear I'll make him suffer, then kill him for everything he's done to her. God, how could I have been so blind!"

"Alex, calm down. I know what you're thinking, but you know as well as I do there has to be proof."

"Proof! Go look at my daughter. What more proof do you want!" Alex's voice shook as he leaned against the wall.

"You know Sarah is like one of my own kids. And I'm angry, even tempted to take off this badge and go after him myself. But that's not the way and we both know it. How are you and I going to help Sarah if we're in jail? Let's find Greg and bring him in for questioning. I'm sure he'll deny any of this and even pretend to be the distraught husband. Sarah's the only witness we have, and the doctors are saying she may not remember what happened." Jeff put a hand on Alex's shoulder and looked at him with compassion.

"All these years, I've represented people who felt the law was unfair and justice hadn't been served. For the first time I'm on the other side and it stinks. My child lies in a bed, fighting for her life, and Greg could get off scot free because there's only circumstantial evidence." Exhaustion plagued Alex again, as he calmed down.

"Why don't you go home and get some rest? The rest of your family needs you. I'm placing round the clock security outside Sarah's room. I'll even stand guard if it will make you feel better. Were going to get him if he did this," Jeff said.

Alex's gaze hardened as he looked at his friend. "Oh, he did it all right. Sarah didn't have an enemy in this world, until she married him," he said bitterly.

"I'll call you as soon as I hear anything. The lake rangers should track him down soon. The duplex has been sealed off until the investigation is over and an officer will be posted there if Greg shows up." Jeff said reassuringly, as Alex prepared to leave.

"I'm going to check on Sarah before I head home. If it wasn't for Cath and the boys, I'd just sleep here. I know they need me right now too." He yawned as he spoke.

"If you're too tired I can drive you home and bring you back in the morning," Jeff offered, noticing how exhausted Alex looked.

"Thanks, but I'm fine. You've got a wife and kids to get home to. I'll see you tomorrow. I appreciate all you and your men are doing." Alex patted him on the back and walked toward Sarah's room. An officer was sitting outside the door drinking a cup of coffee while reading a magazine. Alex nodded an acknowledgment and felt relieved. The anxiety he experienced before was not present as he put his hand on the handle and pushed the door opened. The sight of Sarah was still overwhelming, but he was past the initial shock.

His fingers gently stroked her unbroken cheek back and forth. The nurses were giving her pain shots and he was thankful she wasn't suffering. He leaned over and kissed her forehead. She was alive and for right now that was enough. As long as there was breath in her, there was hope. "I love you, Sarah. We're going to get through this together." Except for the sounds of the monitors, the room was quiet and peaceful. He needed to go home and check on everyone, but Alex couldn't bring himself to leave. If something happened during the night he'd never forgive himself. The hospital would just have to bend the rules this time on his behalf. He would let the nurse know he was spending the night and call Catherine, too. In the morning she could bring him a change of clothes and personal items. She would understand and probably be glad he'd decided to stay.

The sofa wasn't long enough for his long frame, but Alex made the best of it. As tired as he was, sleep wouldn't come at first. He repeatedly opened his eyes to make sure Sarah was all right. But as the minutes passed, his body relaxed in conjunction with his steady breathing. Images filled his mind as he sank deeper into the subconscious where dreams live. Pictures of Sarah slowly faded, while Alex desperately attempted to hold on to her, though she slipped hopelessly away. Another face suddenly appeared. It was blurred except for the dark, wild eyes.

Alex wanted to call out for Sarah, though words wouldn't come. The unfamiliar form approached him, seething and yelling out profanity. The stranger was so close, Alex could see smoke pouring from his enraged nostrils. As the thick haze cleared, his son-in-law emerged like a maniac, ranting and raving. Rage overtook Alex as he attacked him with vengeance, purely consumed with hatred. His knuckles began to bleed as he pounded Greg's face over and over until he was unrecognizable. "I'll kill you, I'll kill you!" he screamed over and over.

"Mr. Matthews, Mr. Matthews, wake up." The night nurse shook him gently as he jumped and sat up abruptly.

Fear seized him. "What's wrong? Is Sarah okay? " he demanded looking over at the hospital bed.

"Yes, she's fine. You were having a bad dream. I heard you yelling," she said quietly.

His shirt and hair were soaked with perspiration. "I apologize if I disturbed any of the other patients," he said, leaning back against the couch.

"No need to apologize. You've been through a lot. If there's anything I can do or get for you, just let me know. My name is Nurse Talley." She smiled as she took the blanket and pillow off the couch. "Let me get you some dry ones." The nurse checked Sarah's monitors before she left the room.

The memory of that dream was still vivid in Alex's mind as he watched Sarah. He could still see Greg's mangled face and it made him feel good. Never once had he committed such an act of violence as he had done in his gratifying dream. Alex felt that if he came in contact with his son-in-law, with no one else around, he would lose control and kill him. But even Greg's death wouldn't be enough satisfaction to make up for what had happened. One thing he was sure of, Greg would get what he deserved, one way or the other, and Alex would make sure to witness his demise.

Chapter Twenty

The sun streamed through the blinds with pretense of warmth, for the winter weather was cold and frigid. Alex's eyelids opened slowly, taking in his surroundings, which were foggy. But the reality of what had happened the night before quickly jolted his recollection. The past hours had been like a death watch. He had dozed off and on, but always woke with dread that Sarah wouldn't make it. The fears that tormented him through the night dissolved when he saw a nurse changing the IV. Though Sarah's appearance hadn't changed, and her body remained unmoving, she was still alive.

He silently thanked God and walked over to the nurse. "How's she doing this morning?" He looked with pity at his daughter.

"Her vital signs are a little stronger. The doctor will be in soon and he will be able to tell you more."

"Could you tell me if there is a restroom with a shower, nurse—?" Alex paused and looked down at her name badge.

"Nurse Hensley. It's right across from the waiting area." She checked the monitors and changed the empty IV bag.

He thanked her as she left the room. When Alex kissed Sarah's forehead, he noticed her skin wasn't as cold. Even though the temperature change in her body was a small improvement, it encouraged Alex. The recovery process could take awhile, and he would try not to set his expectations too high, although he welcomed any positive signs. "Keep fighting sweetheart. We all love you."

Outside the room, Alex spoke briefly to the officer and then went to the waiting room. It was a quarter past seven, and he wanted to call Catherine to check on everyone. After the second ring, Josephine's worried voice answered.

"Josie, it's me." He wanted to come across as being in control and collected.

"Oh, Mr. Alex, how is Sarah? I've been so worried." Josephine's concern was apparent.

He wasn't sure how much Catherine had told her or the boys, and didn't want to cause any undue stress over the phone. "Did you see Mrs. Matthews when she came home last night?"

"Yes, she was extremely tired, but Will and Carter were waiting and wanted to know what was going on. I fixed everyone hot chocolate while she filled us in. We just couldn't believe it. Mrs. Matthews tried to answer all our questions before she went to bed." Josephine sighed, as though remembering all the details.

"How are the boys and Mrs. Matthews this morning?" He didn't want to sound impatient or cut Josephine short. He just didn't want to answer any questions.

"Pretty quiet. Miss Catherine is going to bring them to the hospital this morning while I take care of Katelan. She's in the shower and said to tell you if you called that she would see you there. Oh, I almost forgot. Sheriff Parkerson and Mr. Winslow called early this morning. They both want you to call them."

"Do me a favor, please. Remind Mrs. Matthews to bring me a change of clothes and the personal items. I know you want to see Sarah, too, and we'll work it out in the next couple of days. I've got to go. I don't want to miss seeing the doctor. Give Katelan a kiss and hug for me." He hung up the phone and thought about who he should call first. Frank and Marina probably didn't have a clue yet that their son was the prime suspect. Perhaps Jeff would have some information as to Greg's whereabouts. Maybe Frank had heard from Greg and that's why he had called so early. Alex decided to call the Winslows.

After the fourth ring, Alex was about to hang up when Marina said "Hello."

"Hello, Marina, this is Alex. Josephine said Frank called this morning. Is he in? Have you heard from Greg yet?" he asked, trying not to sound hostile.

"You'll have to talk to Frank about that," she replied rudely.

Before he had a chance to say anything further Marina began yelling for Frank to pick up the phone. "Did you hear me? Pick up the phone, now!"

"Hello," Frank sounded embarrassed.

"Frank, it's Alex," he said, thinking about the bombshell that would be dropped on the Winslows today. He felt sorry for Frank, who was nothing like his wife or son. Marina didn't even ask about Sarah, not that Alex expected her to. She was a cold, heartless, and ruthless woman, who cared only for herself and Greg.

"How's Sarah doing? I would have come back up last night, but the hour was so late, and I knew you were worn out," Frank said apologetically.

"That's okay, Frank, but I appreciate the thought. Well, she made it through the night, which is a small victory. I ended up spending the night in her room. I just couldn't leave her alone. And now I'm waiting for the doctor to come by."

"That's great to hear," Frank said, relieved. "I know she'll pull through. She's surrounded by people who love her."

"Thank you, Frank. I know how much you have grown to love Sarah, and she feels the same about you." Alex meant every word, but couldn't include Marina in his sentiment.

"I've got some good news. The lake ranger called early this morning. They were able to locate Greg's campsite and get word to him. According to the ranger, Greg was going to pack up and head out right away. I'm assuming he'll go straight to the hospital but I've been unable to reach him on his cell phone. It must still be out of range."

Alex thought of the officer outside Sarah's room. He also wanted Jeff close by in the event that Greg might show up. The Winslows would find out anyway, so Frank might as well be here too. "Were you planning on coming up here anytime soon? I wanted to talk to with you about something." He tried to keep his tone nonchalant.

"Give me about an hour and I'll be there. Marina's just now getting around. She'll be up later."

After what would transpire today, Alex doubted Marina would ever come up. Not that he cared. "Okay, I'll see you then. Bye."

After making his phone call to Jeff, who made himself very clear that Alex was not to do anything stupid if Greg showed up, he went to alert the guard. They were talking about the situation and what precautions to take when his wife and two sons walked into the ICU unit. The distraught looks on the boys face made Alex's heart heavy, knowing the hell they were going through. He hugged both of them and held them briefly, as he looked at Catherine and smiled. The sadness in her eyes was still there, but she seemed stronger.

Carter was the first to speak and the distress he exhibited was intense. "Dad, where's Sarah? I've got to see her. Is she going to be okay? Have they caught the guy who did this, yet?"

"Son, slow down. Both of you will see her soon. Sarah is going to be fine. Her recovery will take some time and she'll need all of us to help her get through this. The sheriff and his men are working round the clock to find the person who did this."

"How could someone do this to her! For God's sake, everyone liked Sarah." Will's eyes filled with tears as he clenched his teeth. "When they catch him, I'm gonna kill him. He's not going to get away with this!"

Alex put a hand on both his sons' shoulders. Will was so much like himself it was like looking in a mirror sometimes. "I know how you both are feeling, believe me. We will get him, and he'll pay for what he's done. I know you're angry, and I'm angry, but right now we need to help Sarah get through this. Not just physically, but emotionally, as well. She's going to need a lot of love and support." He looked at both boys seriously. "Can I count on the two of you?"

"Yea, Dad, you can," Carter replied, followed by a nod of Will's head.

"Your mother probably told you Sarah doesn't look like herself. She's severely bruised and swollen. The initial shock is the hardest. Well that's about it, so if you're ready, let's go in." Alex ushered everyone past the guard and into the room.

The Matthews family stood at the foot of the bed with arms wrapped around each other. Carter buried his face in his mother's hair and wept while she held him. Tears flowed down Will's cheeks, though he never uttered a sound. As a family, they had been through trying times before, but their strength had always pulled them through. This tragedy would only make them stronger and closer. Alex's eyes became moist as he looked at his daughter who seemed so frail and helpless. Hidden beneath her fragile form, courage and the will to survive would bring her back to all of them.

* * *

"Where do you think you're going?" Marina slammed her coffee cup down on the table, spilling the hot liquid.

"You know good and well where I'm going. And if you had any decency you would come with me." Frank walked out of the kitchen with car keys in hand.

Her bare feet slapped down against the cold linoleum as she went after him. "Go with you," she mocked. "I've never been able to stomach that family. I told you they would get theirs someday, thinking they were better than everyone else. Sarah got exactly what she deserved!" Marina sneered, but fear filled her eyes when Frank lunged at her, grabbing her around the throat.

"I could kill you for that! I wish it would have been you instead of Sarah. Hatred and jealousy have totally consumed you. Your life's mission is to destroy everyone around you, at any cost." Frank released her and stepped back. He took in deep breaths as his temper decreased. "I believe you would even hurt our granddaughter if she got in your way."

Marina quickly regained her composure. "How do we even know Katelan is really our son's child?" she declared boldly.

Frank thought he had heard it all from her as he glared at her in disbelief. "You'll stop at nothing, will you? How low will you stoop to ruin lives? Sarah is the best thing that's happened to this family, and you can't stand the fact she's everything you're not."

"I hate you! Why don't you just die so I can collect the insurance money? That's the least you can do for me since you've never given me anything else of worth." Her sarcasm was so thick, Frank could taste it.

"I feel very sorry for you, Marina. You could have had a life full of love and fulfillment, but something happened to you along the way. I can't live like this anymore. I thought if I stayed you would eventually change, but I was only kidding myself. I'm leaving you Marina. I want a divorce. The last years of my life may be spent alone, but they will be peaceful ones. I'll be by later to pick up some of my things." Frank turned away from her, picked his coat off the chair and walked out the front door.

"You're leaving me? No, you're not, because I'm throwing you out!" she yelled running after him. "All you are is a worthless loser! I should have gotten rid of you years ago. Do you hear me, Frank!" Marina stood on the porch shivering as he opened the car door. "Give my warmest regards to the Matthews family," she taunted. Her eyes darkened when Frank turned to look at her. "Tell them I hope their tramp of a daughter dies! I hope she dies!"

Frank got in his truck and shut the door. He could hear Marina screaming and shouting profanity as he backed out of the driveway and pulled onto the road. Her words echoed through his mind as he thought of Sarah. Prayer had never been a part of Frank's life, but he managed a simple prayer, "God, please don't let Sarah die. If anyone deserves to die, it's Marina. Amen."

Chapter Twenty-One

A hot shower was just what Alex needed to be revived, while Catherine and the boys went to the hospital cafeteria for breakfast. Will and Carter held up better than he'd hoped. Now that everyone was past the initial shock, they would be able to focus on Sarah getting better. Dr. Andrison had been very hopeful this morning and was encouraged with her steady vital signs. Alex emerged from the bathroom to find Jeff Parkerson in the waiting room.

"Good morning, Jeff," Alex said as he walked toward the sheriff, while combing his wet hair back. "Did you speak to your man on duty?"

"Yes, he told me there's a good chance Greg will show up. I've posted another officer in the main lobby who will be notified by the information desk if anyone asks for Sarah's room number." Jeff looked intently at Alex. "You've got to promise me, if he does come here, you'll let me handle this."

"Don't worry, I'm not going to do anything stupid. I would like to be there when you question him, though. Listen, Frank Winslow will be here soon. He doesn't know about our suspicions regarding his son. We need to talk to him as soon as he arrives. Frank is a good guy and I want him to know beforehand." Alex wished he could spare him the pain this news would bring.

Officer Bohner poked his head in the waiting room interrupting the two men. "Sheriff, Mike just called from downstairs. A white male matching the husband's description is on his way up to the ICU unit. He asked for Mrs. Winslow's room number, but didn't give a name."

"Thanks, Carl. Go back to your post and wait for him. We'll be watching from here."

"Yes, sir." Officer Bohner went back and sat down in the chair and pretended to read a magazine.

"So much for breaking the news to Frank," sighed Alex. Catherine and the boys would be back soon. This wasn't how he wanted to confront Greg. The situation could get heated.

"I'd like to question him in here, but if he doesn't cooperate, we'll take him back to the station. Remember, let me do the talking. When his father gets here, he can stay as long as this situation stays under control." Jeff was always a professional, but this time was harder because Alex was like a brother to him.

Alex began to say something, but Jeff put his finger to his lips and motioned for him to step back as the elevator beeped and the door slid opened. Greg approached the nurses, stated he was Sarah Winslow's husband and asked where her room was. A nurse directed him toward the room where the guard was sitting. Greg shifted uncomfortably and his eyes narrowed when he saw the uniformed officer. Officer Bohner rose and glanced briefly toward the waiting room.

"May I help you?" The officer's tone was harsh as he stared at Greg, who looked liked he'd been up all night with his disheveled hair and five o'clock shadow.

"I'm here to see my wife. Why is she under guard?" he demanded.

Jeff approached undetected and stood next to Greg. "I'm Sheriff Parkerson. Mr. Winslow, I would like to speak with you in the waiting room."

"What's going on here? I want some answers now." Greg crossed his arms, indicating he wasn't moving.

"Then we want the same thing. There are very critical patients on this unit and I won't discuss it out here with you. The waiting room, Mr. Winslow." Jeff turned and waited for Greg to follow.

"This had better not take long. I've been on the road all night and I have the right to see my own wife." he exclaimed arrogantly. With reluctance, he followed the sheriff into the waiting room.

"Take a seat, Mr. Winslow," Jeff said, shutting the door.

The minute his loathsome son-in-law entered the room, Alex's body tensed as his jaw tightened. He gripped the arms of the chair to keep himself from attacking Greg. At first, Greg looked surprised at seeing Alex, but his expression changed to one of contempt.

"What's he doing here?" Greg made no effort to conceal his hatred.

Alex could barely contain himself and didn't know how he would be able to stay in the same room with Greg and remain civil. "What do you think I'm doing here? My daughter's lying in a bed fighting for her life!" He could feel the blood pumping through his veins.

Jeff threw Alex a warning glance. "Mr. Winslow, your father-in-law has every right to be here. Sarah is your wife, but she is also his daughter. Now, there are some questions I'd like to ask you. From the information I've been able to gather you were the last one to see your wife yesterday before the assault. What time did you leave to go to the lake?"

Greg turned back to face Sheriff Parkerson and eyed him with caution. "I left around noon with some friends."

"What are those friends' names?" Jeff held a pencil and pad in his hand, waiting for an answer.

"What's going on here?" Greg threw his shoulders back defensively. "What do my friends have to do with anything?" He looked from Sheriff Parkerson to Alex. The look in his father-in-laws eyes was all the answer he needed. "You think I did this, don't you?" Greg pointed his finger at Alex. "You've hated me from day one, and now you're trying to pin this on me! You can cram your accusations right up your—"

Alex stood up angrily and lunged toward Greg whose fingers curled into a fist. "I know you did it! You beat Sarah and left her for dead, you miserable son of a bitch!" He tried to grab Greg by the throat, but Jeff quickly intervened and stepped between the two men.

"That's enough! Now back off, both of you. Alex, sit back down," he ordered as he pushed Greg toward a chair. "This is an investigation and will be treated as such." Jeff faced Greg who was seething with hostility. "We can either do this here and be civil or go down to the station. It's your choice."

Three brisk knocks struck the door. Jeff opened the door to find Frank and Catherine standing there. "Please come in and have a seat." The atmosphere was polluted by animosity, making the room uncomfortable.

Alex stood up when he saw his wife. "Where are the boys?"

"They're in with Sarah." Catherine glanced at Greg before walking over by her husband.

"It might be better if you stay with them." Alex nudged her toward the door, but she sat down on couch.

"No, I'm staying right here," she said firmly.

Frank looked from Greg to Alex. "What's going on here?" he asked as he sat down on the couch next to Catherine.

"Dad, they think I did this to Sarah," Greg blurted out tapping his fingers on his knee.

"Alex, is that true? You actually think my son could do something like this?" He asked in disbelief.

"I'm sorry, Frank. I didn't want you to find out like this. I wanted to talk to you first." He wished he could have spared Frank any grief.

"Mr. Winslow, before you arrived I was attempting to ask your son some questions. I'm hoping to shed some light on this situation." Jeff meant to keep control and prevent any more outbursts, physical or verbal. "This is very serious and I only want to get to the truth."

Greg started to speak, but Jeff interrupted. "Let me finish, then everyone will have a chance to comment or ask questions. Now, these are the facts. The duplex where you live was not broken in to. There was no forced entry anywhere. Nothing is missing, and Sarah was not sexually assaulted. That only leaves one conclusion. The person who did this was someone she knew and trusted."

Alex surveyed the room as he did in a courtroom when the accused heard the evidence presented against them. Immediate reaction was everything, revealing innocence or guilt. Frank looked stunned as he sat back against the couch looking up at Jeff. But Alex's eyes rested on Greg who popped his neck and shifted in his seat. Nothing had been said that his son-in-law didn't already know. He was guilty. If the law didn't get him, Alex would, whatever the cost.

"So, of course, that makes me guilty. I may not be an officer of the law or a hot shot attorney," he said sarcastically glaring at Alex, "but I've got rights and you've got no real proof, so I really don't care what you think!" Greg directed his hostility toward Jeff. "Now, unless you're going to arrest me, which I don't think you are, I'm out of here." Greg stood up, walk toward the door and reached for the doorknob.

Jeff blocked the door and noticed the bruises and abrasions across Greg's knuckles. "I'm not finished. Sit back down," he said with authority.

"I'm not saying another word without a lawyer," Greg lashed out.

"Son," Frank said. "Why don't you calm down and answer the Sheriff's questions. If you've got nothing to hide, you don't need a lawyer," Frank said, hoping to keep Greg's temper from erupting.

"If you want an attorney present," said Jeff, "that's your right. So, if you would like to contact a lawyer you can have him meet us down at the station."

"No, my dad is right. I've got nothing to hide." Greg sat back down casting a smug look in Alex's direction.

"Please, Sheriff Parkerson, continue. I'm sure you will find out my son had nothing to do with this." Frank sounded like he was trying to convince himself.

"Sheriff," Greg said, "I'll save you a lot of time here by just telling you about yesterday. The guy whose car I rode in is Ryan McCormick. He picked me up around 12:15 PM. He honked the horn and I met them outside. Sarah was fine when I left. Now, I don't know what happened to her because I wasn't there. Maybe she opened the door to someone and they forced their way in. I don't have any answers. And all you have is presumption." Greg spoke with an insolent look on his face.

"You've thought of everything, haven't you?" Alex lashed out. "How convenient that Ryan honked the horn giving no one a chance to come inside. Sarah always keeps the storm door locked when she's there by herself. Why didn't she lock the door after you left? Because she wasn't able to, was she?" Alex's cold stare and his undeniable accusations caused Greg to flinch.

"I don't have to listen to this. You've got no proof and you know it." Greg stood up to leave. "I'm going to see my wife."

"I can't allow you to do that, Mr. Winslow." Jeff stated, never taking his eyes off Greg or his bruised hands.

"You can't stop me," Greg said through clenched teeth.

"Yes, I can. When a crime of this nature has been committed, the spouse is a usual suspect." Jeff spoke with full authority. "A restraining order has been filed against you, and until I prove you're not a threat to your wife, the order stands. Your home is also off limits until the investigation is over. I have one more question before I'm finished here. What happened to your knuckles? They look like you've been in a fight." All eyes in the room looked to Greg's hands.

An immediate change settled on Greg's face as he gazed down at his hands. Seconds past as he remained speechless. He avoided all eyes except for his father. "I scraped them against some rocks in the brush trying to set traps."

"Had to think about that one, didn't you?" Alex stood and took a step forward as rage crept up his neck. Every bruise and abrasion on Greg's knuckles represented the blows Sarah had suffered. He could have thrown his career away and everything he'd worked for to have one minute alone with

Greg. All the respect he'd earned didn't matter if he could end this sorry excuse for a human being's life.

Catherine stood and put her hand around her husband's forearm. "No, Alex. Leave it to the law." Tears filled her eyes as she turned and faced Greg. "When Alex first told me about his suspicions of you, I didn't want to believe it. I always tried to smooth things over when my husband had misgivings about you. I gave you the benefit of the doubt, even when I sensed something was wrong with Sarah. But after sitting here, listening and watching you, I believe with all my heart, you did this to our daughter." She began to tremble as she reached out and slapped Greg's face with full force. "You are an evil person and you will pay for what you have done to my child."

No one could have been in shock more than Alex over his wife's behavior. He had never seen her like this before. Everyone seemed to be in a trance for a brief second until Greg spoke with retaliation and broke the spell. "All of you can go straight to hell." He glared at Alex with such hatred, it was felt by everyone in the room.

"Son, wait, I want to talk to you." Frank rose from the couch as Greg brushed past the sheriff and left the room. He looked out the door but his son was already gone.

"Alex, I'd like to talk to you." Frank's voice was strained.

"Of course." Alex would have to reveal all of his reasons as to why he believed Greg was guilty. It was only natural for a father to want to defend his son and believe the best of him. But when the facts were laid out, even Frank would have to begin to wonder about his son's innocence.

"Unless you think I'm needed here, I'll head on back to the station," Jeff said.

"No, you go on. But thanks." Alex waved him on and sat back down in the chair.

"Mr. Winslow." The sheriff nodded his head and then left.

Catherine walked over to Frank with tears still in her eyes. "I'm so sorry you had to hear me say those things to your son. I wouldn't want to do anything to hurt you. Our family has been under enormous emotional stress. This situation is hard for all of us, and apologize you had to find out this way. Please, just hear Alex out as to why we believe Greg did this."

Frank sat down and settled against the couch. "I will, but would like to say something first. In addition to being in-laws, I consider you two as friends. I'm not a man to make rash judgments of people or situations. I respect you, Alex, but you better have a good reason as to why you think Greg could do something like this."

With a heavy sigh, Alex leaned forward and begin to share what he had perceived over the past year of their children's marriage. He told of Sarah's continual withdrawal from her family and her frequent mood changes. When the topic of her marriage would come up, Sarah had become apprehensive and evasive. Looking back now, he believed his daughter's fall on the ice was not an accident. And did she really fall. Frank's face took on a downcast expression when Alex continued to recount his hostile encounters with Greg on the night that Katelan was born, and at the emergency room when Sarah fell.

"I don't know what to say," Frank said. "I can understand now why you might suspect my son. There were times when I did notice tension between the kids and just figured whatever was wrong, they'd work it out. I never imagined Greg could be hitting her." Frank's voice broke as he leaned forward. "I just can't believe this."

"No matter what happens, we don't hold you responsible for Greg's actions. He is a grown man and accountable for himself. You love your son, as you should, but Sarah is my daughter, and I will see justice served."

As both men stood and faced each other, Frank spoke. "I just want you to know one thing. If my son truly did this unspeakable horror, I won't protect him. But if he's innocent, I'll defend him to the end." Frank put his hand on Alex's shoulder. "I need to ask you a favor. I believe you're a man of principal and integrity. Your profession requires you to seek out the truth everyday. Find the truth, Alex, based on the facts, and not your emotions. Then justice will be served."

"I will, and that's a promise." Alex shook Frank's hand before they parted. Catherine stood and hugged Frank. They agreed to talk later, after Frank had a chance to talk with Greg. Alex could only imagine the impact this would have on Marina. If it sent her over the edge, there was no telling what she would do. Catherine took the boys home, but would return a little later. She planned on staying the night with her husband at the hospital. Alex walked into Sarah's room and stood by her bed.

"Well, sweetheart, you've made it through the night. We all love you so much." He gently took hold of her hand. "You just rest and know I'm here, and no one is ever going to hurt you again. Do you hear me? Never." Suddenly Sarah's fingers moved. Tears filled his eyes as he lightly squeezed her hand. "I'm here. Keep fighting and come back to us." Alex bowed his head and wept, not out of sadness, but joy.

Chapter Twenty-Two

The past three days dragged for the Matthews family, especially for Alex and Catherine, who stayed with Sarah around the clock. It was as though life had been placed on hold while they went through the motion of living. But for them, their lives were non-existent without their daughter. They tended to the things that needed their attention, but it was done without enthusiasm. Their main focus revolved around Sarah and getting her better.

Josephine came to visit between caring for Katelan and her regular household responsibilities. The baby sensed something was amiss and Josephine did her best to keep the child as occupied and happy as possible. It wasn't an easy task trying to appear to be cheerful when she felt sad and overwhelmed with sorrow. The boys went back to school, but called the hospital often. To be kept updated about their sister helped to relieve the anxiety they felt. The news of Will and Carter's sister had spread through the school halls and the rumors were rampant. A few close friends had asked the brothers directly what had happened, but for the most part the students were giving them their space.

Dr. Andrison was confident Sarah would make a complete physical recovery. Her vital signs were growing stronger, her eyelids had fluttered occasionally, indicating she was trying to wake. The doctor said it would take time and not to expect too much at first. Sarah's prognosis was encouraging, and this got the family through each long day. Every ounce of hope that was offered, they clung to with fervency.

Sheriff Parkerson came by often, more of a social call than a professional one, as no new evidence had turned up. Greg was still denying any involvement. Hopes of an arrest seemed dismal, but as long as the case was open, the restraining order would stay in effect and an officer would remain at Sarah's door. A policeman was also posted at the Matthew's home in case Greg attempted to take his daughter.

Every evening after work, Frank came to the hospital and ate dinner with Alex and Catherine. He wanted to see Sarah and he enjoyed their company. It helped to take his mind off his own personal affairs. Frank opened up a little about his separation from Marina. He told them there had been problems in their marriage for some time though he didn't go in to detail. There were deep rooted issues that were too painful to bring up. Frank had always been a private person and it wasn't easy for him to talk about this situation. The Matthews expressed their sympathy, but were secretly glad that Frank was getting away from Marina. From what they had witnessed first hand, he would be better off without her in his life. Frank tried to apologize for his wife not coming to the hospital, although Alex told him it wasn't necessary. Both the mother and son were cut from the same piece of rotten material and now that Greg was a suspect, Marina's hatred for the Matthews family became fully revealed.

After Frank had gone back to his hotel room, Catherine fell asleep on the couch, leaving Alex to his thoughts. He was restless and couldn't stop thinking about Greg, which only caused his temper to rise. His son-in-law was living back at home doing whatever he wanted. There wasn't a shred of evidence to convict Greg, let alone put him in jail. The case was at a standstill, and it was maddening not being able to do anything about it. His good friend, Adam Barnes, the district attorney, told Alex he would have to have more than just circumstantial evidence.

Alex looked over at Sarah. Next to the white sheets and white walls the slight color that had returned to her face was hardly noticeable. This hospital room, with its IV's and needles, seemed as hopeless as this case. The only person who could bring light to the situation was his daughter. Alex walked over to her and stroked her hair. But would she be able to remember what happened? The doctors had said it wasn't likely. He was convinced this was not the first abusive incident. If she couldn't remember this one, perhaps she would remember other attacks.

Greg would get his, one way or another. Alex, besides being one of the most respected citizens in Seaside Cove and owning a most prominent law firm, had connections on a personal and professional level. There wasn't a place in the city that his loathsome son-in-law could show his face where everyone wouldn't know what he had done. This wasn't the justice Alex wanted, but it was a start. Hell took on many shapes and forms, and Greg was about to experience them one at a time. Maybe Alex would refrain from touching him physically, but he would attack him in every way legally possible.

Though the temperature outside was still frigid, the sunlight which filtered through the mini blinds seem to bring a ray of hope for a brighter day. Alex's long, lean legs extended even farther past the end of the recliner when he stretched. He rubbed his eyes and looked at the clock on the wall. The time was 6:30 and he wanted to shower and shave before the doctor arrived on his morning rounds. The couch was empty except for the blanket Catherine had folded with the pillow on top. He knew she had gone home to shower and see the boys before they left for school. Alex picked up his own blanket and began to fold it when he heard a soft moan. He dropped the cover and turned toward the bed and held his breath. Seconds passed as he made his way to Sarah's side. His eyes never left her face as he waited. Could he have imagined the sound? "Sarah, can you hear me? It's Daddy."

Alex grasped her hand and looked for any sign of movement. "Please, sweetheart, just wake up." He shut his eyes and prayed, "God, oh God, let her wake up." He concentrated on those words as they went over and over in his mind. Tears filled his eyes as her hand moved slightly beneath his, followed by another low moan. Her eyelids opened a little and then shut. It was hard to contain his excitement as he leaned forward and kissed her cheek.

Her lips began to move, but she uttered no sound. But then he placed his ear close to her mouth and could hear her whisper the word, "Thirsty."

He quickly pushed the button to call the nurse. Within seconds a nurse entered the room. The look on Alex's face made her hasten to the bedside. "Mr. Matthews, is something wrong?" She checked the monitors and IV carefully to make sure everything was working.

He smiled broadly. "My daughter said 'thirsty'."

The nurse checked Sarah's pulse and raised her eyelid as the door opened. "How's my patient doing this morning?" Dr. Andrison, inquired walking around to the other side of the bed. He flipped opened the chart and checked the updated information. "She's growing stronger everyday."

"Doctor, she spoke. I heard her say 'thirsty'!" Alex beamed. "She moaned twice and opened her eyes."

"She's a fighter. Nurse, start her on very small ice chips and keep me posted of any changes throughout the day." The doctor smiled and shook Alex's hand before he left the room.

Within the next three hours, Sarah woke up to the smiling, tearful faces of her mother, father, brothers and Frank. She was groggy from the pain medication, but understood who was there. Everyone gathered around the bed, wanting to be close to her. It was an emotional time, yet a joyous occasion for the family. Alex and Sheriff Parkerson were anxious to ask some questions, knowing they would have to be patient. Dr. Andrison had instructed them not to pressure Sarah because her state of mind could be fragile. The conversation should be kept light and short.

Being careful not to jostle her, Alex sat down on the bed next to his daughter. Her auburn hair was still matted together with blood even though a nurse had tried to remove as much as possible. He took her hand in his and tried not to be overly anxious. "Sweetheart, you're in a hospital. Do you know why you're here?"

Sarah looked from one face to another and then back to her father. "I um, I don't know." Her emerald eyes looked glazed and as confused as her voice sounded.

"There's no need to worry about anything right now. You need to rest." Catherine ran her fingers across Sarah's forehead. "We can talk more about it later."

"Where's my baby?" she asked. The effort to sit up, only caused her head to throb. A pained expression settled across her face as she lay back down. "I want to see Katelan. Is she okay?" Panic filtered in her tone.

"Just take it easy. Katelan is being spoiled by Josie and your brothers. As soon as you're up to a visit, we'll bring her to see you." Alex reassured her as he adjusted the covers to make her more uncomfortable.

"Daddy, what happened to me? I hurt all over." Sarah groaned when she tried to move her broken arm.

Looks were exchanged between Frank and Alex, while Catherine gently put a pillow under the cast for additional support. "There was an accident." Alex lied, in hopes that it would satisfy her for right now. "We'll talk more about this later, after you've rested."

Sarah put her hand to her forehead and frowned. "Why can't I remember? Everything is just blank. It's like looking at a book with no pictures or words, just empty pages. I'm so confused."

"You've been through a severe trauma. The doctor said memory loss is common in this type of injury." Alex didn't want to reveal the extent of her injuries.

"Will I ever remember? Mom, Dad, will I?" Sarah looked at both parents.

"I don't know, sweetheart. The doctor said it can go either way. Don't think about that right now. We need to concentrate on you getting well." Catherine smiled and patted her daughter's arm.

"Where's Greg? Was he in the accident, too?" She asked with a shaken voice.

"Calm down, sweetie. Greg is fine. He was here earlier." Alex lied again. Until he knew what she was going to remember, Alex wanted to tell her as little as possible. Risking her emotional state was not an option, no matter how bad he wanted to get Greg.

That little bit of information appeared to settle her for the moment. A nurse entered the room with a syringe; Alex sighed with relief. He wasn't prepared to answer any more questions.

The pain medication began to take effect and Sarah's eyes soon closed in sleep. Catherine felt it was time to take the boys home to give Josephine a break from Katelan, although it was hard for her to leave the hospital. Catherine put on a good front for everyone, but on the inside her heart was broken. Every time she looked at her battered child laying in that bed, hopelessness seized her. As Sarah grew from infancy to being a toddler and on to an adolescent, Catherine had been there to wipe away the tears and bandage scraped knees. It was a mother's job to protect her child. Because Catherine had wanted to see the best in Greg, Sarah was almost beaten to death. Even Alex, more than once, had voiced his concerns about their son-in-law. But she ignored what was staring her in the face. She felt responsible for what had happen to her daughter and knowing she might have prevented this would torment her the rest of her life.

Alex and Frank stayed in the room. Both men agreed that Greg shouldn't be given any information about Sarah. Now with Marina and Greg accusing him of consorting with the enemy, being a traitor to his own family, Frank spent more time at the hospital when he wasn't at work. He moved into a cheap motel on the outskirts of town. Because the room was drab and it depressed him, he went there only to shower and sleep.

Throughout the afternoon, Sarah slept on and off, while Alex checked in with his law office and returned calls to friends and associates who wanted to know how his daughter was doing. Frank went back to work with the promise of returning with a bottle of red wine and Italian food for dinner to celebrate. By the end of the day, Dr. Andrison placed Sarah on a liquid diet. If she continued doing well, he would move her off the ICU and down to a regular floor in the next couple of days.

As difficult as it was, Alex refrained from questioning his daughter. He would give her time to gain back more physical strength. Maybe by then her memory would return, although he tried not to get his hopes up. Even with the doctor's orders not to pressure Sarah, he didn't know what he would say to her when she started asking for Greg again. He could only put her off for a while. But the sight of Greg could trigger her memory of that horrible day. The pros and cons of what to do troubled Alex. He wanted to spare his daughter further pain and heartache, but knew that was impossible. The only thing he could do was to be there for her, and make sure Greg never hurt Sarah again.

Just as Dr. Andrison promised, within the next two days, Sarah was moved off the ICU. Even with the bruises starting to change colors and the swelling subsiding, she still looked battered. The day came when Sarah wanted to see her daughter. She longed to hold her baby in her arms, to feel the softness of her skin. She could smell Katelan's hair and hear her sweet voice. Tears filled Sarah's eyes as she envisioned her child. But she had to see herself in the mirror first. Her mother protested, "Sweetheart, I've told you it would only upset you. Every day you're looking better, but it's going to take some time for your body to heal." Catherine persisted, knowing Sarah wouldn't back down.

"Mom, you told me I don't look bad, but I must if you don't want me to see myself. How can I let Katelan see me if I look awful? I'm a big girl, Mom. Let me make the decision, okay?" She reached out her hand while her mother held tightly to the mirror.

Reluctantly, Catherine laid the mirror face down on her daughter's stomach and put a hand on Sarah's shoulder. Grasping the handle, Sarah took a deep breath and raised the mirror to her face. A gasp escaped her lips as her mother's hand tightened around her shoulder.

Sarah dropped the mirror and lay back against the pillow. What kind of accident could have done this to her? Over the past couple of days blurred images had appeared in her mind. No matter how hard she tried to remember, everything was still hazy. Things didn't make sense at all. The last thing she vaguely recalled, was folding Greg's clothes and a bag. "Mom, what happened to me? Daddy said I had an accident, but I feel there's something he's not telling me."

Catherine sat down on the edge of the bed and took her daughter's hand in hers. "Your father only wanted to protect you and keep you from any more trauma. The doctor said we needed to wait until you grew stronger, which I feel you are," she said looking into Sarah's questioning eyes. "What is the last thing you remember?", she asked, being careful not to push too hard.

"Folding clothes, a bag, something about a trip, I think." Sarah said, gazing up at the ceiling, then looking back to her mother. "Please, tell me what you know. I'll be fine, honest. I need to remember." There was a piece of her life that had been lost and she needed to get it back.

"Remember a week ago Friday, you and Katelan were coming over for the weekend while Greg was going to the lake with friends." Catherine said, searching her face for any flicker of recollection.

"The lake. Yes, he was going ice fishing." Sarah prodded her mind farther. "I remember doing Greg's laundry for the trip and...," she closed her eyes as thin lines appeared on her forehead. "The next thing I remember was waking up with everyone looking at me." She opened her eyes and let out a deep sigh. "Almost a week of my life gone that I can't recall. And I don't know if I ever will remember or not. Please, Mom, tell me the rest." Her eyes pleaded with her mother. "I've got to know, no matter how painful it might be."

"I'm going to tell you everything we've been told." Catherine decided to proceed with caution and see how Sarah reacted. "Your father and I would never lie to you unless we felt it was absolutely necessary. When your father told you that you'd been in an accident that wasn't exactly the truth. At the time you were in no condition to hear the truth. Now, I think you're ready, or I wouldn't even consider telling you." For a moment Catherine remained quiet and looked at Sarah's battered face. "Late Friday afternoon your next door neighbor heard Katelan crying. She knocked on the door and when there was no answer, she opened the door and went in. She found you unconscious on the bedroom floor. She called 911 and you were brought here to the emergency room."

There were so many questions Sarah wanted to ask, but her mind was racing, grasping at any familiar image. It's like there was something, and then it was gone. The pained expression in her mother's eyes caused her uneasiness. "Finish telling me," she urged.

Catherine swallowed and put her other hand on top of Sarah's. She knew her daughter needed her to be strong, but she felt weak at this moment. This was still very hard and to relay the facts was difficult. "You were almost beaten to death." Catherine's voice broke as tears ran down her cheeks.

Sarah squeezed her mother's hand as tears filled her eyes. Beaten to death.

Someone tried to kill her. The news hit hard and then another thought tortured her. "Mom, was I…" She couldn't bring herself to say the degrading word.

"No, no, you weren't," Catherine reassured her.

Both women were quiet as they looked at each other with love and sadness. Sarah just wanted to lie there. She felt numb and dead inside. There was no point in asking her mother who would do this to her. Deep down she knew. She didn't need to remember. Only one person could have done this. The person who had threatened to kill her, had sent her to the emergency room once before. There was no doubt in her mind that her husband, who had become a living nightmare, was guilty. Greg had attempted to carry out his threats. The revelation devastated her. How could her life have gone downhill in such a short time? She thought of her wedding day and how happy she had been. She was going to prove to her father that he was wrong about Greg.

Sarah grieved in the deepest part of her heart where only a woman can understand. She had loved him with all of her being, given herself to him in every way and had been completely committed as a wife. To know that he wanted her dead would haunt her for a long time, if not forever. In a strange way though, Sarah was relieved. It was like a heavy weight had been lifted. No more lying to her parents, hiding the bruises, or living in terror every day. Everything could be out in the open now, even the shame and guilt she had lived with for months. Sarah wasn't worried anymore about what her parents might say or think, because she was free now from the fear that had plagued her day and night.

An inner strength and courage rose up, suppressing the pain of her physical wounds. She knew the trouble was not over yet. Greg had told her he would never let her leave their marriage alive. She didn't want to think about that right now. For this time she would rest so her body could mend. And when the right time came, Sarah would be ready to do whatever it took to make a new life for herself and Katelan. With the love and support of her family, she knew she could make it, no matter what Greg might try to do. She wasn't sure what would happen, but knew she'd have to be on guard at all times until her husband was out of her life for good. But for now, she knew she was about to go through the toughest battle of her life.

Chapter Twenty-Three

All night Sarah had been unable to sleep. The nurse thought it was because of pain, but it wasn't. She was nervous about telling her parents the truth. Her breakfast remained on the tray cold and untouched. Sarah pushed the tray away, got out of bed and walked with small, easy steps to the mirror. She brushed her hair with her good arm and adjusted her nightgown. Though her body and face were on the mend, it still hurt sometimes when she moved. Nine days had passed since the assault and she would be going home the day after tomorrow. Excitement was mixed with anxiety. The reality of what happened to her kept her emotions in constant turmoil.

As hard as this was, she decided against seeing her baby until she went home. Sarah was afraid her battered appearance would be too frightening. Her eyes became sad as she picked up a picture of Katelan from the night table. She missed her daughter so much it hurt. The separation seemed longer than it really was. Each day Sarah called to talk to her, but it wasn't enough. Her thoughts were interrupted when her parents walked into the room.

"Are you okay? You look so pale." Catherine walked to her side and put an arm around her waist. "How long have you been out of bed? You're not that strong yet. Come on and get back in bed." Catherine helped Sarah back to bed.

Alex straightened the covers and pulled them back before he helped her sit down. "Lie down, now."

"Mom, Daddy, I'm fine. Just a little weak, that's all. You don't need to worry so much." Sarah scooted back and rested against the pillow.

"We're your parents. It's our job to worry." Alex laughed and kissed her on the forehead. "You look better every day."

"You'd say that even if I didn't. But I love you for it." Sarah smiled briefly, then became solemn. "I want to talk to you about something and I'd appreciate it, Daddy, if you let me finish before you say anything."

Alex would have kidded with her except he sensed this was no joking matter. He pulled up a chair for Catherine, then stood at the foot of the bed. Catherine had told Alex that Sarah knew about the assault and that she couldn't remember it. Was her memory coming back? Or did she just want to talk about the ordeal in general? Whatever it was, he must stay calm and not react in anger. Sarah needed his love and support to get through this.

"I've been doing a lot of thinking about what I'm going to tell you. I don't expect you to understand because I don't even understand myself." Sarah let out a breath and looked from her mother to father. "I still don't know what happened, but I believe Greg did this to me." Tears ran down her cheeks and Alex started to walk around the bed. "No, Daddy, please, just stay there. I need to look at your face, to see what you feel about me."

"Oh, Sarah. No matter what you tell us, nothing could ever change how much we love you. Don't you know that?" He wanted to reach out and hold her like he did when she was a little girl.

"I've been so ashamed," she continued. "I didn't want you and Mom to be disappointed in me. I know I let you down when I married Greg. I should have listened to both of you. I'm so sorry for everything." Sarah reached out as Alex embraced her. He stroked her hair while she sobbed against his chest.

Catherine stood up and put her arm across Sarah's back. "We love you sweetheart. Everything is going to be okay. We're going to get through this."

Using the sheet to wipe her face, Sarah sat back into the pillow. "I need to finish telling you. This is just so hard to talk about."

Alex sat on the side of the bed while Catherine stood next to Sarah. "You take all the time you need." He held her hand and smiled.

"It all started on our honeymoon. I thought Greg was angry with me because he gambled and lost too much money. I had never seen him so mad before. After we got back, everything went okay at first, but then he changed. No matter how hard I tried to be a good wife, he was always angry with me. The first time he hit me, I told myself it was my fault. That was how he made me feel. The situation went from bad to worse. I didn't fall on ice. Greg beat me." Her heart broke as she looked at her parents and saw the agony in their eyes. "I don't want to talk about each incident. It's just too painful." Sarah sniffed and pushed her hair behind her shoulders. "The reason I think he did this is because he threatened to kill me if I ever tried to leave him." Well, everything was out in the open now. There was no turning back, not that she wanted to. She waited patiently for her parents to say something, anything, but her father stood up and walked over to the window staring through the glass.

With clenched fists he pressed them hard against the pane. "My God, he told you he'd kill you." The anger rose in his voice as he turned around to face his daughter. "You've lived in this hell for months, being brutalized verbally and emotionally."

There had never been any doubt in his mind that Greg was guilty. All the signs had been there. But to hear his own daughter talk about her abusive marriage, to confirm all he had suspected, stirred up all the hatred he felt for Greg. Feelings of guilt smothered him. He had failed to protect her, to keep her safe from harm. The past could not be reversed, yet he had the ability to change the present and future. And he would make sure his soon to be ex son-in-law never hurt her again.

"Daddy, I just want to put this all behind me and get on with my life." Sarah looked to her mother for support.

Alex walked back toward the bed. "I'm glad you told us. I don't understand though why you didn't think you could come to us. Did your mother or I do something to make you think you couldn't?"

"No, Daddy, you guys haven't done anything but be supportive. I guess it was a lot of things. I was afraid of Greg. He threatened to take Katelan away if I ever said anything." She paused and sighed, "And I was so ashamed. My pride, I think prevented me, too. You didn't want me to marry Greg, and I wanted to prove to you that I could make my marriage work. I know now I was wrong and stupid. Can you ever forgive me?" She asked looking at both her parents.

"Forgive you for what? Wanting to love your husband and make him happy? Sarah, you've done nothing wrong. Don't you ever forget that." Catherine leaned over and hugged her as she looked up at her father.

"I love you, Sarah," he said, thinking he should be the one to ask for forgiveness. He let her down as a father and somehow he needed to make atonement. "I want my firm to handle your divorce. I'll call Jeff and tell him what you've told us so he can arrest Greg." Alex notice the distressed look on his daughter's face. "You don't need to worry about this. I'll take care of everything."

"You've taught me a few things about the law, Daddy. There won't be a case against him. I can't remember what happened, and the other times I never told anyone. No one saw the bruises, and Greg will deny it all. It will be my word against his. Case closed." How could she have let him manipulate her as he did. There was no evidence of any previous abuse. Greg's attorney would get her on the stand, rip her testimony apart, and make him look like the victim. Sarah felt the whole situation was pretty hopeless.

Alex realized she was right. Without any proof, there was no case. Greg would walk away if he didn't do something. "I'll worry about that later. I'll get the divorce papers filed awarding you temporary custody of Katelan. The restraining order will be extended based on your complaint of domestic violence. Judge Thurman owes me a favor. He'll make sure Greg can't come near you or Katelan. And if he does, he'll go to jail."

"I just want this to be over so I can get on with my life. I know I can't until this is all over for good." But would it ever be over? Would she ever be free of Greg? He had said he'd never let her go. Fear gripped her as she relived his threats. Had she escaped one prison only to be placed in another? He was still in control and she wondered what dangers awaited her.

"Your mother and I will go to the duplex and pack up all of yours and the baby's belongings. Sarah, you will get through this. Someday this will only be a bad memory. Life will be good for you again. You'll see." Alex walked around to the side of the bed and hugged her. "I'm going to go now. I want to call Jeff and then go over to the courthouse to get this thing filed. I'll come back later and have dinner with you, okay?"

Sarah kissed him on the cheek. "I'll see you later. Bye, and thanks, Daddy, for everything."

"You're welcome." As he left the room, he struggled to control his rage, to think rationally. There had to be a way within the law to put Greg behind bars. If only Sarah had confided in someone, but she hadn't. The thought of Greg going unpunished made him fill with rage. He took in deep breaths while he waited for the elevator. Justice would find a way to vindicate his daughter. It was Alex's belief in the system which kept him from taking the law into his own hands. And if the system failed, God help Greg, because no one else could protect him from the vengeance he would carry out.

The morning flew by as Sarah had rested after her mother left. There was so much to think about to do, but she felt helpless in her current physical condition. She was anxious to leave the hospital and be home with her child and family. Her parents were being wonderful as usual, and she was determined to get her life back in order. Maybe this time she would return to school and find a career, so she could eventually take care of herself and Katelan without assistance from her parents. The phone rang making her smile. Would it be Will or Carter? Between the two of them, they called about ten times a day. She teased them about it, knowing they only wanted to make sure she was okay. "Hello," she said, prepared to answer the same questions the asked everyday.

For a brief moment silence hung in the air. "Hello, Sarah." The tone was icy.

At the sound of her husband's unfriendly voice, Sarah's heart skipped a beat. "Greg, I—"

"You told your father everything and then he went straight to my old man. I told you I don't make idle threats. I would have thought after this visit to the hospital you'd have taken me a little more seriously." His sinister implication caused panic to seize her. "I warned you not to ever say a word to anyone. Didn't I!" His breaths came fast and heavy as he yelled into the phone.

"You admit it? You almost beat me to death. How could you do this to me?" Sarah trembled with fear.

"It's your word against mine. Just like that stupid sheriff, you've got no proof." He sneered, "You've just made the biggest mistake of your life. You don't walk out on me. Ever! This will never be over! You're gonna wish you'd died in Intensive Care. Where ever you go, I'll be there, watching and waiting." He began to laugh like a maniac, sending Sarah over the edge.

The phone dropped from her hand as she frantically looked at the door, screaming, "Please, someone help me. Oh, God, please." The guard rushed in followed by a nurse, as Sarah broke into hysterical sobs.

"What's wrong?" The nurse asked as she put an arm around her shoulders, trying to assess the situation. The officer noticed the receiver off the hook, picked it up, listened, and then hung up the phone.

"He, he…," her words were muffled by her continual crying.

Alex walked through the door, each hand holding a take out container filled with Chinese food. The color drained from his face when he saw Sarah. His hands released the bags as he hurried over to his distraught daughter. The nurse stepped back to allow him to sit on the bed. He took her in his arms and held her close. "It's okay, I'm here. Sh, sh," he spoke with reassurance. His voice soothed her and she began to calm down.

"Oh, Daddy,…he,…he's going,…" She uttered the words between sniffles. "to kill me." With her head against his chest, she clung to him like a frightened child. "I'm so afraid."

Alex pulled her away from him and held her at arms length. "He's contacted you?"

His expression hardened when he looked at the officer.

"Mr. Matthews, I heard your daughter cry out for help and rushed in here. The receiver was off the hook, but there was no one there."

"Daddy, he called me. He knows I told you because you went to his father and Frank confronted him. He basically admitted to beating me and said that where ever I go he'll be watching and waiting." The tears had stopped but she was still shaken up.

"There's no proof and he knows it." She put her head back against her father's chest. "What am I going to do? I'll never be safe from him. I just want to go home."

"You listen to me. We're going to get him. And you'll never be by yourself until we do." Alex reassured her. He could kill that pathetic excuse for a human being. Greg's arrogance would be his downfall, and sooner or later his son-in-law would slip up enough to hang himself.

"Nurse, would you call Dr. Andrison? I would like Sarah to be discharged in the morning. Unless there is a medical reason, I don't think one day early should matter. After what's happened today, Sarah would probably feel safer at home."

"I'll let you know as soon as I get hold of him." The nurse checked to see if Sarah needed anything before she left.

Alex addressed the officer as he was about to leave the room. "I'm not sure how long the sheriff can provide around the clock protection. Are there any officers who moonlight? I would like to hire an officer to be at my house when I'm at work. I'll make it worth their while."

"I'll check around at the station when I get off duty. Some of the guys are always looking to make extra money." He left the room to return to his post.

"Daddy, please don't leave me alone tonight." The fear she still felt was evident in her voice.

"I won't sweetheart. I'll be here when you wake up." He stood up and walked over to retrieve the food containers which sat on the floor. "Let's not let Greg ruin our dinner."

All through dinner Alex kept the conversation light, away from the subject of Greg, as the mood was pretty somber. Sarah nodded her head occasionally and smiled somewhat at her father's tales of his law firm, but her mind was somewhere else. She had thought the hard part would be telling her parents the truth, but knew now, what lay ahead didn't even compare. There was only so much her parents and the law could do. To Sarah, her future seemed grim. Would she have to live the rest of her life in fear? How could she live through each day having to look over her shoulder everywhere she went?

Greg's words haunted her. Any hopes she had of a new life were gone now. Her days would be filled with uneasiness and the fear of not seeing another sunrise. Not a day went by that she didn't live with regret. If only she could turn back the hands of time and start over. But there was no second chance. Sarah had chosen her own destiny and she was reaping the consequences of her decision. If it wasn't for her child, she didn't know if she would have the will to go on. In death there would be timeless peace, compared to a life of terror knowing she was being watched, as her husband waited for the precise minute to end her life.

Chapter Twenty-Four

Four weeks had passed since Sarah left the hospital and moved back home to The Pines. Each day was uneventful, and except for three visits to the doctor, she hadn't left the estate. Greg had made no attempts to contact her, yet she still felt afraid. Her father hired off-duty police officers to be there when he was at the office, which brought her some peace. But every time the phone rang or someone knocked on the door Sarah tensed up. The officers offered to walk with her along the beach, but she couldn't bring herself to venture out. The last phone call from Greg still played over and over in her mind, emotionally crippling her. She had become a prisoner in her parents home, shut away from the world.

Sheriff Parkerson had made a personal visit to Greg, ordering him to stay far away from Sarah and the baby until the hearing that was scheduled for April 25th. The judge would rule on temporary supervised visitation of Katelan until the divorce was final. The assault case was at a stand still, as she knew it would be. There was no solid evidence and Greg still denied everything. He had hired a lawyer by the name of Curtis Beaman, who, according to her father, was the sleaziest attorney in town. His specialty was divorce and he won his cases by digging up every piece of dirt he could uncover. Alex had told Sarah to be prepared for the worst case scenario. By the time Beaman got through, he would have her made out to look like the bad wife. But don't worry, her father had said, Greg's attorney didn't stand a chance against him or his partners. Alex had gone up against Beaman more than once and was successful.

Stretched out on the den sofa, Sarah flipped aimlessly through a Cosmopolitan magazine. She was restless and nothing much interested her. Boredom was fast becoming a constant companion. Her brothers were spending the night with friends and her parents had retired to their room. Katelan even fell asleep earlier than usual, leaving Sarah to herself. She got off the couch and walked around the spacious room looking at nothing in particular. This was ridiculous. She might as well go to bed rather than stay up and be bored. Sarah turned off the lights in the den and made sure the French doors were locked. This had become a ritual she did every night without fail before she went to bed, even though her parents already locked up.

As she headed out of the den toward the front door to shut off the remainder of the downstairs lights, Sarah heard a soft thud outside on the front porch. She froze in her tracks, unable to move, as footsteps pounded down the steps. "Daddy! Daddy!" she screamed in terror and turned to flee up the stairs.

Alex came running frantically down the hall, followed close behind by Catherine. "Sarah, what's wrong!?" They met halfway, almost bumping into each other. His arms went around her as he surveyed the foyer.

"Somebody's outside. I heard them at the front door." Her whole body shook as she clung to him.

"Stay here with your mother. I'm going to take a look." He released her and headed down the stairs toward the front door. "Don't worry. I'm sure they're gone by now." Alex approached the door with caution, turning on the outside lights. He looked out the window to make sure no one was there before he opened the door. At first he didn't see anyone or notice anything unusual. The only noise that could be heard was the sound of the ocean as waves crashed against the rocks. But when he stepped back to close the door, a long and narrow, white box on the welcome mat caught his eye. For a few seconds he stood there looking down at the box.

Alex decided to call Jeff and have him come over and look at it. If Greg was up to something there might be fingerprints which would prove he violated the restraining order. For that he could go to jail. He shut the door and told his wife and daughter what he found and then called the sheriff. Within an hour Jeff Parkerson arrived, wearing blue jeans and a Maine University sweatshirt. Catherine had brewed a pot of gourmet coffee, filling the room with the aroma of vanilla.

"I appreciate your coming out on such short notice." Alex stood in the doorway with Sarah and Catherine behind him while Jeff put on latex gloves before opening the box, which remained on the doormat.

"You did the right thing by calling me. With all that's happened you just can't be to careful." Jeff used both his index fingers to lift the lid from the box. A puzzled expression crossed his face as he looked down at dead, long stem, black roses. A small, white envelope was on top. Holding the envelope between his index fingers, he slid out a white card inscribed with black letters. The ink had run from each letter, but you could still make out the dangerous message, Till Death Do Us Part. He showed the card to Alex before putting it back into the envelope.

"Cath, would you please serve the coffee in the den? Sarah, you go with your mother. We'll be there in a minute."

"What did it say, Daddy? It was for me, wasn't it? They're from Greg, aren't they?" The volume in Sarah's voice rose to the level of hysteria.

As much as Alex wanted to protect his daughter, he knew this couldn't be kept from her. There was no point in putting her off. She had a right to know. Keeping her in the dark could make her more vulnerable and unsafe. "Sweetheart, calm down. You're safe with us. Nothing is going to happen to you." His efforts to reassure her failed.

"Tell me. I have to know." Tears filled her eyes. "Daddy, please."

"The card wasn't addressed to anyone or signed. I believe the roses are from Greg and they're intended for you because of what the card says." His heart broke at the torture he saw in his daughter's eyes. He wanted to take her pain away, but he couldn't. "It says, Till death do us part."

Sarah clutched at her shirt and stepped backward. "He's never going to give up until I'm dead." Tears ran down her cheeks as Catherine embraced her. "I can't live like this anymore! What did I do to deserve this?" She cried on her mother's shoulder as Jeff put the box in a clear plastic bag, being careful not to deface evidence.

"Sarah, we're going to get him. He will slip up, sweetheart." Alex didn't even know if he really believed that or not. Was Greg really stupid enough to leave fingerprints? Sarah couldn't stay inside forever. Every day that passed she became more like a hermit. If he had to hire a full time bodyguard, so she could have some peace of mind then that is what he would do.

She wiped her red, blotchy eyes and sighed. "I just want to go to bed. Mom, will you stay with me until I fall asleep?" she pleaded.

"Of course, I will." Catherine thanked Jeff for coming over and put an arm around her daughter's waist as they walked up the stairs.

When they were out of earshot, Alex spoke in anger. "There has to be something we can do to stop him. You know as well as I do those flowers are from him! And if there are no fingerprints, again no proof."

"My hands are tied until a crime can be connected to Greg that I can arrest him for. The message on this card is loud and clear. I believe eventually he will try to kill her again. We have to be smarter than he is, Alex. We've got to stay within the boundaries of the law or it will work to his advantage. You know that." Jeff took off the latex gloves and stuffed them in his jean pocket. "I'm as angry as you are. And I'm determined to get him, but the legal way."

"Sarah's going to lose her mind if she stays cooped up here another day. I'm going to hire a bodyguard to be with her when she's away from the house." Alex looked away, thinking. "Maybe I can talk her into working part time at my firm as an office assistant. Her emotions are running pretty high right now, and it would do her a world of good to get out of here and be with people besides us."

"I'll go see Greg tomorrow and question him about the roses. I'll let you know the outcome of the box. Maybe we'll get lucky." Jeff said hopefully, then left.

A miracle wouldn't hurt either, Alex mused, as he locked up and turned off the lights. Greg was a sorry excuse for a human being, and he belonged in prison, right along side the lowest form of mortal garbage that lived behind those concrete walls. And Alex would do his best to make sure his detestable son-in-law took up permanent residence there.

"I'm coming!" Marina shouted as the door knocker banged against the front door. She hurried from the kitchen and wiped her hands on the dish towel before opening the door. Her expression hardened when she saw the sheriff.

"May I come in? I need to speak with your son."

"You got a warrant?" Her tone was contemptuous as she glared at him.

"Mrs. Winslow, I don't need a warrant to speak to Greg." Jeff was losing patience.

"What do you want to talk to him about? Haven't you already asked enough questions?" Marina's eyes narrowed. "And you still don't have any proof, do you?" The sarcasm in her voice was clear.

"You and your husband are welcome to be present when I speak to Greg."

"My husband doesn't live here anymore, thank God. He was as worthless to me as Sarah is to my son."

"I'm not here to discuss Sarah..."

She interrupted, "Well, you should be. "You're so positive my son beat Sarah up, not that she didn't deserve it. Why don't you question one of her boyfriends?" Marina sneered at Jeff's surprised expression. "That's right. Her boyfriends. Greg told me all about them. In fact, he caught one of them in his own home one night when Sarah thought he was working late. I'm sure I don't need to draw you a picture, Sheriff, as to what they were doing," she mocked.

"Mrs. Winslow, I'm going to give you a piece of advice that I suggest you take. You could be sued for spreading malicious slander. It would..."

"It's not slander. It's the truth!" Marina cut him off again. "My son didn't realize he married a whore until it was too late. She probably messed around with the wrong guy and he let her have it. If you live that kind of life style, what do you expect?"

Never in his life had Jeff hit a woman, but he could definitely make an exception in this woman's case. If it were not for his badge he didn't know if he could have restrained himself. Marina Winslow was the most spiteful, vicious person he had ever encountered. He had his suspicions that domestic violence had occurred in this home more than once. Greg's behavior was a possible result of what he had seen and learned, or experienced first-hand. He breathed deeply to stay calm. "Need I remind you that I am the sheriff and am here on official business. Now, for the last time, I would like to talk to Greg."

Marina put her arm up to block the door. "He's not here. And his attorney told him not to speak to you or anyone else about this case without him being present. The next time you come over you better have a search warrant because you're not getting in without one." She stepped back and slammed the door as hard as she could.

Jeff walked back to the patrol car in utter amazement at Marina's behavior. Alex had warned him about her, but to experience her first hand was an eye opener. This family had some serious issues which were probably deep rooted. If Greg was capable of the brutal assault he inflicted on Sarah, then it was a terrible thought to ponder what his mother could do to someone she hated. Before he got in the car, Jeff glanced back at the house to find

Marina watching him from an upstairs window. He got an eerie feeling as he remembered a scene from the movie *Psycho* when Norman Bates' so-called mother was standing at the bedroom window. Next time I come out here, I'll bring backup, he thought to himself, as he got in the car and pulled away.

Chapter Twenty-Five

After Alex convinced Sarah he had obtained the services of a highly recommended, experienced bodyguard, she finally agreed to the arrangement. First, she wanted to get the cast off her arm before she started to work at her father's law firm. Second, she made it very clear that under no circumstances was she to be given special treatment because she was the boss's daughter. The day finally arrived to cut the cast off, and Sarah had to admit she was excited about going to work part-time. Being a mom was still her number one priority, but this change would be good for her. And besides, Katelan was in good hands with her mother and Josephine. She had come to terms with herself. If she wanted her life back, then she was going to have to take control, starting now.

To have a protector gave her a new sense of bravery in venturing out, but she was still nervous and didn't plan on taking any unnecessary risks. But at least, this was a start and she was going to make the best of it. Since the incident with the dead roses, there hadn't been any more contact from Greg, though she still suffered from an uneasiness, making it hard for her to relax. But today she was going to do her best to enjoy her so-called new found freedom.

Katelan giggled as Sarah sat down on the bed and tickled her on the tummy. "What is mommy going to do without you today, my little pumpkin?

I'm going to miss you." Sarah picked up her child and held her close. "You are growing up too fast." She kissed her daughter on the head and stood up with Katelan in her arms. "Let's go see grandma. Mommy has got to go to work." They laughed together and headed for Catherine's bedroom.

"Sarah, we need to be going." Alex stood at the bottom of the stairs looking down at his watch. "You don't want to be late your first day. The staff might think you're getting preferred treatment." He laughed out loud as his daughter came down the stairs brushing her hair.

"Oh, Daddy." Sarah playfully punched him in the arm. "What?" she asked, as her father looked at her.

"I'm just happy to see you smile."

"It feels good to smile. Well, shall we go?" Sarah said putting her brush in her purse.

"Right on time," he said when the doorbell rang. Alex opened the front door to meet the man who would make his daughter feel safe when she left the house.

"Hello, Mr. Matthews. Nice to see you again." The men shook hands and turned to face Sarah.

"This is Ross Sammuels. Ross this is my daughter, Sarah." Alex made introductions and watched his daughter's face.

Sarah shook Ross' extended hand. Nice firm handshake she thought as she looked him over. She guessed him to be about thirty. His brown hair was combed straight back pulled into a pony tail at the nape of his neck. His facial features were plain except for is expressive brown eyes which held her attention. He was of medium build and appeared to be solid. She instantly liked him and felt at ease in his presence. He was dressed in blue jeans, a white crew neck shirt, and a lightweight jacket, nothing like what she had expected.

"Well, do I pass your inspection?" Ross laughed, and as if reading her mind, pulled his jacket back to reveal a gun in a shoulder harness.

Sarah blushed a pale shade of pink. "I apologize. I didn't mean to stare. You're just not what I expected."

"No need to be embarrassed. It happens all the time. I guess people think I should look like the CIA or something. Believe me, the less attention I draw to myself, the better." Ross grinned, then asked, "Well, what's on the agenda?"

"Why don't you follow us to work in your car. I'll be working late tonight, so you can bring Sarah home. She's only going to work three days a week at my firm and the rest of the time you'll take her where she wants to go. Your hours may vary from week to week. Most of the time you'll be needed during the day. Well, shall we be on our way?" Alex walked out the front door, followed by Sarah and Ross.

The morning weather was perfect, with a cool April breeze. May was right around the corner, and the flower beds were in full bloom. Sarah breathed in the fresh, spring air and smiled. She knew this was just another day, but for her it was different. She felt elated, rested and was ready to take on the day. Sarah got into her father's Lexus, while Ross stepped into his black Pathfinder. The vehicles drove down the winding cliff road and turned onto the main road that would take them to town. No one noticed a tan, Ford Escort parked behind a group of pine trees. When the other vehicles drove till they were almost out of sight, the car followed at a safe distance.

"Open this door! Marina, I mean it. You either open the door, now, or I'll kick it in!" Frank had been pounding on the door for five minutes. He knew she was home because her car was in the garage. He had every right to come by and pick up the rest of his things. His attorney said if Marina wouldn't cooperate, the police would come out to assist. "You let me in or I'll call the police."

The door was jerked opened by his wife, who stood there outraged. Her eyes were wild with fury as she shook. Frank expected her to foam at the mouth any minute. "Go ahead, call the police! I'll have you arrested for harassment," she threatened.

"I have every right to be here. My attorney called yours. You knew I was coming. I only want to get my things and then I'll be gone." Frank pushed his way past Marina and headed for the staircase. The house reeked of cigarette smoke and he noticed an empty bottle of Jack Daniels on the kitchen table. He turned to face Marina and looked at her. There was no love left between them, yet he pitied her. "Is this what you're going to do now? Die of lung cancer or drink yourself to death?"

"What I do is no longer your concern," she responded hatefully. "There is no need to pretend we care what happens to each other."

"That never was an issue, was it? The only thing you've ever cared about is Greg. But your love is tainted with hate and jealousy, and now, it's destroyed him too. My God, Marina, don't you see what has happened?" Frank was bitter, and he wanted to hurt her as bad as he'd been hurt. Greg wouldn't have anything to do with him now. His own son called him a traitor because he was still friends with the Matthews. But Frank blamed his wife more than Greg. She had filled their son with her poison till it consumed him. "You have turned Greg into you, but worse. How do you sleep at night knowing he may have been the one who almost killed Sarah?" Frank had not cried in years, but felt he could breakdown at any moment.

With slow steps, Marina approached Frank with her venomous hatred. "I hope he did do it. I live for the day when he tells me he did it," she hissed in a malicious whisper. "I want to know every detail of how Sarah suffered." Marina grabbed Frank's arm and began to squeeze. "I lie awake at night trying to visualize the attack. I wish I would have been the one to beat her." Marina began to laugh like a lunatic.

Frank jerked his arm away and shook his head. "What has happened to you? I don't even know you anymore," he said in despair. Maybe he was to blame. He should have taken control years ago when Marina began to manipulate and twist everything. Guilt and regret would haunt him daily in his own private hell.

As Frank went up the stairs, he could feel her eyes bore into his back as she continued to laugh. He now believed his wife capable of horrors he never thought she could do. She might be dangerous, and he was afraid for Sarah. With Marina and Greg feeding each other's hate and anger, the outcome could be disastrous. As soon as he finished collecting the rest of his belongings he would go see Alex. He felt it was his responsibility to warn them about Marina's behavior. Overwhelmed by grief and humiliation caused by his wife and son, Frank's shoulders drooped. He took a final look around the bedroom. He couldn't recall one happy memory he had shared with this woman.

The day went fast for Sarah. Her job title, office assistant, meant glorified gofer, but she didn't mind. It kept her busy, and she enjoyed the varied duties. She made sure her desk was straightened before she picked up her purse and headed for her father's office. The door was open so she went in. "Daddy, I'm going."

"Is it four o'clock already? How did you like your first day?" He smiled and walked out from behind his mahogany, executive desk.

"I liked it. Everyone was helpful and made me feel right at home."

"I told them they'd be fired if they didn't." Alex laughed whole heartedly.

"I'm surprised you can keep good help around here." Sarah teased back. "What time should I tell Mom you'll be home? Will you make it for dinner?"

"I don't know. Tell her I'll call her later. Where is Ross?" Alex asked.

"He's waiting for me in the reception area. I just want to thank you for everything. I mean the job, and Ross. I had such a great day." Sarah embraced her father.

"You're welcome. Now don't you have a daughter to get home to? She has probably missed you." Alex walked her toward the door.

"I've missed her, too." Sarah planted a kiss on her father's cheek and waved goodbye. "See you at home."

Ross was on his cell phone when Sarah approached him. She waited until he finished his call and then they stepped out into the afternoon air. "How was work?" Ross walked at a medium pace so Sarah could keep up without any effort.

"I liked it. It was a nice change. Where are you parked?" Sarah looked down the street.

"I parked in back of the building."

They walked around the building and headed toward the Pathfinder. Ross unlocked Sarah's door, and opened it for her to get in. She was about to get in when she saw Greg standing across the street in front of a restaurant, watching her. The color drained from her face as she trembled.

"Sarah, what's wrong?" When she didn't answer, Ross looked across the street to where her terrified eyes were fixated, though he didn't see anything.

"Greg was there, in front of that restaurant. I saw him." Her voice was shaky.

"Well, he's gone now." Ross helped Sarah into the Pathfinder, then shut the door.

He walked to the edge of the parking lot and looked up and down the street. He had a feeling even though Greg was out of sight, he was still watching from somewhere. The restraining order couldn't keep Greg from being in town. Ross had seen this type of case before. Greg would push the boundaries as far as the law would allow. Stalking her from a distance was a way to intimidate and keep her frightened until he made his move.

He got back into the drivers' seat and reassured Sarah that Greg was gone. Ross had been in this business a long time, and he knew no matter how much protection a person had, there was always a way to get to someone. This could go on for months before Sarah's husband attempted to carry out his threats. Ross liked the Matthews and hoped this situation wouldn't turn from bad to worse. Greg sounded psychotic and that made him more dangerous. Ross looked over at Sarah as he started the car. The radiant smile that had been on her face earlier was now replaced with a look of despondency.

The vehicle pulled out of the parking lot with ease and edged its way down the street, as Greg sat at the bar looking out the restaurant window. With eyes glazed over from the three shots of whiskey he had already downed, he never blinked while watching the vehicle turn on to the street and drive away. His lips parted in to a sinister grin. "No one can protect you from me," he said in a low, sadistic voice. "Your days are numbered." Greg turned back around and drank a final shot of whiskey before going back outside. The tan, Ford escort pulled up next to the curb. Greg opened the door and got in, exchanging words with the driver. Minutes later, the car drove down the street, headed in the direction of The Pines.

Chapter Twenty-Six

The full moon floated above the ocean and illuminated the waters. Sarah leaned against the granite pillar of her bedroom balcony and gazed out at the sea. The French doors off the den below were open, and she could hear Katelan laughing as Will and Carter played with her. Being back home with her family meant everything to Sarah. There was a serenity at The Pines that had been present as long as she could remember. Being there was like living in two different worlds. The Pines represented love, safety, and security. But the other world apart from here, meant fear and anxiety, where Greg watched and waited for her.

Sarah looked up at the stars, remembering how as a young girl, she would pick one out of the thousands to make a wish upon. She had never doubted that her wish would come true, no matter how long it took. If only she could become that innocent child again, with no cares or worries. But that was an impossible dream which could only live in her heart. For now she had a small child who needed Sarah to make her world free from worry and care. How was she supposed to do that with a husband who wanted to kill her? She and Katelan couldn't hide out at The Pines forever.

She harbored an intense anger in addition to the fear she lived with every day. Sarah hated Greg for all the pain he had caused her. At first she had endured the abuse to save a marriage that was doomed from the start. Then, had separated herself from her family to hide her shame. He had manipulated

Sarah in every way possible to fulfill his need to be in complete control. And that still wasn't enough to satisfy his twisted desires. Greg wanted her dead, and she knew he would stop at nothing to make that happen. No matter what he might do to her physically, he could never hurt her on the inside again. Any feelings she may have had for him were dead forever.

All Sarah was concerned about now was their baby. As horrible as he was, Greg would always be Katelan's father, whether he wanted to be or not. He made it clear at the custody hearing he wanted nothing to do with his daughter. Sarah never looked at Greg through the entire hearing, yet could still hear his allegations of how she got pregnant so he would have to marry her. He even claimed that Katelan might not be his. The judge stated that a DNA test would have to be done before the court could grant child support. Sarah declared that if her husband wanted nothing to do with their child, then she wanted to file for termination of his parental rights and waive any of her rights to child support.

As brave as she had tried to appear that day in the courtroom, her heart broke, not for herself, but for Katelan. She would be a year old next week and had a father who didn't love her. What would she tell her daughter when she grew older? That her father was a detestable monster, or make up some lie to spare her any feelings of hurt and rejection. This was a question she couldn't answer right now. The time would come some day and she'd have to deal with it then.

"You must be a million miles away. I knocked three times and you still didn't hear me." Catherine said, as she walked out onto the balcony to join her daughter. "Are you okay?"

"I'm fine, Mom. Is Katelan being good?" Sarah asked.

"Your brothers are wearing her out. She'll sleep soundly tonight. They love having her here. We all do," Catherine said, resting her arms on the ledge.

"Since we're on the subject of Katelan, I've been wanting to talk to you about something," Sarah said.

"What is it? You sound so serious." She looked at her daughter and waited.

"I've just been doing a lot of thinking about the present and the future. I never thought my life would be in such a mess. I used to have my whole world planned out." Sarah looked away from her mother.

"You do have a good future ahead of you." Catherine put her hand on Sarah's forearm.

"Do I really, Mom? Greg wants me dead. I'm afraid to leave the house without Ross. Even at night when I try to go to sleep, I'm afraid. And when I finally fall asleep, he's in my nightmares. I'm never going to escape him. What kind of future is that?" Sarah wiped the tears from her eyes. "I know this is a terrible thing to say, but I wish he were dead. Then I would be free."

Catherine put her arm around Sarah's shoulders and looked up at the pine trees that towered over the estate. "Greg has done unspeakable things to you, not just physically, but emotionally as well. And it's apparent he's not changing. You are still going through a lot, and I understand what you're feeling. I have to pray every day for God to help me not to hate Greg. We will get through this, Sarah. You've got to believe that."

"I want to believe that, more than anything. Some days, it seems so hopeless. I wonder if I will even see tomorrow. Mom, I have to know that, if something happens to me, you and Daddy will raise Katelan and never let Greg or his mother near her." Sarah fell into her mother's arms and began to cry. "Promise me."

Catherine held her tight, rocking back and forth. "That is never going to be an issue because nothing is going to happen to you. Do you hear me? Now, you stop thinking like that. You're going to have a good life with your daughter. And no one is going to take that away from you." Catherine stroked her hair as Sarah hugged her mother tighter.

With all the hatred Catherine had in her heart for Greg, she felt she needed to go to confession. There were times, she even wished her son-in-law would die. It wasn't fair he could still torment Sarah, from a distance. When she looked at her daughter, it was like looking at a familiar stranger. She looked the same as far as her facial features. But it was her character that had changed. A girl who was once confident and vivacious was now afraid and unsure. And for that, Catherine despised Greg. She knew it was wrong to feel this way, but if something were to happen to him, she wouldn't care. Even though she felt justified, she hated her feelings. This was not her normal disposition. Maybe someday, when all this was behind them, she would be able to forgive him. But not now. Mother and daughter held each other, cherishing the peace for the moment as a cool breeze rolled off the ocean.

In the shadows below, only a few feet away, Greg lurked among the midst of the trees, watching the two women. A sneer appeared on his face as he drank from a bottle of scotch. "Soon, Sarah," he said in a low, dangerous voice. "Soon."

"Mom, Daddy, you guys need to go out and have a good time. It has been a long time since you've done anything together." Sarah stood in her parents' bedroom doorway watching her mother as she put on a pearl necklace. "I don't want you to worry about me. Josie is here. Will and Carter will be home by ten, and an officer is outside, as always."

Alex walked over to his daughter and put a hand on her shoulder. "I'm a worry wart. What can I say? Until Greg is behind bars, I'll worry."

"You know, it's been three weeks since I saw him in town. Maybe he's gotten bored with this whole thing," Sarah said with false hope.

"You don't believe that and neither do I. Let's just continue to use good judgment and never underestimate him, okay?" Alex kissed his daughter on the forehead.

"Well, I'm all ready. Sarah, are you sure you'll be okay? We don't have to go out tonight." Catherine turned from the mirror to face her husband and daughter, whose eyes were filled with admiration. With her auburn hair swept up in a French twist, and the way the black, backless, chiffon evening dress adorned her figure, she looked like royalty.

"Mom, you look like a million dollars. And yes, I'm sure. You guys need a break away from here. Honest, I'll be okay. I'm going to watch romance movies, eat junk food and gain ten pounds." Everyone laughed as they walked down the stairs.

"I have to admit I'm excited about going to the Chardonnay Room. That is my favorite place." Catherine smiled as she looked at Alex, who looked exceptionally handsome in his black, silk Armani suit.

"You guys have a great time and remember your curfew," Sarah teased, as good-byes were exchanged. She watched her parents go down the walkway and stop to talk with the officer before they left. Sarah locked the front door and went into the den where Josie was playing with Katelan. "Josie, is she wearing you out? This room looks like a tornado hit it." Sarah laughed, as she began to pick up toys and throw them in the toy box.

"Would you like for me to get this little one ready for bed? I'll read her a story and rock her to sleep." Josie looked affectionately at Katelan.

"I appreciate the offer, Josie, but I'll do it." Sarah never wanted to take advantage of the devoted housekeeper who had become one of the family. She was like a grandmother to Sarah and her brothers. And besides, bedtime was a special time for her and her daughter.

Josephine kissed the baby goodnight before handing her to Sarah. "If you don't need anything else, Miss Sarah, I think I'll turn in too."

"No, you go on to bed. Thanks for all you do." She hugged Josie, then carried her sleepy child who was rubbing her eyes up the stairs to the nursery. After changing her wet diaper and putting on her pajamas, Sarah hummed Brahms' *Lullaby* and rocked Katelan until she went to sleep. Turning on the monitor and the night light, Sarah closed the bedroom door and headed back downstairs to pick up the rest of toys, which seemed an endless chore.

Throwing the last stuffed animal into the toy box, Sarah sat down on the sofa and listened to the silence. She was looking forward to having a peaceful evening, but there was an uneasiness she couldn't shake. Get a grip, she told herself. The guard's right outside, the doors are locked, you're safe. This is one night, Greg, I'm gonna try and forget you.

The grandfather clock in the foyer chimed out eight thirty. She would have time to watch most of a movie before her brothers came home. Sarah decided to watch the romantic drama, *Return To Me*. She put the video on top of the television and was about to go to the kitchen for food and a Dr. Pepper, when the telephone rang. Her heart stopped for a brief second, as it often did when the phone rang. She picked it up and pushed the talk button and hesitated before she spoke. "Hello."

"Sarah, are you okay? You sound funny," Carter said with concern.

Breathing out a sigh of relief, she laughed. "No, I'm fine. I guess I've just got a case of the jitters. Why are you calling? Is everything okay with you and Will?"

"Yeah, we're fine. I wanted to let you know we won't be home until around eleven instead of ten. The guys are wanting to go out for pizza after the game. But if you want us to come home, we will."

"No, you go eat pizza. I'll let Mom and Daddy know if they beat you guys home. Have fun. Bye." Sarah pushed the off button and set the phone back down. It was stupid, but knowing they wouldn't be home until eleven made her feel a little less protected. "Stop it," she said out loud. "Everything is fine." Before she went to the kitchen, Sarah stopped at the front door and looked out the window. The police officer was standing next to his patrol car smoking a cigarette. All the outside lights were on and nothing seemed amiss. Sarah sighed deeply and headed toward the kitchen.

Holding a bag of Doritos, a jar of salsa, and a Dr. Pepper in her hands, she pushed opened the kitchen door and walked back to the den. She set the soda and food on the coffee table then put the video into the VCR. Sarah settled against the comfort of the leather sofa, ready to enjoy a good movie which would allow her to escape reality for a couple of hours. At first, she didn't pay attention to Butch, the family bulldog, barking. He was always barking at something. But when he wouldn't stop, it put her on edge. She stood up and looked around. The lights from the back patio were on, and she didn't see anything.

Trying to stay calm, Sarah proceeded to the foyer and looked out the window. The police car was there, but she didn't see the officer. Maybe he went to the back of the house to check out the dog's barking. Fear gripped her, and she started to tremble. She was afraid to move. Should she yell for Josephine or call 911? With the housekeeper's living quarters on the third floor, Josephine would be unable to hear her. Don't panic, she told herself. Take in deep breaths. Go find the officer. Sarah forced herself to walk back to the kitchen where she would be able to see the dog's kennel. She left the light off and approached the French doors with caution. Butch had stopped barking and she couldn't see him. She moved to the other side of the room and looked out the window over the kitchen sink, but there was still no sign of the guard or the dog.

The blue digital clock on the microwave showed it was nine forty five. No one would be home until at least ten thirty. If something was wrong, the police officer would have come up to the house, that is, if he was able. Terror seized her as she crouched down on the floor. "God, help me," she whispered the words and saw the phone on the counter top. She crawled across the floor and reached up to the phone, with tears streaming down her cheeks. Her hand shook as she pushed 911. The phone rested against her ear only to disclose a dead silence. Sarah's hand went to her mouth to muffle her cries as the phone fell to the floor.

Greg was out there somewhere. Or was he already in the house? She felt she was losing control. She wanted to scream and run as fast as she could. Every horrible thought invaded her mind. Had her deranged husband killed the guard and their dog? Would he stop at nothing to get to her? Sarah took in deep breaths and tried not to hyperventilate. "Use your brain, don't let fear control you." She breathed in deeply as she talked to herself. She had to think of Josephine and Katelan, because Greg could hurt them, too. Her eyes searched the shadowy kitchen for a something, anything. In the corner on the countertop, Sarah saw the butcher block filled with an array of knives. Slowly rising to her feet, she pulled out the biggest butcher knife and clutched it with all her strength.

She was afraid to remain still, but even more afraid to move. Intense anxiety, mixed with deep-rooted fear, clouded her thoughts. "Think, Sarah, think," she whispered, as she looked at the basement door. Of course, the lights. She could get around this house in her sleep. In the basement was the breaker box. If all the outside and inside lights were shut off, she would have Greg at a disadvantage. The house would be in total darkness. With each step she took toward the door, her fear increased. She bit the inside of her mouth to keep from making any sound. Sarah grasped the doorknob and prayed the door wouldn't make any noise when it opened. She willed her feet to move, praying for God's help and protection.

Halfway down the stairs, the faint sound of glass breaking shattered any composure Sarah had left. She fell against the wall as the knife dropped from her hand and clanged onto the cement steps. Sarah covered her mouth with her hands to muffle the sounds of her cries of terror. Her heart was hammering in her chest, loud with every breath she attempted to withhold. Her eyes fixated on the opened door, waiting for Greg to appear. Soon, it would all be over.

Chapter Twenty-Seven

Alex and Catherine glided with ease across the dance floor in each others arms. The Chardanay Room was elegant with a live orchestra composed of men in white dinner jackets and black bowties. A huge, crystal, chandelier with dimmed lights, glowed above the dance area. The atmosphere provided a long overdue romantic evening for the couple. Being alone together was exactly what they needed. "It seems like forever since we've had time for ourselves. I've enjoyed this so much." Catherine was radiant and happy. "And I don't mean to put a damper on tonight, but would you mind if we called home to check in? I'm sure everything is fine, but I'd feel better just knowing."

"This is your night, darling. Your wish is my command," Alex teased, as the music ended. He led his wife back to their table and took his cell phone from his inside pocket. He wanted Catherine to have a good time and he had given her his full attention. But he'd wanted to call home, too, so he was glad when she brought it up. Catherine sat down and sipped her champagne, looking around to see if she knew anyone while Alex punched in their home number. He looked surprised when a recording informed him this was not a working number, please be sure you're dialing the correct number. He ended the call and tried again, only to hear the same message. Immediately he called Jeff at home who answered on the second ring.

"Hello." He sounded preoccupied with the noise of children in the background.

Catherine turned back around and was caught off guard by her husband's disturbed expression. "What is it? Is Sarah okay?"

"Jeff, this is Alex. Get hold of your officer at my house. I've tried to call my home number and it's not working." The urgency in Alex's voice was obvious.

"Don't panic. It could be anything. Dave is one of my best men. I'll get him on the car radio right now. And I'll go out there myself to make sure. Where are you?" Jeff asked and grabbed his jacket out of the hall closet.

"We're at the Chardonnay Room. We can be home in thirty minutes. Call me on my cell phone as soon as you talk to your man." Alex stood up and motioned for the waiter to come over. He handed the gentleman one hundred dollars and told him to keep the change.

"Alex, what is going on?" Alarm crept into Catherine's eyes as she searched his face for answers.

"I'll explain in the car. We need to leave," Alex said, and pulled her chair out. Minutes later, Alex's Lexus was speeding down the highway. Catherine was looking out the window, but he could tell she was praying. He squeezed the gear shift as his anxiety level climbed. In his gut, he knew there was something very wrong. Alex clenched his teeth and tried not to dwell upon the thoughts that ran rampant through his mind. If Greg was there, Sarah was not the only one in danger. He pushed the accelerator harder as he thought of Katelan and Josephine. If Greg harmed any of his family, he would kill him with no regret. Right now, the law meant nothing to him as he raced down the highway. In minutes, he would be at The Pines, and the dread of what he might find tortured him.

Sarah wasn't sure how long she stood on those steps, paralyzed with fear. As hard as she strained her ears, she heard nothing. She still felt her only defense was to shut off all the lights. With what little courage she could summon, Sarah edged her way down the remainder of the stairs and crept along the basement wall until she found the breaker box. Not sure which to turn off, she flipped them all. When the doorway to the kitchen became black, she knew the lights were off. The dark was frightening, but it could be her only salvation. The concern she felt for Katelan and Josephine empowered her to persevere.

Hanging onto the rail, she moved with extreme caution up the stairs, listening for any sounds of impending danger. She gasped when her foot stepped on the knife she had dropped. With a sigh of relief, she picked it up and held the weapon tightly. Upon reaching the final step, Sarah stood still and listened to the silence. But the lack of sound gave her no reassurance, for it seemed to hold all her terrors in it's dark hand. Her heart raced as she stepped onto the kitchen floor and walked slowly beside the wall, feeling her way. By the time she reached the door to the foyer, she was shaking. Sarah became nauseous as she reached out and pushed the solid wood door open. The only noise which could be heard was that of her own shallow breaths.

If she could only make it upstairs to where her cell phone was, in her bedroom. The distance from the foyer to the bedroom was a perilous journey. Greg was somewhere in the dark, waiting, just like a predator hidden from view. She inched her way over to the stairway, with one hand stretched out while the other clutched the knife. Her fears were confirmed when she stepped on broken glass and wind blew through her hair. He must have shattered the window and unlocked the front door. Greg could be anywhere. Not knowing where he was hidden was as terrifying as if she were face to face with him.

Sarah froze at the sound of foot steps coming from the upstairs. She struggled to hold back screams which rumbled deep in her throat. If she moved, the glass beneath her feet would reveal her presence. The footsteps came to a halt at the top of the staircase, releasing a deadly silence.

Her skin crawled when Greg whispered her name. "Sarah. I know you're down there. You thought you were so smart by turning off the lights. But nothing can protect you from me." His voice penetrated the darkness and engulfed her. "You see, I waited for the right time for everything to fall in to place." Greg laughed in a low malicious tone. "Even that stupid cop outside couldn't stop me. One blow to the head and he's out for the night. There's no place for you to hide, no where for you to run. You could scream and wake up your child, or that fat, pathetic housekeeper. But then I would have to hurt them, too." He descended a couple of stairs.

Her limbs were immobile as terror seized her. She believed Greg would hurt Katelan and Josephine. If she could only get out of the house and make it to the woods, she might have a chance. The sound of his heavy breathing only fed her fear. She needed to make a run for it now, before it was too late. The front door was closer, but there was the broken glass and steps. The den was straight ahead. Through the French doors was a clear shot in to the woods. The thought of her daughter living without a mother, and her own desire for survival, gave Sarah the strength to run. She had nothing to lose and everything to gain. Her leg hit the corner of an end table. She groaned, but didn't stop. Greg's feet pounded the stairs hard as he came after her. She unlocked the doors as he ran into a table knocking a lamp to the floor. "I'm gonna kill you, you bitch!" he screamed, kicking the lamp.

Sarah threw open the door and ran as fast as the rough, uneven ground allowed. Her breathing was rapid and heavy with the strong wind blowing against her face. The light from the quarter moon was not enough to see more than a few feet or the tree branch which struck Sarah's face. She put her hand to her cheek, but kept moving because the sound of Greg's feet beating against the earth was terrifying. Every twig that snapped, each branch that rustled in the background, made her keep running, despite the ache in her side.

"I'll get you, Sarah," Greg kept screaming at her between short gasping breaths.

Sarah grabbed her side and screamed. He was gaining on her. Tears streamed down her distraught face. The trees became a blur as she thought of her family and child. What if never saw them again. Would they even find her body, be able to have a funeral to say their final good-byes? Katelan would never know how much she was loved by her mommy. Sarah would never get to watch her daughter grow up and get married and have children of her own. How could it end like this without putting up some kind of fight? She owed it to Katelan and herself. There was nothing to lose now.

Even though consumed with fear, her will to survive was stronger. Sarah saw a group of trees ahead clumped together, which would provide some concealment. She could hide there until somebody came to look for her. Maybe Greg would keep going deeper into the woods and she could run back to the house. No plan seemed perfect, but it was all she could think of. If he found her, she was dead. The opening between the trees was not very wide though she managed to squeeze through them. Sarah squatted, crouching as far from the opening as possible. She gasped when Greg ran by. Afraid to move, she peered through a slit and couldn't see him. "God, please let him keep going," she prayed under her breath.

Minutes dragged by and Sarah's legs were cramped. She needed to stand up, but was afraid to make a sound. Unable to bear it any longer, she quietly rose to her feet. The only thing that she could hear was the wind and the ocean. Again, she looked between the trees and saw no sign of him. Sarah turned around and looked toward the house. Her heart leaped when she saw lights that seemed so far away. Breathe deep, stay calm, she told herself. You can make it. When she got close enough she would scream and yell for help.

Danger lurked in the night shadows and she was at great risk. But it was a risk she had to take if she wanted to live. Her body trembled as she squeezed back through the trees. Apprehension smothered her as she edged her way around the trees. The sight of the lights brought tears to her eyes. All she could think about was home and being safe. The last thing she saw were the lights that represented hope, fade away until there was only blackness.

The Lexus sped up the winding road to the estate. Before the car got to the drive, Alex and Catherine saw two squad cars with the red and blue lights flashing. An ambulance was pulling out as they pulled into the driveway. "Oh, God," Alex cried out as he got out of the car and ran up the steps to the house, followed by Catherine, whose long dress slowed her down. He burst through the open front door to find Jeff Parkerson trying to talk with Josephine, who was crying and holding a sleepy Katelan. He had tried not to fear the worst at the sight of the police cars and ambulance, but to see the housekeeper in this emotional state and no sign of Sarah was more than Alex could take.

Catherine rushed in as her husband's eyes flooded with tears. If it hadn't been for Katelan reaching out to her, she would have collapsed. She clung to her granddaughter and wept grievously for Sarah. Jeff put a hand on Alex's shoulder. The situation was grim and there wasn't much hope he could offer. "I don't know where Sarah is. We can't…"

"But the ambulance." Alex stared at Jeff in shock, wanting to grasp at any hope. "That wasn't Sarah? She's not…" He couldn't bring himself to say a word so final.

With the baby cradled in her arms, Catherine stood close to Alex in a daze.

"I never could get hold of Dave on the radio. I called for backup when I turned off the highway to your place and saw there were no lights on. I found Dave unconsciousness in the patrol car with his head busted open. We woke up Josephine and Katelan with the sirens; she was frantic about Sarah, and then you got here. One of my men went down to the basement and found the switches all off in the breaker box. The telephone wires have been cut, and it looks like there may have been a struggle in the den." Jeff wished he could be more encouraging, but the situation didn't look hopeful.

"We never should have gone out. Greg was waiting all this time for the perfect opportunity and I hand delivered it to him." Alex ran his fingers through his hair while guilt overwhelmed him. He'd cut off his arm if it would bring his daughter back safely.

"It's all my fault. I wanted to go more than you did. Sarah needed me and I let her down. And now it's too late." Catherine began to cry again. "Oh God, Sarah, Sarah."

Alex took Katelan from his wife and handed her back to the housekeeper, whose devastation matched their own. "Josie, please put Katelan back to bed and stay with her." Alex put his arms around Catherine, although comfort was something he couldn't offer. He watched Josephine carry his granddaughter up the stairs. If Sarah was gone, their lives were changed forever, including Katelan's, whose life had barely begun.

"Both of you listen to me. No one is to blame, but Greg. We don't know that it's too late. I sent my men out into the woods to look for Sarah. There is no trace of blood in the den or anywhere else. She could have gotten away from him. A tan, Ford escort was spotted off the road parked behind some trees. If Greg drove that here, there's a good chance he's out there somewhere. We're going to find her and we've got to pray for the best." Jeff put his hand on Catherine's arm and fought back the tears. "I love you guys. Sarah has always been like my own daughter. I'm going to go join the search, and I'm not stopping until I find her. I'll leave one of my men here at the house just in case Greg comes back."

"I'm going with you. I can't sit here and do nothing." Alex pressed his lips against Catherine's forehead before he released her. "You go check on Katelan and Josie. Make sure they're okay. They need you right now."

Her lips quivered as she wiped the smeared makeup from her tear stained face. "Promise me you'll find her safe. Bring her back to me."

"I won't come home without her. I promise, Cath." Alex and Jeff went out the French doors off the den and headed into the woods. They could see flashlights waving around in the distance and could hear the men yelling for Sarah. Alex wanted to believe they would find her alive. His heart felt as though it was ripping through his chest. Tears stung his eyes as he yelled, "Sarah." Darkness and hopelessness surrounded them as they plodded deeper into the woods. The sound of the waves rang in his ears and he knew they were near the cliff. Sarah could be anywhere, and the clock was ticking. Every second was crucial and the more time that passed, the chances of finding her alive decreased.

"Sheriff, are you there?" Officer Yant's voice came through the police radio. "We found something."

Jeff depressed the talk button and brought the radio close to his mouth. "We're not far behind. What did you find?" Alex and Jeff's faces tensed as they walked faster toward the flashlights.

"It's the sleeve of a shirt with blood on it."

"We're close to where you are." All Jeff could think was, please, God, let her be okay. He had never seen his best friend fall apart, but if something happened to Sarah, he didn't believe Alex would survive this.

The color drained from Alex's face when he saw the shirt stained with blood. "It's Sarah's." His voice broke as he picked up the sleeve and hung his head down in defeat.

"Yant, you and the other men keeping looking and spread out farther. Radio me if you find anything else. I'll be along in a minute." Jeff was about to let Alex know he knew this didn't look good, but it didn't mean the worst was true either. Then a blood curdling scream pierced the night air.

Chapter Twenty-Eight

Fiery pain wrenched through Sarah's bruised body as she came to while being dragged by her hair across the merciless ground. For a split second, she was confused, but then she regained her senses and struggled to free herself from Greg's punishing hands, which only caused him to jerk harder. A jagged branch caught Sarah's arm, tearing the flesh and ripping her shirt sleeve off when Greg jerked her free from the tree limb. She cried out in agony as warm blood oozed out, and Greg continued to pull her in the direction of the cliff.

"Stop! Let me go," she begged through tears, knowing he wouldn't listen.

"I warned you, but you wouldn't listen." He panted heavily and swore at anything in his path. "I've made a believer out of you now, haven't I!"

A rock struck her in the back, inflicting more distress. She had fallen victim to his abuse once again, but this time she was conscious and would remember every part of his wrath. If she was going to die, let it be now. She couldn't take anymore suffering.

"What are you waiting for? Just kill me and get it over with!" Sarah didn't care anymore. There was nothing left to be afraid of. Not even death, who she sensed was near by.

The cliff came into view as Greg dragged Sarah past the rest of the trees. He let go and dropped her at his feet. "Since you love the ocean so much, I thought this would be the perfect burial place for you." He looked down at her and sneered. "And there won't be any trace of your body. It will be washed out to sea with the tide. No body, no murder, no conviction." His eyes narrowed and became dark. "No one saw me here, and I've got an air tight alibi. It's the perfect murder that even the great Alex Matthews won't be able to prove," Greg said sarcastically. He leaned over and grabbed Sarah's wrist jerking her to her feet.

"You're crazy! You'll never get away with this!" She spit in his face and tried to pull lose from him.

Greg squeezed Sarah's wrist until her hand went limp. His eyes became wild as he grabbed her hand and wiped the saliva off his face. "Take this to the grave. A little something to remember me by." The impact of his fist knocked her head backwards. Sarah fell to the ground, blood pouring from her mouth. There were no more tears to shed. All she could think about was Katelan and her family. Would God allow her to look down from Heaven and see them? She hoped so.

For the last time, Greg seized her arm and dragged her to the edge of the cliff. She knew he was going to push her off. She would be washed out to sea, never to be found. She had no false hopes of saving herself from her husband, who had evolved into an evil force she couldn't overcome. But if she had to die, he would die with her. When Greg stooped to put his hands under Sarah, she reached up and grabbed his groin. She twisted and pulled with all the hatred she felt for him as he in screamed out in shocked agony. He tried frantically to free himself, but Sarah's teeth clenched as she dug her fingers deeper into his testicles. Greg fell on top of her writhing and thrashing in severe pain. The smell of his sweat and the heat from his body sickened her. She despised him with every fiber and his touch made her want to vomit.

Sarah tried to scoot out from under him, but he was too heavy. And then she knew what she had to do. They went in to this marriage together, and they would leave their marriage together. There was no fear of death now. To know that Katelan would be safe from Greg, was all the peace Sarah needed to take her from this life into the next one. She continued to hold tight to his tender, tortured flesh and started to roll to the left. The pressure from his body increased as he moved slightly, only adding to her own physical torment. She groaned out loudly along with his verbal outcries of anguish, using all her strength to turn over. Sarah's foot hung off the edge as she struggled to push Greg off of her.

He didn't fully understood what was happening, until it was too late. It happened so quickly. Greg rolled off the cliff edge head first, and let out the most horrific scream she had ever heard as he plunged downward into the ocean below against the rocks. Sarah grasped desperately at a branch that stuck out from the ground as her legs slipped over the edge. She clung to the branch with the last hope she had in her. Heavy sobs poured from her mouth when she heard voices yelling her name through the darkness. Tears soaked her blood stained face at the sound of one voice she thought she would never hear again. God had spared her life. Death, would have to wait for her another time, another place.

Sarah walked along the beach enjoying the sunrise as she had done for the past six months. She was grateful for every moment and never wanted to take the beauty of life for granted. Autumn mornings were exhilarating and the smell of pine was thick in the air. Her long, auburn hair blew in the wind, and the mist from the sea dampened her skin. With her arms crossed over her chest she stopped and looked out at the ocean, searching for answers that never came. Her question was always the same. Why? The memory of Greg's death would remain with her forever. She was tormented by remorse over his wasted life and untimely death.

Not a day had passed, since that horrible night, that she didn't wonder whether she could have done anything different to make Greg happy. His behavior had deteriorated so quickly throughout their relationship, that there didn't seemed to be a coherent reason why he descended into madness. Sarah had gone to therapy to relieve her troubled soul and find peace, but it didn't help. Hopefully, in time, she would come to terms with herself, and realize there was nothing she could have done to change the outcome.

The day of Greg's memorial service had been emotional for the whole Matthews family. Alex and Catherine had sat down with Sarah to discuss what she wanted to do. They had made the decision not to go, because of the circumstances surrounding his death and felt it best that they didn't make an appearance. She was inclined to agree with them, but was torn between guilt and feeling she needed to be there. But the decision was made for her when Frank called early that morning and requested that their family not show up, not even Sarah. The sadness in his voice made Sarah's heart ache. Frank had come to understand what his son had done, and as a parent he was suffering the greatest loss, his only child.

He explained that Marina was taking this very hard, to the point of having a breakdown. She blamed the Matthews for everything and swore if they showed up at Greg's memorial service, she would throw them out.

If Sarah had been the one to fall off the cliff and die, in Marina's eyes, it still would have been her fault. Greg could do no wrong in his mother's mind. Deep down, Sarah felt sorry for her. She was a lonely, bitter woman who wasn't happy when Greg was alive. In all honesty, Marina had driven her son to his bizarre behavior.

Frank had asked if it would be okay if he came by later in the day. He didn't want to be by himself and he wanted to see his granddaughter, who brought tremendous comfort to him. Frank knew Sarah was not to blame for any of this. He had learned the truth about everything. His relationship with the Matthews had grown, in spite of all that had happened. If it hadn't been for their love and support, he couldn't have made it through each day. He had no one now except for his grandchild, Sarah and her family.

Sarah doubted any of their lives would ever be the same again. She eventually would put all this behind her, not to forget, but to go on with her life. One memory that would haunt her for a long time, if not forever, was what occurred the day after Greg's memorial service. Everyone in the house was still asleep when Marina showed up at The Pines. The sun was just beginning to rise above the horizon, and the wind was blowing very strong. Sarah had been agonizing in a nightmare when she awoke, drenched in perspiration, to sounds of high-pitched screams coming from the front yard. She jumped out of bed and ran out of her bedroom to the nursery. Catherine and Alex were already up, heading downstairs. Sarah looked in on Katelan who was still sleeping before she followed her mother and father down the stairs.

"Murderer! Murderer!" Marina shouted over and over. "You killed my son! Your day will come and you'll pay for what you've done!"

Sarah and her parents opened the front door to Marina, whose haggard appearance shocked them. She was dressed in a two piece, black linen suit which looked as if it had been slept in. Her short hair was oily and lifeless, matted beneath a silk scarf. Dark streaks of dried mascara soiled her face, along with smeared red lipstick. Marina's eyes were wild and glazed over, as hatred erupted from them. Alex had wanted to call the police, but Catherine's compassionate nature wanted to reach out. But the minute she tried to approach Marina, the woman only became more enraged. She continued to yell vicious threats and shout profanities, leaving Alex no choice but to call the police. Before they arrived, she got into her tan Ford Escort and sped away down the winding road.

Those accusing words of "Murderer, Murderer" still echoed in Sarah's mind. She hadn't seen her ex-mother-in-law since that dreadful day and hoped she never would. There was something in Marina's eyes that had frightened her. It was the same look Greg had when he lost control and became abusive. Even after six months, Sarah still shuddered at the memory of that morning.

Sarah looked back up at the house and saw her father out on his bedroom balcony watching her. Though Greg's body was never recovered, and Alex believed no one could have survived that fall, he couldn't entirely escape the slight doubt which dwelt in the back of his mind. But Sarah wasn't plagued by fear anymore. By facing what she had feared the most, she managed to overcome the situation and beat the odds. It was hard to imagine life dealing her another ordeal as horrendous.

The morning was going to turn into a gorgeous day and she was going to make the most of it. Sarah had enrolled at the local community college in August and was enjoying her classes. Between going to school, working part-time at her father's law firm and being a mom of a very active eighteen month old, her life was full. Sarah walked backed to the house to be greeted by Will and Carter, who were on their way to school. "Hey, sis. You coming to the big game tonight?" Carter yanked her hair playfully.

"I wouldn't miss it for anything. It's not everyday you get to see a bunch of guys go crazy over a piece of pig skin." She laughed and went up the stairs to take a shower.

By the time she came back downstairs, dressed and ready to go, Alex had left for work and Katelan was in the breakfast room eating breakfast. Sarah kissed her daughter on the forehead. "You're a mess," she said, as the baby giggled. "Well, I better go or I'm gonna be late." She kissed her mother and Josephine goodbye before she picked up her purse and keys then went out the patio French doors, followed by the bulldog. "Butch, go back. Go on, boy." With a gentle pat to his head, she shooed him toward the house.

The morning air was cool and crisp, and Sarah breathed in deeply as she went down the steps toward her car parked in the driveway. She had been in the habit for months of locking her car, and was surprised when she put the key in the lock to find the door unlocked. She was positive she had locked the car the night before, and wondered if her father had been in it before he left for work. Sometimes he would put money in the cup holder in case she needed to get gas.

Shrugging it off, she opened the car door and froze. The color drained from Sarah's face as her eyes widened in horror. The fear which had taken months to bury, instantly resurrected itself. She began to shake as she stared at a dead, black rose lying on the tan, leather seat next to a small, white card. She couldn't breathe or move as panic set it. Sarah didn't want to look, but she had to. Tears poured down her cheeks as she made herself reach for the card. A force was driving her that she had no power to control. She lowered her eyelids and saw the unforgettable, smeared, black letters and deadly message. Grabbing the sides of her head, she fell against the car screaming in terror, "God, no!" as the card dropped relentlessly to the ground.